THE BLACK UGLY SPIDER

Bernie Unwin Spencer

Grosvenor House
Publishing Limited

This book is published by
Grosvenor House Publishing Ltd
Link House
140 The Broadway, Tolworth, Surrey, KT6 7HT.
www.grosvenorhousepublishing.co.uk

This book is a work of fiction. Any resemblance to
people or events, past or present, is purely coincidental.

A CIP record for this book
is available from the British Library

ISBN 978-1-80381-171-0
eBook ISBN 9781803811734

To Phil

A personal gift

from me to you

Bennie

Z.

My daughter

I would like to dedicate this book to my beautiful daughter, Charley. This amazing little girl, (not so little now) who changed my life all those years ago. You made me a better man, a nicer man, a man who is proud to be your father.

I would also like to thank my wonderful wife Sheena; without her unwavering support this book would still be in my imagination and not in print for you all to read.

My reader

I would like to dedicate this story to my reader, in parts this story will make you laugh, it will make you go ah, it will scare and terrify you in many ways, but this story will definitely make you cry. I have been asked on many different occasions to get my story professionally edited so that the grammar and punctuation are 100% correct, to make it look and feel like every other book out there. But no, this book, my story is not perfect, its raw, unedited written from my heart to yours. I hope you enjoy reading it as much as I did writing it.

THE SPIDER'S ARE HERE!!!

The black ugly hairy deadly creatures have finally ascended from the blackness below. Hundreds and thousands are slowly and deliberately infesting every school, hospital, police station, apartment block, every building in a three mile radius of the Royal Archie Memorial. Creeping and crawling under floorboards, up the insides of the walls, every nook and cranny, every tiny little space that they can fit their black terrifying bodies through and still these hideous murderous beings still are out of sight. They are strong, fast, intelligent and highly organised, fanning out, hiding, waiting, pulsating with anticipation. Only attacking when they are all in position, this unstoppable, uncompromising black wave of death and destruction is almost ready to unleash itself upon the good people of Manhattan.

If

ye is of faint heart

I implore **you**

do **not** trun this page

You have been **warned!!!!!**

THE BLACK UGLY SPIDER

My name is Professor Charles Henderson, I am the leading authority on arachnids, I teach at Cambridge university in England, and I have been seconded by the American government to oversee these devastating events that are unfolding on Manhattan Island. This story that I am about to tell you may sound totally unbelievable, but it's not. The story itself is still ongoing and only started a mere two months ago. We are about to drop several genetically engineered mustard bombs, into the heart of Manhattan and New York city killing every living thing. We cannot afford for anyone or anything to be left alive, after the dust has settled. Let us go back to the start the very beginning or as close to the beginning as we can.

THE CURE FOR ALZHEIMER'S

Steve and Jerry are two bright enthusiastic early 20s doctors/scientists who thought that they would be the ones who would find the cure for Alzheimer's. They had both qualified from medical school at the same time and had remained great friends ever since. Steve is a jolly chap, coming from more working class upbringing, while Jerry was born and bred into the medical world. His father is a well renounced surgeon. They had been working tirelessly collecting the animals they needed and then harvesting their D N A. Day after day, month after month, they toiled with hardly any sleep, trying to find the answers they craved. Unbeknown to them they would be the two men who would kill millions of men women and innocent children in the most agonizing and terrifying way imaginable in the months to come.

Let us go back to Tuesday morning the 26th of July 2037, it was like any other day that our scientists Steve and Jerry had been working frantically away in Jerry's dirty damp basement. They had acquired a small amount of funding for their research into Alzheimer's and had managed to hire two slightly under qualified research assistants, fairly new equipment, as their meagre budget wouldn't stretch to a properly equipped laboratory. Their aim was to extract DNA from a range of lots of different animals then combine them together and hopefully find a cure.

Day 132, up until now they had tried many different combinations but to no avail, Jerry said to Steve, "today's the day I can feel it in my bones". Today's combinations are DNA from a dolphin because of its intelligence, a crocodile because of that killer instinct, a cockroach because they have been here since the dawn of civilization, and they are almost impossible to kill. A grass worm because of its remarkable ability to regenerate itself, and an elephant for its remarkable memory. Their test subject is a chimpanzees called George, he was getting old now and nearing the end of his long, lonely life. He is a very gentle old chimp with a thinning grey coat and a wispy metallic grey beard with remarkable intelligence. Jerry gave Steve the syringe" come on "he said" it's time, this is the one. "They are strapping old George to the blood-soaked table and injected him with their latest batch .. Within seconds George starts rolling around in agony pulling at the straps that bind him, growling showing his sharp pointy teeth and making this horrendous grunting noise, knocking the syringe to the dirty basement floor, smashing it into a hundred pieces, leaving what was left of batch in a small pool on the dirty floor." Look at George's eyes Jerry", they seem to be rolling around and trying to pop out of his head. George was in absolute agony his whole body going into spasms. He was thrashing left then right trying to free himself, then suddenly ... George was free. The straps had snapped under the force and George was up thrashing around the basement growling, snarling, smashing anything in his way. Steve stepped in and tried to calm old gentle George down, but he was like an ape possessed. Holding his grey old head with his massive tree trunk hands, spinning around in absolute agony ...!! Suddenly one of the researchers comes running in with a tranquillizer gun, "quick shoot him", Steve shouts!! BANG!!! ... a dart shoots out the gun straight into old

George's grey chest, he staggers back then stumbles forward and with a moan and a groan, George falls to the dirty basement floor, his ape like face twisted and contorted in excruciating pain, trying to grasp hold of the tranquillizer dart lodged in his aching chest. His poor old body still spinning as he slowly falls into a haunted deep sleep. "That wasn't a success Jerry but there is always the next batch, we better clean up this mess and find out what went wrong."

THE SPIDER AND THE FLY

The house fly ...... flying around minding his own business doing what fly's do, around and around the basement he goes, as gentle George is going berserk below him. Then suddenly our innocence little fly spots a small pool of liquid on the dirty, chaotic basement floor. Below him Steve and Jerry are frantically trying to keep old grey-haired George from hurting himself, they were blissfully unaware of this insignificant little fly, flying about their heads. This little fly that would cause millions of men, women, and children to die in agonizing and terrifying pain, all because of what Steve and Jerry had put in motion. Our little fly then descends towards the basement floor avoiding Steve and Jerry and a thrashing George as he goes, making a bee line for the small pool of liquid. Within seconds of his sucker penetrating the fluid, our little fly goes absolutely crazy flying around the room at supersonic speed, hitting the walls, hitting the ceiling, spinning around and around his eyes spinning and spiralling out of control .... Then our little fly is still !! stopped dead in his tracks, stuck solid unable to move, he has flown straight into a spider's web .... Then down it comes, this dirty ... black ... ugly house spider, its fangs glistening, salivating at the meal that is to come. In a flash the dirty ... black ... spider pounces on to the fly, quickly wrapping it round and around and round in its Webb, tighter and tighter until the fly is ready to be devoured. The spider then slowly and deliberately drags his trust up meal out of its Webb and into his Lear, to consume at its leisure. The dirty ... black ... spider cannot wait to devour its prey, it's been slim picking down in the basement for a house spider since Steve and Jerry's experiments begun. The spider pinned down the helpless cocooned fly with its black front hairy legs, it then lifted its black ugly body high above the fly, its glistening razor-sharp fangs protruding downwards dripping with anticipation. Then with a sickening crack it smashed through the cocoon straight into the fly's soft flesh before feasting on its blood ... Then suddenly the spider was off the fly spiralling around its Lear, its eyes are rolling, almost popping out of its head, the spider was going crazy like it was possessed by a demonic demon. It was spinning around and around and around, its whole body was going into spasms, flexing then contracting at a hundred miles per hour, then as suddenly as it started the spider stopped moving, it then curled itself up into a tight black ball and lay motionless.

PATIENT ZERO

In the apartment directly above the basement lives a beautiful, sweet couple called Tina smith and Sam Goodwin. They are both 28 years old and have been together for five years, they met on one of those internet dating websites. Sam is a handsome strapping young man, with short dark hair, piercing blue eyes and a well-toned 5-foot 10 physique. Tina loves nothing more than rubbing her petite well manicured little hands all over her man's muscley body. They are one of those couples that you make fun of across the room because they are silly, giggling, laughing, sitting way to close together, always holding hands and telling each other I love you xx but secretly you wished you had what they had. They lived a good life, Sam is a construction worker and Tina is a nurse, she spends all day on her aching little feet walking up and down the wards. At 5 foot 2, with long curly mousey hair and enchanting green eyes, Tina looks divine in her little nurse's uniform. They didn't get a lot of quality time together but when they did, they made the most of it. Sam is up in the morning at 4.30 am and out the door by 5 am, then home again by 6 pm. Tina worked shifts, working 7 am till 7 pm on different days. But Sunday was their day, as they called it, our P J Day, making love in the morning then breakfast in bed, Sam always cooked, then up late morning snuggled up on the sofa watching a good film having a coffee and there was always cake. They had nick names for each other, Tina called Sam ... my Samoji while Sam called Tina my little pudding because she loves cake. Tina's family called her tin tin because she always had cake at her nan's house and nan kept the cake in this great big green cake tin on the top shelf of her Welch dresser. When Tina was a toddler, she would run into her nan's kitchen look up to the top shelf pointing her little finger, shouting tin tin , tin tin. So, Sunday is their incredibly special day, Tina gets lots of cake but best of all she gets to spend the entire day with her favourite person in the whole wide world ... her Sam. Every morning when Sam is leaving for work, he would always have Tina's coffee mug ready, and he always left her a lovely message with a big smiley face on the chalkboard by the front door. They made the most of every day, they were happy and in love.

Tina rolled over in her warm cosy bed, with a yawn and a stretch she leant over to see what the time was on her phone, 9 o'clock she mutters to herself, it was Friday she had worked the last four days straight and she was having a well-deserved day off. The other side of the bed was cold and empty, Sam had gone to work at five as normal. I know she thought, I'll cook Sam his favourite meal tonight when he gets home, it will be a surprise she giggled as Sam did most of the cooking. So up she got, straight into the shower to get the day on the go. Before long it was nearly 5 o'clock, everything was almost ready for Sam's arrival. She had spent the day shopping, cleaning the apartment and getting herself all glamorous. All her hairy bits removed, her makeup was done to perfection, and she had on Sam's favourite blue and yellow summer dress on, the one with the big slit up the front. Smiling she poured two classes or red wine. Then there was a noise at the front door, Sam she thought as she quickly walked swishing her hair on the way to the door. No, it wasn't Sam, it was Tibby, Tibby was their ginger cat, they'd had him for 4 years, he was getting old now, a bit overweight and half his left ear had been chewed off by a stray Alsatian dog some time before. They had rescued him from a shelter, and they still loved him to bits. "It's almost 5 o'clock" she said to Tibby Sam will be home any time now. With that there was a key in the door and Sam was home, taking his muddy boots off, hanging his work coat on the hook he shouts,

"I'm home my darling and its Friday. I love Fridays when your off work, we get to spend lots more time together my Hun. "Tina raced to the door to give her man a big hug and a big welcome home kiss. Sam stopped in his tracks as Tina comes to greet him," I think you're a beautiful woman my little pudding, but you look absolutely scrumptious today." She stood there looking deep into his deep blue eyes giggling like a little schoolgirl," you always make me feel loved Sam", stepping forward, she gave her big strong man the biggest deepest welcome home kiss ... "I've got a surprise for you my darling Sam," "mmmmm I can smell something lovely coming from the kitchen", yes you can Sam, I've been cooking and not just cooking but your favourite. Yes, ribeye steak, onions, mushrooms, and homemade fries." Sam's face lit up with the biggest smile imaginable, "I love you my honey". He picked her up in his strong muscular arms and gave her the biggest squeeze and swung her around the hallway." Have I got time for a quick shower" he asked, Tina replied with a stern but smiley NO ...!! "You haven't, I've got plans for you after dinner," then with a cheeky wink and a spring in her step she returned to the kitchen quickly followed by an incredibly happy Sam. Dinner looks and smells divine darling as he picks up the wine glasses and hands one to Tina," cheers my beautiful little pudding", "yes cheers my handsome samoji here's to us" ..." Dinners ready my darling let's take a seat." As they sat down at the tatty old brown 4-seater dining table that used to belong to Tina's mum they were blissfully unaware of the horrors that were beginning to be unleashed right under their feet in the dingy dark basement below ......!!!

THE TRANSFORMATION

The spider had lay dormant in its lair for a full three days, during this time it had not moved at all, no signs to show that it was still alive but something strange had happened. Its entire body had been encased in a dark grey shell, just like a butterfly's chrysalis. It was about as big as a tennis ball, with these creepy looking purple pulsating veins covering the entire cocoon. Then at the exact same moment that Tina and Sam were sitting down for their lovely meal just feet away, the shell begins to CRACK ...!! CRACK ...!!

CRACK ... there was movement coming from inside, there is something starting to emerge. Slowly and methodically the spider started to emerge from its cocoon, standing upright on all of its 8 spiny hairy legs, the spider begins to pulsate up and down. It was nearly twice the size of an average house spider and blacker than the pits of hell. Covered in long bristly sticky black hairs, it looked more like a tarantula than a house spider, it was truly horrifying, a killing machine. It began running up and down the walls of the now empty dirty dark basement at electric speed, jumping 2 feet into the air. It was bigger ...!! faster ...!! stronger and more intelligent than before and eager to go in search for its first victim. The spider could sense movement above, vibrations coming down through the floorboards. The sound was Sam and Tina enjoying their beautiful meal, not knowing what unspeakable horrors that were about to unfold. With slow and deliberate movements, the 8 hairy bristly claw like legs lifted the black ... ugly... spider up to its full height. Its black body glistening and pulsating, its razor-sharp fangs dripping with anticipation.

Then it was off, searching in the darkness upwards and upwards towards the vibrations above.

SAM AND TINA

"That was truly scrumptious,"" yes, I enjoyed mine too Sam, the steak was done to perfection mmmm."" Tina, you know that we are getting married in 3 week's time and you gave me one job to do. You played me two songs and I had to pick one for our wedding dance, well I've picked one "Tina was all exited, jumping up and down rubbing her little hands together with the biggest smile on her face," come on Sam which one have you picked ???" Sam took Tina's hand "come on," as he led her to the sofa, sitting her down he smiled intently looking into her green eyes. Sam pulled out his phone, a few taps later, "this one my darling wife to be." As the music begins to fill the living room Tina's face beams with excitement," aw Sam that's my favourite,"" I know" he said. "Tina you are my Bella" and" Sam you are my Edward." The song that was playing was from the film twilight Tina's favourite film in all the world. Sam reached out his strong muscular arm," come on my future Mrs. Goodwin shall we dance". She leaped from the sofa glowing like a Cheshire cat barely containing her overwhelming excitement. "Come on then my husband to be, let's dance." They pulled each other close, wrapped their loving arms tightly around one another and with an enormous smile on their faces and a loving squeeze they were swooning around the room with her blue and yellow dress swishing against her newly shaven bare legs." It's funny isn't Sam we are smooching to Edward and Bella's wedding song, the one she walked down the aisle to, where Edward was waiting for her. Their love is nearly as strong as ours, I'm so lucky I found you ... my Sam "" Yes, and you are my Tina, I'm the luckiest man in the world." As they danced around the living room smiling, giggling holding each other so very close as they began to sing .... I have died every day waiting for you, darling don't be afraid. I have loved you for a thousand years ... I'll love you for a thousand more ...!!!!!!!!

"Right my darling I've got a surprise for you !!!"
Tina loved surprises", what surprise, what is it",
as she jumped up and down squealing like an
excited little girl." I love surprises Sam, I want it
now" as she grinned from ear to ear. Tina had
no patience at all, that's one of the things that
Sam loved about her. As he sat her down on the
edge of the sofa, he gently squeezed her hand
and looked longingly into her green eyes." Ok
my little pudding, I'll go and get it, but you must
be patient"." Me be patient Sam, don't be silly"
and with a wink of an eye and a spring in HIS
step Sam leaves the room." Come on Sam I'm
waiting "as she bounced up and down on the
sofa. Rifling through his work bag …" I've got it"
he shouts!! As he walked to the kitchen Tina was
still bouncing up and down shouting," I'm ready,
I'm waiting.""" I'm on the way my Hun", unwrapping
the small package in his hands revealed Tina's
favourite lemon drizzle cake with extra drizzle,
grabbing two small plates he cuts and places a
piece on each, but he always cut Tina an extra
big wedge because she loved cake so much." On
my way" he shouts, eyes tightly closed" no
peeking, hold your hands out."

As he enters the living room Tina is still sat on the sofa with her eyes tightly closed, still bouncing and smiling." Come on, come on I can't wait", he places the small plate onto her hands," can I open them now" she squealed," ok tin tin I suppose so," she flings her eyes open wide," lemon drizzle cake my absolute favourite, mmmm thank you Sam, I love it but not as much as I love you my samoji." Putting the lemon drizzle down on the arm of the sofa Tina stands up putting her arms around Sam's neck and gives him a long sensual kiss," that's because I love you so much. Come on, I'm taking you to the bedroom I've waited long enough, we can have cake later." Taking Sam by the hand Tina starts to lead her strong handsome man out of the living room but before they can leave Tina spots something!! Then suddenly she stops, frozen solid, not moving a muscle, her eyes wide open fixated onto the corner of the room." What's wrong Tina, come on my darling what's up you're scarring me." Lifting her shaky right arm and pointing towards the TV." There is a spider" her voice trembling, her whole body was shaking, Tina had always hated spiders. To try and cure her of her phobia of spiders, Tina's father had held her down when she was only 4 years old and put a spider on her outstretched little hand thinking it would cure her. But as he did so, the spider run from her hand and up her arm towards her terrified little face. She remembers screaming uncontrollably, shaking violently, her whole body going into shock. Poor little Tina had nightmares for years after that, Sam knew all of this, so he was the one who got rid of all the spiders that invaded their apartment. A frightened Tina jumped onto the sofa, shaking and starting to sob" spider … spider."

Taking Tina by the hand Sam looked deep into her eyes, wiping the tears from her frightened little face," Tina your Sam is here, I'll get rid of the spider for you. This is an old apartment, you know we get spiders sometimes and I'll do what I always do, I'll keep you safe my darling. Go into the bedroom, close the door behind you and I'll get rid of that horrible beast, ok my Hun, don't be scared" …." but Sam this one is so ugly and so black, it's like its looking deep into my soul."" It will be alright my darling it is just a horrible house spider, I will sort it ok, I love you, now go into the bedroom, everything will be fine." Closing the door behind her Tina felt safe in the bedroom, my Sam will get rid of that horrible thing she thought and that seemed to calm her down a little. Sam waited for Tina to close the bedroom door before going into the kitchen to get an empty glass and some paper. Sam didn't mind spiders, he always gets a glass and some paper and would scoop up the spider and put it out of the window, he didn't like to squish them. Coming back into the living room Sam spots their ginger tabby cat Tibby, Tibby is stood there staring into the corner of the room. Its ginger fur standing up on end, hissing with its beady eyes transfixed on its pray.

Go on Tibby get it Sam shouts, as quick as a flash Tibby is behind the TV, hissing and thrashing around trying to catch the ugly black spider. With a loud meow, a scared Tibby comes shooting out from behind the TV and scarpers into the hallway with his ginger tail between his frightened legs. With half a bemused smile Sam calls out to his courageous cat," thanks Tibby, I suppose I'll have to get it." Sam looks at the wall but there is no spider, looking around ... where are you, suddenly he spots the spider on the carpet by the sofa, ah wait there you little spider. ... it's not that little at all!! It is nearly twice the size as normal and black, really black, bloody ugly he thought. With the glass in one hand and the paper in the other he moves in, holding the glass above the spider ready to quickly put it down to trap it, right here goes. Down with the glass but as he moved the glass downwards the spider moved to one side. Sam tried again but again the spider moved out of the way, Sam tried again but still the same. Sam stood there scratching his head thinking what the fuck is going on, a spider had never done that before, come on I need to get this spider out of here ... So down with the glass once more but to no avail, the spider was too quick, then with a flash it was gone, nowhere to be seen. Sam searched high and low, but he could not find it, so finally he gave up, putting the glass back into the kitchen, right let's go and see how my beloved Tina is.

Sticking his head around the bedroom door,"
how are you my Hun"". Have you got rid of that
horrible spider Sam"", yes" he said," it's gone."
With a sigh of relief Tina looked up," thank you
Sam my Saviour, come here and give me a big
hug. I'm sorry I was so scared,"" don't be silly I'm
your Sam and it's my job to look after you and I
will always be here to do just that". With a cheeky
wry smile and a glint in his eye," are you still up
for a bit of .... !!!" Tina smiles and with a glint in
HER eye," I've been looking forward to getting
you, my strong handsome man into bed all day.
but Sam, it's going to have to be a quickie tonight
as we have both got work in the morning, we
haven't got time to be making love for hours like
we do on a Sunday morning." Quickly ripping
off one another's clothes, naked they both
jumped beneath the duvet, Sam shouts," fuck
me your freezing ...!!!" "Come here Sam let me
steel your heat." As they snuggled closer and
closer their hands begin to roam beneath the
covers, stroking each other's naked bodies. lay
side by side facing each other their hands
roamed deeper and deeper, kissing passionately
their tongues entwined. Sam's hand slides down

Tina's inner thigh, rubbing up and down and then back up until he reaches Tina's soft incredibly wet, smooth pussy. He slowly caresses her, slipping one finger between her soft moist lips. Then with a purposeful thrust forward his finger penetrates deep inside her. Tina let's out a very pleasurable mmmmmm, kissing harder and harder, Tina's small, manicured hand moves slowly from caressing Sam's beautifully shaped bum to rubbing his inner thigh.

Then moving up and wrapping her little fingers around the shaft of Sam's hard throbbing cock, the more Sam moans the tighter she grips and the faster she moves her hand up and down his throbbing member. Sam moves his hand away from Tina's, now dripping, pulsating pussy and climbs on top of her. Still kissing her deeply his knees sink between hers and slowly start to push her legs apart, slowly her legs move further and further away whilst gyrating his stiff hard cock against her groin. Tina's hand moves slowly down between Sam's legs and grabs his unbelievable stiff cock and manoeuvres it into position, then with one almighty thrust Sam's rock-hard cock is deep inside Tina's pulsating, soaking wet pussy. Deeper and deeper, faster and faster, harder and harder, their sweaty beautiful bodies smash into one another, becoming one. Rising and falling in unison, quicker and quicker until the passion overwhelms them, moaning, panting, grunting, they are both on the verge of climaxing, Sam's hard cock going in and out. Tina's back arching pushing her bum high into the air, in and out, in and out, faster and faster until their bodies explode as they climax together, their bodies shuddering, pulsating, sweat dripping, heavy breathing and lots of satisfying moaning and groaning as they fall motionless back into each other's arms.

Tina looks up wiping the sweat away from her face as she gives Sam a loving sensual hug, their sweaty bodies entwined, at this moment right now she thinks to herself this is true love, I'm deeply in love with this man, my man Sam. With an enormous beaming smile, she looks deep into her Sam's exhausted sweaty face, her wet pussy still quivering and pulsating ..." Sam, I bloody

love you and that's what you call a quickie !!!"
Looking back at her with his stormy smoky grey
eyes (normally blue) they always changed
colour when Sam orgasms," yes, my darling that
was a fabulous quickie." Giving her an extra big
loving squeeze and a quick kiss on the lips," can
I have my shower now you have had your wicked
way with me !!!" With a cheeky smirk and a
contented look on her face," of course you can
Mr. Goodwin my future husband, you deserve
it." Dragging himself out of the moist warm bed
his muscular toned body still quivering from his
exertions. He staggers towards the bathroom,"
love you Hun" he shouts," love you too, leave
the shower on, and I'll jump in after you ... and
then I can have my lovely cake you bought me."
As Tina lay there totally naked all warm and
fuzzy inside, listening to Sam whistling in the
shower, no one had noticed that something
despicable evil in its nature, blacker than the
pits of hell had been watching them.

THE HORRIFYING ORDEAL

The spider had quickly scurried away from Sam
in the living room. The black ... ugly ... spider

had followed Sam into the bedroom, crept up the wall behind the wardrobe, then concealing its black glistening hairy body in the shadows and waited and watched for the perfect opportunity to strike!!! Sam had gone, Tina was all alone, now is the time, my perfect opportunity!!! vulnerable ... alone ... naked, she is all mine. Slowly one spiny hairy leg after another the hideous spider begins to decent down from the shadows. Down the wall it crept slowly and quietly, its black hairy body pulsating with anticipation. Then onto the bedroom carpet scurrying across the floor towards the bed where Tina was lying, totally naked and contented. Then up it climbed, up towards the duvet, slipping its Black gruesome body under the covers, wriggling its way slowly towards its oblivious victim.

Tina was lying there stretching mmmm, relaxing listening to Sam's happy whistling, thinking of the wedding that was to come. Suddenly she felt a strange sensation on her stomach, thinking it was the bobbles on the duvet catching her she casually lifted up the duvet .... Her eyes opened wider than they had ever done before, her mouth dropped dramatically open, and her breathing became very erratic.

Tina's brain couldn't comprehend what her eyes were seeing, she was in shock, this cannot be happening, this can't be real!!!! The black ... ugly ... terrifying spider was on her stomach looking straight into her eyes, looking deep into her soul ... !! ... Suddenly the spider lifted itself up to full height with its eight spiny hairy legs, its black glistening hairy body quivering with anticipation, the spiders long razor-sharp pointy fangs protruding downwards dripping venom onto Tina's belly. Tina couldn't move, her traumatized terrified body was in total shock .... !!! Then with a sickening crack the spider sinks its razor-sharp fangs deep into Tina's belly button, injecting venom straight into her naked body. Tina let's out a blood curdling scream, she screams and screams like she had never screamed before. But there is no sound, nothing, absolute silence, she screams again but still nothing, only silence. The spider's venom had instantly paralysed her body, she was frozen solid, her eyes and mouth were still wide open. Her body is stiff and rigid, Tina could still hear, see and feel everything but she couldn't move a muscle. The screams, the terrifying panic, the unbelievable horror that was happening to her was all inside her head. Tina was running around at a million miles an hour, screaming frantically trying to get away but it was all in her mind. She could still hear Sam whistling in the shower just feet away, but she couldn't move or make a sound ... !!!

Then the spider begins to move, slowly and methodically one spiny hairy leg after another. Up Tina's terrified frozen body it went. Crawling up her trembling stomach, then up over her left naked left exposed breast and onto her neck, its black bristly thick hairs scratching at Tina's hypersensitive skin as it went. The black hideous beast then puts its two front hairy legs onto Tina's left cheek, then another and another, up towards her wide-open terrified eyes it crawled. The spider stopping for a moment, its ugly black hairy body pulsating, quivering as it hovers over Tina's wide open frozen eye. A terrified Tina was staring straight at the body of this hideous jet-black creature, only millimetres away, oh my God the smell, it was absolutely putrid, like

1000-year-old baby vomit that had been left to dry in the summer sun. Wanting to be violently sick but her body wouldn't and couldn't move, the spider was just hovering and vibrating. Tina's screams grew louder and louder, she was hysterical, biting, kicking, screaming, racing around at unbelievable speed around and around inside her terrified confused head. Tina could still sense and feel everything, the hairs on her entire body standing rigid, up on end, her skin covered in hundreds of goose bumps. Shouting at the top of her terrified voice ... Sam ... Sam ... Sam, please help me, please, you said that you would always protect me. With tears rolling down her pain ridden agonized distorted face, her horrific ordeal was too much to bear but bare it she must, bare it she did, with nowhere to hide. Screaming, agonizing, crying, shouting and still absolutely hysterically with no end in sight.

Then suddenly the spider started to move, spinning its black hideous body around it started heading down her distorted traumatized face, stopping at Tina's wide open, screaming mouth. The spider then puts its front two black hairy smelly leg into her mouth, resting them on her dry limp tongue for a moment, then quick as a flash its whole black glistening hairy body was inside. Tina was freaking out her breathing became more erratic, her chest rising and falling very rapidly, her heart beating out of her chest, God ... God almighty please help me I can't take any more. The spider then rammed it's two front hairy legs down Tina's throat, spreading open her windpipe and pushing downwards. Gagging the sound was unimaginable, a gurgling rasping sound as Tina tried to breathe. Deeper and deeper, the spider descends down Tina's gurgling rasping throat. Her body going into involuntary spasms as she gasped for air, her wide open eyes streamed with tears. Her naked body stiff and rigid, her terrifying deafening hysterical screams only heard inside her own agonizing mind. Gasping for air as the spider kept crawling deeper and deeper.

Then suddenly Tina could breathe a little easier, her throat was clear, breathing deeply in and out she could feel the spider wriggling around deep inside her chest going down slowly into the pit of her aching stomach. For a time, it was still

... then the spider began to move once more, upwards out of her stomach towards her chest. Then the rasping and gagging started as the spider began to ascend back up Tina's gasping throat. Her violated naked body going into violent spasms as she struggled to breathe once more. Tina could feel every single movement the spider was making as it slowly crept back up her battered windpipe, gagging and spluttering as it moved towards Tina's wide open terrified mouth ... !!! then the black disgusting spider was back wriggling and twisting inside Tina's traumatized mouth. Out it came, one sticky hairy leg at a time, until its whole hideous body was back on poor Tina's traumatized face, running down her naked cold frozen body and then it was gone, scurrying away back into the night ... Tina's blood shot teary eyes started to become heavy, her dry aching mouth starting to slowly close, her terrified shaking body staring to relax and just like that, Tina fell into a haunted deep sleep....

"Hello darling" Sam shouts as he strolls naked back into the bedroom," I've left the shower on for you." Stopping dead in his tracks he looks over at the bed and sees that his beloved wife to be is peacefully fast asleep, laying naked on the bed. Aw Sam whispers she looks so peaceful, creeping slowly and quietly over to the bed Sam pulls the duvet up over Tina's frozen shoulders. Giving her a loving kiss on her cheek," I love you, sleep well, see you after work tomorrow." Sam then goes and turns off the shower, turns out the lights and with a big smile on his face closes his eyes and falls into a deep dreamy sleep.

Beep ... beep ... beep it was 5.45am on the Saturday morning and Tina's alarm was sounding. Sam was already up and hard at work. Slowly stirring, Tina awoke with a big stretch and with one eye half opened mmmm ... Suddenly with a sickening gulp Tina let out the blood curdling scream that she had held in from the night before. She screamed and screamed and screamed again, her whole body shaking with the realization of what had happened to her last night. Tina ripped back the covers to expose her bare naked battered body, she began frantically hysterically scratching, ripping away at her stomach, her well-manicured sharp nails gouging out her flesh while screaming hysterically over and over again. Then moving her hand up towards her face, ripping and scratching, blood pouring down her hysterical face. Her fingers going deep into her screaming mouth, searching, probing deep inside like a mad demented crazy person. Then holding her face tightly with both ofher bloodied hands. Tina begins to sob, louder and louder she cries, the tears cascading down her red bloody cheeks, her whole body was shivering and aching at the ordeal that she had faced. Jumping out of bed and running to the bathroom Tina stands and stares into the big bathroom mirror hanging on the wall. Breathing heavily her hands start pulling at her stomach looking for signs of what had happened to her last night, searching, pulling her mouth wide open, still sobbing Tina looks but there is nothing only the deep scratches that she had just made herself.

Wiping the blood away from her frantic face Tina pulls at her cheeks, her eyes and then with her fingers her mouth, she pulls her lips wide apart to look deep inside but there is nothing anywhere apart from all the marks and scratches she had just made herself. Sinking to her knees on the cold hard floor, still naked Tina sobs become less and less. I didn't dream all of that did I .... a dream it was a fucking nightmare, surely not, I'm confused, I don't know what to believe. Still sniffling her body still aching from all the hysterical screaming and crying Tina stumbles back into the bedroom. Sitting on the edge of the bed looking around the room with disbelief, wiping the snot away from her runny nose. Come on Tina she thinks, stop being silly, that ugly black spider you saw in the living room last night must of giving you that horrendous nightmare, something that horrific could never be real, come on pull yourself together girl. After phoning work to let them know that she would be a little late, Tina then jumps into the shower, a quick change, applies a little makeup, coat and bag and out the door to work she goes.

Tina spent the whole day in a daze, patients came and went, the hospital seemed to carry on as normal, Tina is a good nurse, caring, compassionate and good at her job but she just didn't feel herself today. 7pm finally came and it was time to go home, Tina was looking forward to getting home but also a little scared, a little apprehensive. Sam had to work late so Tina would be alone in the apartment waiting for him to get home. As Tina headed home on the subway she rang Sam," hi darling, I'm just leaving work now" he said," how was your day, I will tell you all about it when I see you" … "Sam its Saturday night do you fancy a drink at O'Rielly's", "yes Hun that sounds great I can be there by 8 o'clock,"" ok Sam, I'll meet you there, I can't wait to see you, it's been a strange long day." "Ok darling see you soon." At bang on 8pm Sam comes strolling through the door, walking over to the table where Tina was sat with his usual beaming wide smile and his piercing bright blue eyes. "Hello, my darling girl," Tina springs to her feet flinging her arms tightly around her strong handsome man. Squeezing him tight," I love you, missed you today my Sam,"" missed you too my Hun, good idea about the drink, it has been a hard long day today." Sitting down, lifting his vodka and lemonade Sam clinks his glass against Tina's …" to us" he says, Tina's smiles" yes to us." As Tina sat there sipping her double gin and tonic, she contemplated telling Sam about her nightmare, it was a nightmare she thought, it certainly couldn't be true. Having had many nightmares about spiders over the years starting way back when Tina was a small child, she thought this was just one of them but fuck me, so much worse. Putting it to the back of her mind she sat contented smiling and laughing with the only thing that mattered in her life, her wonderful man Sam.

As the days rolled by Tina had sort of forgotten the events of that terrible night, hardly speaking to anyone about what she thought had or hadn't happened to her that evening. Her life with Sam was wonderful, the perfect couple, not one argument in all the time they had been together, life was good. It was nearly two weeks later, Tina had woken a few times in the night in a cold terrible sweat and in a blind panic but quickly put her fears to one side. It was Thursday night Tina and Sam had only just arrived home from work, having a well-deserved glass of red wine in the kitchen. "Tina its finally here we have got a long weekend off together,"" yes, we have Sam, I've been looking forward to this for ages". "Me and you time but don't forget my Hun you're trying on your wedding dress this Saturday morning,"" I haven't forgotten Sam, I've just been feeling a bit sickly these last few days and I have put on a little weight. Marrying you Sam will be the happiest day of my life, I can't wait, I've just been feeling a bit out of sorts this week, I've been having some cramps in my stomach." "Darling why didn't you tell me, are you ok, you're not pregnant are you?" Sam said with an enormous smile on his face. "No Sam I don't think so, but I'll ring the doctors on Monday just to be sure." After a wonderful evening together Tina and Sam got ready for bed, going to the toilet then cleaning their teeth, after taking all of their clothes off ... they always slept naked, the closeness of their naked skin touching, made them feel safe and secure. As they snuggled naked in bed tightly wrapped under the covers their arms and legs entwined Tina kisses Sam's strong muscular arm that was wrapped lovingly around her," yes good night my darling girl, sleep well and I'll see you in the morning." With that the pair snuggled up and fell into a deep sleep.

The next morning at 7am Sam awoke stretching, scratching, letting out the biggest yawn and an even bigger rasping fart. He then noticed his beloved Tina was not by his side, her side of the bed was cold and empty. So up he got, putting on his PJs, yawning and scratching on his way to find his wonderful Tina." There you are what are you doing on the sofa." Ashen faced, Tina slowly raises her exhausted head off the sofa, where she had spent most of the night curled up in pain under her white fluffy comfy blanket. "Morning my honey I've been up most of the night, I couldn't really sleep, these stomach cramps are getting worse I'm knackered."" Why didn't you wake me" as he stroked the top of Tina's exhausted brow." I didn't want to my honey, you looked so peaceful."" I'll go and make you a nice mug of hot chocolate with lots of milk and then you can snuggle up in bed and try to get some sleep."" That's a lovely thought Sam but I'm whacked I'll just climb back into bed if that's ok with you."" Of course, it's alright my sweet" and with that Sam scooped his beloved Tina up in his big strong arms and very carefully carried her to the bedroom. Softly laying her down, covering her with the duvet sitting beside her stroking her very tired head."

"I hope you feel better soon my Hun," half lifting her head off the pillow and with an exhausted smile …" I hope so Sam, I am excited to try my wedding dress on tomorrow morning."" Is your big sis still going with you,"" yes, my big sister Martha and her daughter Skye are both coming, they are both really excited. I love little Skye, she is only five, every time I see her, I just want to pick her up in my arms and swing her around, she is a lovely child."" Tina, I hope we have one just like her after we are married." "Only one Sam, I want lots of kids after we are married."" Me too my darling but you need to get better first." As Sam continue stroking Tina's tired head, wiping the hair away from her eyes Sam confesses …." I know you're not feeling very well but I'd planned a couple of surprises for you today my wife to be." With that Tina perked up a little," surprises … surprises you know I love surprises, come on Sam, you must tell me now."" Ok my darling I have organized" …. "Come on, come on tell me!! "" ok … right I have arranged to go and pick up some of your favourite foods from the deli you love for our picnic in the park at lunchtime, I have also picked up your favourite bath oils so you can have a good long soak when we get back and then .... I have spoken to your mum and dad, and they are putting on a late dinner for us so we can finalize all of our wedding plans ...... plus your sister and Skye will be there too, everyone is really excited to see us but especially you my little tin tin. It is really your wedding day my darling, it was kind of Martha to organize the whole day."" Awe Sam you've organized all that for me, I must be the luckiest woman in the whole wide world to have you." Giving Sam a big sloppy kiss," I love you so very much,"" I love you so very much too my little pudding. Now please try and get some sleep, I'll just be in the living room if you need me, just call." Sam puts his hand on Tina's soft cheek, leans forward and kisses her gently on her forehead," love you, now sleep."

He then leaves the room and half closes the door behind him. As Tina lay there with the cramps slightly easing, her mind spinning with all the wonderful things that Sam had planned for that day, especially going to see her parents. Tina also felt a little sad for Sam as his parents had died in a house fire when he was only two years old, his aunt had brought him up, but she had also sadly died some years earlier. When Tina met Sam five years ago, he was all alone in the world, she thinks that is why they have been so inseparable ever since. Right come on she says, I need to get to sleep, turning over and snuggling up Tina finally closed her eyes and drifts off to sleep. Meanwhile Sam was pottering around, tidying, dusting, washing up the dishes making the apartment presentable for when his beloved Tina awoke. After watching tv for a short time Sam looked at his phone. Its 11 o'clock, I'll just check on my darling, popping his head quietly around the bedroom door he sees that his beloved is still sound asleep. Staring longingly at her, it's sad that Tina wasn't feeling very well, I know he thought I have got a fabulous idea?? After gathering some clothes from the bedroom, he pulled the bedroom door gently behind him. Getting dressed in the hallway, Sam grabs his keys, and he was out of the front door closing it really quietly.

Thirty minutes later Sam returns carrying two shopping bags, into the kitchen, then with lots of rustling between the kitchen and the living room his job was done. Smiling Walking slowly into the bedroom Sam sits softly onto the bed," are you awake my honey." With a stir and half a smile Tina looks at Sam," yes, my darling, I had a pretty good sleep and I'm feeling a lot better now. "Giving Tina a big but tentative squeeze Sam asks" do you fancy a coffee and perhaps something to eat?"" What time is it Sam, it feels about 6pm,"" no its only 12.30 its lunchtime, are you hungry?"" I am actually, I'm starving,"" ok my darling I'll go and make us a coffee." As Sam is in the kitchen Tina drags herself out of bed, has a wee then joins him in the kitchen." I know you're not feeling yourself today, Tina, so I have cancelled our picnic in the park."" Oh, a picnic in the park sounded lovely Sam but I suppose your right, I am not fully myself today."" Come on my darling let's go and sit on the sofa, go on, I'll carry the coffee." As Tina walked towards the closed living room door Sam walks quietly behind, laughing and sniggering to himself.

As Tina opened the living room door, she freezes in her tracks ... Sam had put the big comfy picnic blanket on the carpet, and he had laid all of Tina's favourite finger foods on it.

There were different coloured balloons scattered all around the room, Sam had also made a banner out of some old cardboard which he had placed on the sofa." If you can't go to the picnic, the picnic will come to you, my darling." Tina squealing like a little girl," Sam this is really beautiful I can't believe you have done all of this for me, I love it, I really love it and I absolutely love you," flinging her arms around Sam's neck giving him a big monster kiss. As Tina enters the living room, she notices her banner perched on the sofa .... it read. To my darling Tina ... you are my world ... you are my life ... I can't wait for next Saturday ... because then, you will be my wife XXX." Ah Sam that is absolutely beautiful, I don't deserve you.""
Tina, I have only got two jobs in this world, one is to keep you safe, and the other is to make you happy, you are my world my honey, you and me together forever." Sitting on the floor tucking into their fabulous feast Tina and Sam were happy, smiling, laughing enjoying their time with one another. After they had eaten their scrumptious buffet, they lay on their backs bursting at the seams." Sam, I know you have

spoiled me today, but it is still early, can we curl up on the sofa with the duvet and watch my favourite film of all times."" Of course, we can my darling," so up they got, wrapping the duvet around themselves, snuggling on the sofa, hand in hand as they watched twilight, Tina's favourite film of all time.

As the hours ticked by Tina became more and more agitated," are you in pain again my darling,"

" Yes, just a little, the cramps have come back." By 6pm Tina was in a lot of pain," should I phone the doctor?" Sam asked," no it will be alright they will calm down soon, its only stomach cramps. I'll go and have a nice hot soak to see if it will help, don't worry Sam I'll be fine." As Tina soaked in the bath she called," Sam can you ring my parents and tell them that we can't make it tonight, I don't think I'm up to it, ask if we can do it tomorrow after the dress fitting but don't tell them I'm not well."

"Ok my darling I will do it now, are you still in pain?"" yes, I am Sam, but it comes and goes." As the night wore on Tina's cramps became more intense. By 8.30pm Tina wasn't feeling well at all, she had lied and told Sam she wasn't in that much pain," I am going to bed now my darling, all I need is a good night's sleep." Giving Sam a big hug and a good night kiss Tina got herself into bed, shutting her eyes tight, trying to put the nagging pain to the back of her mind, right all I need is a good long sleep, and I will be fine. Sam relaxed on the sofa watching some TV ... well its 10.30 and I better get myself off to bed. Sliding gently in beside Tina who was fast asleep Sam snuggled down and was soon sound asleep.

At 2.45am Tina started stirring, rolling from side to side, curling her legs tightly up against her aching stomach, moaning and groaning which woke Sam from his slumber." Are you ok my darling, have the cramps come back,"" to be honest Sam they never went away." Slowly but surely the pain became worse, to the point where Tina had her arms and legs tightly squeezed against her throbbing aching stomach." Sam my stomach is killing me, I'm in agony."" Right, I am calling an ambulance," grabbing his phone Sam dials 911," ambulance please, yes, my girlfriend is in tremendous pain," giving their address the ambulance was soon at their door." What's the problem sir how can we help?" "it's my girlfriend she is in the bedroom in agony." "What's your name miss?" "it's Tina, where is the pain, it's my stomach, it is absolutely killing me." Tina started to double over, the pain was excruciating, starting to sweat profusely, swaying backwards and forwards moaning louder and louder," make it stop, make it stop … please … please, it's hurting." All this time Sam was right there at Tina's side holding her hand tightly, telling her everything will be alright. "Right come on we are getting you to the hospital," within minutes Tina and Sam were in the back of the ambulance with the lights flashing and the sirens wailing.

They had given Tina some morphine for the pain, and she was sucking deeply on some gas and air. They lived about four miles from the hospital so were there in minutes, it was The Royal Archie Memorial hospital, the same hospital where Tina worked. Screeching to a halt outside, the ambulance team rapidly wheeled a tearful Tina straight into the emergency room. Sam was right there by her side and was going nowhere, still holding the hand of his beloved wife to be. The doctors came rushing in because by this time Tina was screaming with immense pain, her body going into spasms. They hooked her up to all sorts of machines, with lots of beeping and bonging. Sam shouts" what's wrong with her, help her, help her, my Tina's in agony." Sam was told to leave," I'm not going anywhere" he said," this is my woman, this is my Tina." Suddenly Tina starts violently shaking, her arms, her legs, her whole body bouncing up and down on the hospital bed, screaming in absolute agony, screaming, shouting, its hurting, its hurting, make it stop. All the time Sam stood right there by Tina's side gripping her hand tightly telling her everything will be ok, everything will be ok, I am here, your Sam is right here. Suddenly one of the doctor's shouts," what is that in her eye," looking closely a tiny little black object appears inside Tina's right eye. Wriggling, it starts to move outwards, all the time Tina continues hysterically shouting and screaming out in agonizing pain. Sam holding on with all his might.

Then suddenly the black object pops out of Tina's right eye and sits on her bottom eyelash, it's a tiny black spider, then another appears, and another, they are coming out of her eyes. One then crawls out of Tina's nose and onto her lip, then more and more gushing downwards, little, tiny black spiders are running out of Tina's eyes and nose, covering her chest. One of the two doctors starts screaming, spiders, spiders, Tina's screaming in unimaginable excruciating pain, still bouncing up and down screaming and screaming. Then with a terrifying gush Tina spews thick clotted red blood all over the bed, thousands of little black spiders start gushing out of Tina's mouth, coming out of her eyes, her nose and now her mouth, thousands of them everywhere. The doctors run out of the room screaming with their arms in the air. Then with one last sickening scream Tina's blood soaked body comes to a shuddering halt ...!!! The tiny black little spiders were nowhere to be seen, they had scuttled down the blood soaked bed and disappeared into the night. Tina lay there totally still, her whole body covered in her thick red blood, the room is totally silent apart from one machine omitting a long continuous beeeep !!! .... Tina is dead.

Through all this Tina's brave strong Sam was still standing there beside her, his pale contorted face in total shock. He just stood there all alone with his brain trying to comprehend what had just happened to his beloved Tina. The sound of the continuous beeeep still ringing in his ears, the tears starting to well up in his eyes, welling up and up until they came cascading down his pale heartbroken face. Sinking down to his knees onto the bloodied cold floor still holding the warm dead blood soaked hand of his beloved Tina. He shouts out in anguish, the tears streaming down his cheeks howling with despair he sobs uncontrollably, sobbing and sobbing, screaming into the night .... Tina .... Tina. Yelling through his torment, I was supposed to keep you safe my darling, I was supposed to keep you safe. Putting his blood soaked hands to his tortured face, Sam cries and cries, his entire body aching with unimaginable grief at the pain he felt. Slowly Sam stands to his feet and faces his beloved Tina, still sobbing with tears streaming down his grief stricken face Sam places Tina's still warm soft small hand in his, then with the other he rests it on Tina's tormented brow. He starts brushing Tina's blood soaked matted hair away from her beautiful loving sweet face. Fighting back the sickening heart wrenching sobs he takes a deep breath," I'm sorry my darling for not protecting you, for not looking after you. You are my life, my lover, my best friend, I love you, I will always love you." Squeezing his beloved Tina's hand ......

What am I supposed to do without you by my side. The emotion was too much to bear as Sam flings himself onto his beloved blood soaked chest, my darling he cries don't leave me .... Squeezing her tightly your Sam is here, please don't leave me here all alone. Still uncontrollably sobbing laying across Tina's lifeless body Sam feels a compassionate hand touch his arm, looking up through his anguish, it was a nurse, one of Tina's colleagues. Talking hold of his hand she looks deep into his eyes," come on Sam let's go and get you cleaned up, you can't stay here we need to come in and take care of Tina." "I can't leave my beloved Tina" he sobs" I'm lost without her." Holding firmly onto Sam's hand the nurse very gently eases Sam back onto his unsteady feet, then walks a confused and distraught Sam towards the door. More doctors enter the room and gather around Tina's blood soaked bed, pulling the curtains behind them. As Sam is gently guided to the door he stops, he then turns around taking one last lingering look towards his beloved Tina, Sam then looks straight into the eyes of nurse holding him steady …. "What do I do now without my beautiful Tina." Still sobbing his heart broken into a million pieces the nurse leads a devastated, lost and alone Sam down the long hospital corridor far away from his beautiful, funny, kind, amazing beloved Tina forever!!!!

THE KIRK FAMILY

The Kirk family live just a few miles away, they are a loving but dare I say it a typical modern family. Richard, the man of the house, he is 38 years old and drives his hydrogen powered truck for a living, delivering office furniture all over the place. He is in good shape for a man who, as his daughter would say, sits on his bum all day. Then we have Shona, she is the sweet, kind, caring member of the family. She is 37 years old and works as a nursery teacher. At 5 foot 4 with a very slim petite body, long wavy mousey hair and entrancing green eyes with spectacles to match. Then we have Ryan, he is a typical 16 year old boy. Slightly taller than his mother with thick black short hair, Ryan is a quiet boy, a very sensitive young soul. Then last but certainly not least we have Charlie, she is 9 years old, a little on the small side for her age, with lovely long shiny black hair, lots of beautiful freckles, which she hates, and little Charley looks exactly like her dad. They are a mostly loving family with their ups and downs living in a modern society. Richard is the worker of the family, he is up at silly o'clock in the morning and sometimes away for days on end running around delivering his office furniture for a company that doesn't really appreciate him. But Richard sort of enjoys his job, but you have to pay the bills.

Then there is Shona, she is the one that keeps the family ticking over, Shona is the glue that holds them all together. Shona loves her job, she is a nursery teacher and has been for over 20 years, having that caring compassionate side to her personality makes her perfect for childcare. What can we say about Ryan, he is 16 and is absolutely obsessed with social media. Spending all day and night connected to the world wide web." You don't understand" Ryan repeatedly tells his concerned but loving parents. The problem is, in this modern day society young people don't have what you call a typical mobile phone anymore. the kind of mobile phone that Ryan's mum and dad had when they were teenagers. Today's generation have body phones, it is a phone that is incorporated onto their forearm. You simply put your arm of choice into a 3-D phone printer, then the machine lasers the body phone straight onto your forearm. It is about 4 by 8 centimetre's wide and only 1 centimetre high. No charging needed because the phone gets its power straight from the electrical impulses of the user's body. To look at it, you would think that the skin was slightly raised but as soon as the user taps their forearm, it lights up showing all the functions that a phone has. To hear, they have a very small skin coloured speaker lasered behind each earlobe. Richard and Shona had held off for as long as they could before they let Ryan have a body phone, they are legal at the age of 14 but on his 16th birthday they relented, making Ryan one of the last kids in his school year to have one.

Ryan was the happiest young man in the whole world when he was constantly connected to his beloved web. Richard would often shout at Ryan, moaning to Shona because he was always on that bloody internet." In my day you could just take the phone off him" but not now. Life was so very different when Ryan was born, the world was being besieged by a brand new pathogen called covid 19. The virus had killed millions around the world but luckily by the end of 2021 the scientists had developed an antibody and the people around the world were slowly starting to heal. Today, covid 19 is still prevalent, it is very similar to the flu virus now, yes it can still kill people but with most of the world now inoculated, it's something people have learned to live with.

Little Charley, the apple of Richard's eye. She is a funny little girl, nearly always laughing, singing and doing silly lovable things that make you love her even more. Charley also has a dark side, she can get very, very angry. On one occasion when Charley was only 5 years old the Kirk's were all relaxing as a family watching TV. As the program came to its end, the adverts came on. Richard didn't like watching the adverts so he would turn over to see what else was on. As he did Charley pipe's up … "dad can you go back please because I want to see that advert." "No Charley let's just see what is on this side." With that Charley stands up her little fists were tightly clenched, her body getting stiffer by second after second and her face as red as a tomato. Stamping her feet ...." dad I want to look at it." Her little body rigid and her red face ready to explode, Charley was mad, really mad. Unfortunately, Charley had inherited her dad's affliction, as Richard called it, The Crusty Pie Syndrome. Ever since Richard could remember he sometimes had this anger, this uncontrollably rage deep inside of him, that he found almost impossible to control. As a small boy Richard would often be taken to the local cake shop on the corner, on the counter was a small glass oven containing delicious hot Crusty pies. Steak was Richard's favourite but on this one occasion they had none. Same as Charley Richard's body would become stiff, his hands clenched and his face turning purple as he got absolutely mad. At that moment Richard could imagine himself outside of the shop looking in through the window as it burned to the ground, smiling and laughing to himself as it did so. Richard had named his affliction The Crusty Pie Syndrome but unfortunately Charley had it too. So, when Charley became angry, only her dad understood, everyone else thought that Charley was just being naughty, but it wasn't her fault. So, when Charley became mad her dad would say ...." go to your bedroom." Charley would then stomp off to her bedroom still clenching her hands and her face still red and flustered, stamping her little feet as she went. It only took a few short minutes and Charley would walk slowly back into the room, stand before her dad ...."I'm sorry" she'd say. Then climbing onto his lap, Charley and her dad always had a big cuddle. Charley and her dad had many conversations about their Crusty Pie, the older

Charley got the better she became at understanding and controlling her affliction, as her dad called it.

It was 7 o'clock on a Wednesday night and Richard had just returned home from a long 3 days out on the road. Hearing clattering noises coming from the kitchen Richard goes to investigate. But as he reaches the kitchen Charley comes running out, jumps into the air straight into her dad's arms." Hi dad I thought it was you," giving him a big welcome home squeeze. Carrying her to the kitchen, he gives Charley a big sloppy kiss on the cheek," how was your day at school?" "Yes, it was ok dad but its school ...... it's boring." "I know it's boring, but did you learn anything my cheeky little daddy's girl," "not really dad." Putting her down on the kitchen table Richard looks sternly into Charley's eyes .... I've got something for you, with the biggest, sweetest smile Charley's face lights up with excitement," what is it dad?" Pulling his right hand out of his pocket, Richard's first two fingers are stiff, and they are doing a scissor movement. Charley's excited little face instantly turns to horror .... "No dad, no, not walkie man." With that Richard starts walking his stiff rigid fingers all over Charley's belly softly shouting" walkie man, walkie man." Not knowing whether to laugh or cry Charley is rolling around the kitchen table, "dad, dad stop, I hate walkie man," "I know you do my darling girl, but daddy loves walkie man." Looking up from the sink where Shona was washing up the dishes, smiling she says," daddy leave her alone, quick Charley run" as Shona covers Richard's face in bubbles. Smiling and still laughing Richard putts his hands around his loving wife's waist. "It's nice to be home my darling," "yes, it is good having you home in the week".

Giving each other a welcome home kiss, "coffee Richie," "yes love, that would be great." Sitting at the big round kitchen table drinking coffee asking each other about their day .... "Shona I need to go for a quick shower I'm back up at 2.30 in the morning, I've got a long two day run ahead of me, then it will be Friday." "Yes, Richie it will be Friday, at least we'll get to see one another over the weekend."

Saturday morning quickly appeared, Shona slowly opened her eyes, with a big yawn she putts her arms around Richie, "come on Richard it's time to wake up." Stretching and moaning Richard gradually opens his tiered weary eyes. "What time is it?" its 7am" ...." 7am what time do call this?" "Richard, have you forgotten its Charley's soccer game today. The therapist suggested we try and get Charley involved in some form of sports to help with her anger issues and Charley chose soccer, she has been with the soccer team training twice this week and is really looking forward to today's game. Come on Richard we need to be up and out by 8.15," smiling Shona whips back the covers and cheekily slaps Richard's bare arse," come on I'll go and get the kids up." Getting the family up, washed, dressed and a quick bite to eat they are all in the car by 8.10 am. Charley was sat there all excited with a big smile on her face, "dad, dad it's my first soccer game today," "I know my darling girl are you all excited," "yes, I am dad, I can't wait to get there." The last thing Richard wanted to do after a long hard week in his truck was to go and watch a load of 9 year old girls running around a soccer pitch with all of them judgmental soccer parents screaming from the side-lines. But he thought, this is for my darling Charley and if this makes her happy, it is what I will do.

Putting a big smile on his face Richard turns towards" Charley, we will be there soon Charley, we just need to drop your brother off at his friends first and we'll be there in plenty of time." Turning the key on the family car Shona was off down the road, Ryan was too busy looking at his arm, Richard was daydreaming out of the window, wishing he was still in his warm cosy bed and Charley was all excited. As the car sped along Richard's mind drifts back to when his darling Charley was born. He had met his sweet and caring Shona when he was 20 years old, it was her warm loving smile and her natural beauty that drew Richard towards Shona, but it was her inner beauty, her genuine caring and compassionate nature that Richard slowly and surely fell in love with. Shona is a beautiful person, sweet, kind and always put others before herself. After getting down on one knee and asking his wonderful Shona to marry him life was perfect. Shona makes Richard a better man, learning to stop being so selfish and putting others first.

Then two years later their little handsome Ryan appeared, this bundle of joy, Shona was in her element, caring, feeding, changing and most of all, cuddling. Shona is a fabulous mother and wife, and Richard was so very lucky to have her in his life. Richard loved being a dad, this is my son he would say, the first six years, just the three of them were wonderful, then little Charley was born. Standing there Richard was at the business end while Shona was huffing and puffing. The midwife was busy doing her thing," your baby is coming "she said. Really huffing and puffing by now and an awful lot of moaning Shona sucked deeply onto the gas and air. Push, push, then suddenly Richard saw a thick black mop of hair starting to arrive into the world. Her head was only halfway out, and Richard stared to cry, the tears rolling down his confused face. What's going on he thought, as his baby daughter started to emerge, Richard became overwhelmed, engulfed in this emotional wave emanating directly from his newly born infant. Shona was still panting, sweating and the odd cursing as her little bundle of joy was born into the world. The midwife quickly checked and wrapped the baby girl before handing her over to her emotional dad. Holding his newly arrived daughter in his trembling hands Richard looked down in astonishment.

What were all these new and scary overwhelming emotions I was experiencing, my hands slightly shaking, my legs wobbling, my breathing short and erratic, my heart almost beating out of my chest. I feel pure and deep love, for the first time in my entire life, I was totally smitten. Peering through the tears he looked lovingly into my newly born daughters eyes …." your name is Charley, and I am your dad." Richard finally felt that maternal bond, don't get me wrong Richard loves Ryan and Shona with all of his heart but with Charley it was so much deeper, in that very moment when his daughter was born into the world Richard's life changed forever, becoming a nicer, a more compassionate, a man more in touch with his emotions.

After dropping Ryan off at his friend's house for the night, the rest of the Kirks arrived at the soccer ground. Charley was out of the car as soon as the handbrake was on, Running straight over to her other team mates." Look at her Shona, Charley's not our little girl anymore, she is growing up fast," "yes too fast Richie, she will be off to uni before we know it." "Come on old girl, let's go and join the others" ... through gritted teeth ... wonderful parents on the sidelines. As Shona gets out of the car, she looks at Richard, with half a cheeky smile she says "old girl, I will show you old girl, old man!! I am younger than you." Laughing and smiling they hold one another's hand and joined the other wonderful, judgmental soccer parents." Come on Charley" Richard shouts at the top of his voice, Shona looking all embarrassed, tugs at Richard's shirt," the game hasn't started yet," "I know Shonie I'm just giving Charley some encouragement." Charley looks up from the pitch, elbows one of her teammates," that's my dad" as she waves. The game kicks off and the teams all 9 year old girls fight it out on the pitch. The final whistle blows, and the game is over, Charley comes running over all sweaty and out of breath." Have I got time to say goodbye to my friend's mum?" "Yes of course you have my darling." As Charley gallops away Richard shouts after her," good game my darling girl you played well. I am so glad that Charley's team won Shona, I would hate to think what Charley would be like if they had lost," "angry most probably Richie." After a few minutes Charley comes back a little bit excited ...." daaaad I was wondering!!!

Some of the teams are going for a sleep over at Becky's house, I know it's only my first game but," looking up with these big blue puppy dog eyes, "can I go .... please dad." Asking her dad was a safe bet, Charley knew that she could rap him around her little finger. Richard was just about to open his mouth when Shona takes hold of Charley's hand, "come on Charley let's go and talk to Becky's mum first." 10 minutes later Shona returns alone, "where is Charley?" "She has gone with Becky for a sleep over," giving Richard a big kiss on the lips Shona smiles," that is off Charley, tell dad I will see him tomorrow and give him a BIG kiss from me." Walking back to the car Richard looked a little glum," come on sad face when we get home it will just be you and me. I have got to pop round to Becky's mums and drop Charley some clothes and a toothbrush off but when I get back, we can have a well-deserved glass of wine." On returning home after Shona had done her errands Richard was waiting with two glasses of wine in his hands, handing one to Shona," here is to us Shonie," "yes here's to us, a well-deserved break from the kids." Richard sighed," I will miss my little Charley, it is the first time she has been away from home." "Yes, it is my darling Richard, but she is getting older now, not your little baby anymore, you will have to get used to it."

As the evening wore on Shona was upstairs doing a few jobs, when she came back into the living room Richard was watching a slide show of lots of photos of when the children were young. Sitting beside him Shona put her arm around Richard's shoulders," you miss our little babies, don't you?" Speaking with a slight tear in his eye," yes, I do, that's why I have put the old photos on." "Ok darling, we will sit and watch them together," "budge over." The photos slowly roll by," oh look Richard do you remember, Ryan in those stripped blue shorts," laughing "yes, I do Shonie, he never took them off, he wore them for 4 weeks straight, you even had to sneak into his bedroom when he was asleep so you could wash and iron them and put them back on him before he woke up in the morning." As the photos skipped by, they reminisced, laughing and smiling together about the past. "Look, look there's Charley in the bath all covered in lots of soapy bubbles." "Yes, she was only about three years old there. Do you remember Richard what you used to do with your thumbs, Magic thumbs !!" "Yes, I remember, when Charley used to get soap in her eyes she would cry, stinging dad its stinging. So, I invented magic thumbs, my thumbs would wipe away the bubbles so no more crying." After that every time Charley got water or soap in her eyes, she would cry out," magic thumbs, magic thumbs dad." Charley would then close her eyes ever so tightly, screw her little wet bubbly cute face up and I would use my crafty magic thumbs so there were no more tears."

Oh, look Richie the Kirk family on holiday, I do miss taking the children away on holiday especially when they were young, their little faces full of wonder and excitement. Oh, bless there's Charley with Patrick," Charley was only 5 then. Patrick, the Ps, is a lovely story. Richard and Charley were out doing some Christmas shopping, more looking than shopping. As they were heading back to the subway empty handed Charley suddenly stops, look dad in that window. In the window peeping out was a stuffed black and white toy penguin, he was naked apart from a yellow and blue scarf tied around its neck. Dad, dad, I love it, with that Richard took Charley into the shop and of course bought it for her. As Charley squeezed it tight, she looked up at me and said, "what is its name dad?" I had convinced Charley that I knew everyone's name just by looking into their eyes, that is why, when I looked into Charley's new born face I knew straight away that her name was Charley. Looking deep into the penguin's face, I said," what's your name!!!!" After a few seconds I looked down at Charley excitedly holding her new toy ...." his name is Patrick, and he is a boy," "Patrick, Patrick, I love it and I love you too Patrick" as she skipped holding my hand tightly as we made our way home. About six months later I was out doing one of my deliveries when I saw something familiar peeping out of a different shop window. Going inside the assistant told me that there were two, one bigger than the other, so I bought them both.

Getting home that evening I called, "Charley, Charley dads home and I've got someone very special for you to meet." Racing down the stairs Charley was jumping up and down, "who is it dad" looking around slightly confused. Hiding my hands behind my back, trying to be serious, while looking into Charley's excited little face," look Charley you know that Patrick had a life before we met him," "yes dad." "Well, I had a message on my internet, telling me that I had to meet someone very special today and that someone is ...... Patrick's daughter," smiling from ear to ear and starting to bounce up and down with pure excitement," Patrick's daughter dad !!". Then as quick as a flash I swung my right arm from behind my back, sat on my hand was a smaller version of Patrick, minus the scarf. Charley's face was a picture, her eyes wide open believing every word I was saying." Now Charley there is one more thing," "more dad" holding her hands out getting impatient. Then again quick as a flash I swung my left arm around from behind my back and sat on this hand was an even smaller black and white little penguin. "This one Charley is Patrick's daughters baby," scooping them out of my arms and giving them an enormous hug" but dad what are their names ..." Looking deep into the new penguin's faces, trying not to smile too much ...." Patrick's daughter is called Patricia and Patrick's granddaughter is called Pamela." "Dad, can I take the new penguin's to meet Patrick," "of course you can." As Charley raced up the stairs to show Patrick her new arrivals, she stopped at the top of the stairs, shouting" dad come here," as I got to the bottom step, Charley was giggling," dad we can call them the Ps," Patrick, Patricia and Pamela. The Ps sat in pride of place for years on Charley's bed but now they lived on a shelf, but Charley still loves them.

As more photos rolling by the memories came flooding back," oh look Richard the children in the garden with Easter eggs, I think that was the time when we all had an Easter egg hunt. We had hidden lots of little eggs around the garden for the two of them to find, do you remember

Richard." "Yes, I do, it was a funny day, the two of them were excitedly running around collecting as many eggs as they could find and giving them to you to hold for them. Then when their little backs were turned you were throwing them into the air, and they were landing with a plop. The noise made them turn around … mom I have found another one!! Didn't little Ryan say to you at one point, mommy it's raining Easter eggs." "That was funny Richard, that was, their little excited faces collecting all those lovely chocolate eggs, it was a good day" … Remembering, laughing, lots of smiling and a glass or two of red wine Richard and Shona have had the best night in together in ages.

Sunday afternoon and all the Kirk's were back together enjoying their lunch, Ryan was still engrossed on the internet, Charley full of beans after her sleepover, Richard and Shona are quite contented to have their little family back under one roof. Normal life resumed, working, sleeping, the ups and downs of a modern happy family.

It was now Thursday, Richard had been away from home all week doing his delivers. Every evening at about 6pm Richard would video call Shona if he was stopping out. Ring, ring, ring, ring," hi Richie how was your day, are you parked somewhere safe?" "Yes, my little Shonie I am, and my day wasn't too bad, how was yours?" "Yes, it has been a good day in the nursery today but I'm glad to be home. Richard I'm a little concerned about Ryan, he hasn't been hiding away in his bedroom constantly on his beloved internet, he has spent most of this week down stairs moping around." "He will be fine love, he is just a 16 year old boy, they go through different phases but if you are concerned, have a word with him." "Ok Richie I might do just that, anyway, have you had something to eat?" "Not yet Hun, I've got a curry bubbling away on my little cooker and its nearly ready, mmmm it smells lovely." "Well, you enjoy, and I will see you tomorrow, I miss you when you are away." "Yes, I miss you too my little wifey, love you loads, and I will see you tomorrow, night night my darling." "Night night, I can't wait see you tomorrow."

Turning the video call off Shona walks into the living room, Charley is in her usual comfortable place, on the sofa watching her favourite programs on the TV and Ryan is sat in the corner of the room just looking into space. Sitting down next to him, Shona puts her hand on his knee," are you ok Ryan?" Looking a little lost and confused Ryan looks at his mom and says "not really, I don't really know." "Come on Ryan lets me, and you go into the kitchen for a good mother and son talk. Charley if you need me, I'll be in the kitchen with Ryan, ok darling," nothing, not a Titter, Charley was glued to the TV. Entering the kitchen," would you like a glass of orange juice Ryan?" "Yes, please mom." Shona poured them both a glass," come on Ryan let's sit at the kitchen table and have that chat, come on Ryan everything will be fine. What is troubling you son, you know I'm only here to help, is it school?" "Yes, to be honest mom that is part of it, you and dad keep telling me that I will be a man soon and I need to decide what I am going to do with the rest of my life. To be honest mom, I haven't got a clue. Back in your day there were plenty of jobs but today robots do most of the work, nearly everything else has been automated. It is so much harder mom, especially in today's society, most of the jobs are technical and you know I'm not very technical." Amazon runs the whole world now, back in 2027 the owner of Amazon Jeff Bezos, called a press conference, in it he told the world that Amazon had been making billions of dollars and wasting the money on non-sequential things, like putting a rocket into space etc., things that didn't really improve the lives of normal, everyday people.

So, he has decided to rebrand Amazon, now calling itself Amazon Global. He then hired the brightest and smartest people from all around the world to come and work for his new rebranded Global company. Now 10 years later Amazon Global runs the whole world, with arms stretching out from its gigantic organization controlling every facet of human existence. The new Amazon now has, amz-medical which supplies most of the worlds medicines and vaccines, amz-media that controls all the news reports in the world, amz-social which controls and dominates the whole internet, they bought out Facebook, snapchat, Twitter, they bought them all and they now practically run the entire internet. Amazon also owns loads of other companies, but their biggest achievement is that they mastered hydrogen power, clean efficient energy. Now everything is run by amz-hydro, cars, buses, trains, planes basically all petrol, diesel and electric engines have been replaced by hydro power. There are even mini hydro power stations strategically placed every 10 miles apart that powers everything from homes to the work place." So, mom as you can see, I haven't got a clue what I am going to do when I get to be that man that you and dad say I will be one day" ......

"I'm starving" Charley declares as she trolls into the kitchen, "mom I'm starving, ""you're always starving you are Charley, there is some leftover chicken legs in the fridge, take two, make sure you use a plate and grab some kitchen roll as well," "ok mom I will." "Now go back and watch your program while I finish my chat with your brother, go on and close the door behind you. Right Ryan while Charley's out of the room did your dad mention the cinema?" "No mom," "typical you can't trust your father to do anything. Anyway, you know that your sisters been seeing a counsellor Mrs. Nuttall, for the last 9 months and she said that Charley's been making excellent progress. So, your father and I have decided because of this she deserves a special treat. So, we are all going to the cinema," "oh mum you know I hate going to the cinema," "I know Ryan but we all have to make an effort, come on Ryan we are doing this to cheer up your little sister, she needs cheering up and you'll enjoy it too … "Shoulders slouched, a half painted smile on his face …

"Ok mum I'll do it for Charley, but we better be seeing something good." "Oh, Ryan I have seen the trailer for the movie and its hilarious, you will be laughing all the way through it." "Go on then mom what's it called and what's it about?" "Well, I am glad you asked, Charley has been wanting to watch this movie for ages and when we tell her later, she will be bouncing off the walls with excitement. The movie, how shall I explain it … it's a CGI and it's called The Planet Zoooton," "that sounds rubbish mom," "Ryan just let me tell you all about it, then you can have a moan. Right here we go, The Planet Zoooton , its inhabitants are called Zooodons , they are about 4 feet high with small wobbly arms and small wobbly legs. Their feet are slightly enlarged with three bulbous toes sticking out. Their heads are big and round with pointy ears on top like a bat with big googly lovable eyes and a wobbly quivering mouth. A slightly large belly and its whole body is covered in a very fine shimmering fir. The Zooodons come in all the colours of the rainbow and when they are happy their whole body glows, with their fine fir standing up on end as it shimmers and shines. When the Zooodons laugh, purple gas bellows out of their quivering mouths, it's like blowing enormous purple bubbles into the air. The purple bubbles then float up serenely into the atmosphere making the whole sky bright purple. With millions of Zooodons constantly laughing the sky is always purple, if the sky is purple the Planet is safe and so are the cute and cuddly Zooodons .... but there is a problem !!! the Zooodons have lost their sense of humour and they cannot laugh anymore. Their planet is slowly dying and so are they. The Zooodons are very intelligent creatures, with advanced technology and extremely modern cities. They gather all their best scientists together to devise a cunning plan, to save the planet and to save themselves ...... we will use our super advanced technology to send spaceships out into the universe and hopefully find a cure. Right Ryan this is where the story gets really funny," Ryan shrugs his shoulders, puts his hands under his chin and pretends to be interested," ok mom carry on." "Then one of the spaceships lands on earth, its pilot who is bright blue then jumps out of his spaceship to start his quest. Not very long into his quest the bright blue pilot meets a little 6 year old boy walking his dog called Benji. Who are you asking the bright blue pilot, I'm Tommy and this is my little Jack Russell called Benji. What's your name asked little Tommy, my name is Zaaarow ... Zaaarow then stars telling Tommy all about his home and his frantic quest to save it. Then suddenly Benji starts barking and playfully jumping around knocking poor little Tommy to the floor. With that Zaaarow lets out an enormous bellow, his bright blue little body glowing and shimmering as purple bubbles erupt from his blue quivering mouth, a little startled Tommy jumps back and stubs his big toe on a root of a tree. Zaaarow laughs and laughs, the more he laughs, the more, big purple bubbles explode from his mouth. Tommy, I think I've found the cure ...... it's you Tommy, the cure is you. Please come back with me to my home Planet and teach everyone how to laugh again. Tommy says yes and into the spaceship they go on an unbelievable adventure of a lifetime but the best thing about the film is!!! Ed Sheeran, you know the most famous pop star and my all-time favourite, from England in the entire world, he is the voice of Zaaarow !! ....

What do you think about the movie Ryan, I told you it was funny." "Yes, mom it does sound a little funny, I suppose I'll go. That is funny mom you mentioned Ed Sheeran, you know he is doing a concert at the George Floyd Stadium on this coming Saturday." "I know Ryan I would of loved to have gone but we couldn't get any tickets. I shouldn't tell you this, but dad tried his hardest to get a pair of tickets, but 87 thousand tickets were sold out within 2 hours. So, Ed being Ed put on an early Saturday afternoon concert but that sold out this time within an hour of going on sale." "Please mum don't tell dad that I told you," "I won't tell your dad, I promise" ... ah bless Richard he has got a heart after all." Now Ryan about the cinema, do not mention it ok, mums the word, until I can surprise Charley later" ... Shona takes a second to remember what her and Ryan were talking about before Charley barged into the kitchen ...." Ryan, I understand all that you have said, I do understand love, we can sit down with your dad and hatch out a plan, sound good," "yes ok mom, that sounds good." "Right Ryan early you mentioned that there was more than one thing on your mind, so come on, we are sat here just the two of us, if there is anything still troubling you ... I can help, I know I am only your mother, but you can talk to me."

After gathering his thoughts and taking a deep breath ...." ok mum there is something, it might sound a little silly, but it has upset me a little bit. I know you and dad don't really do social media but about three weeks ago a horrible story appeared on the social network platform about a woman called Tina. Her name was Tina Smith and she died, she was only 28 years old, according to the reports it wasn't an ordinary death. They say she was eaten from the inside out by enormous black African spiders, then they said that tiny baby spiders came pouring out of her dead body and there was blood everywhere. The doctors that were there all made horrifying reports of everything that they had witnessed. They even took Tina's boyfriend Sam down to the police station and questioned him about his girlfriend's death for two days. Well mom social media had a field day, for every one person who believed the story there were 20 who trashed it, its rubbish, fake news, the boyfriend killed her, she was a hooker, and some nasty people were even posting that she deserved to die. After the police let Sam go without any charges social media crucified him. Hounding him saying that he didn't love Tina, that he was a girlfriend beater. The story was only online for two days before it was taken down. And mom it did really upset me but when we were all back home on Sunday the story reappeared. This time someone, allegedly, had got hold of Tina's autopsy report and had published all the grisly details back online.

The usual people have dismissed the story but mom, what has really upset me was, Tina's boyfriend Sam. He had got so much abuse from those awfully people online, he had got to the end of his tether. One week to the day of his girlfriend's death, I think mom that was supposed to be the day him and Tina were to be married ...... Sam was found hanging in their apartment, he had killed himself !!! just leaving a short simply note on the bedside table, it read .... to my beloved little pudding, I am on my way. Your Sam" ..." That is a very sad story Ryan but there is always going to be lots of nasty, vindictive people in this world, unfortunately that's part of our modern day life, being on that internet can't be doing you any good, I am so glad you have stopped it for now but ...... African spiders roaming around killing people, even I think that's got to be fake news." Giving Ryan a big loving hug, reassures her sensitive young son that everything will be fine, that life has a way of sorting things out." Come on Ryan let's get you all off to bed, don't forget we are all having a fabulous day out at the cinema tomorrow morning," giving Ryan a playful dig in the ribs. "Come on son, you will enjoy the cinema I promise. "Walking into the living room arm in arm," come on Charley, bed time." "Oh mom, can I just finish watching" ...." no, come on, its bed time." The rest of the Kirk family slowly climbed the stairs and with a loving kiss on the cheek they are all tucked up into their nice warm cosy beds for night.

SALLY WAINWRIGHT

Sally is 48 years old, she has never been married or had any children, but she once had a boyfriend and didn't much like it. Sally is a hard working woman and she has worked her way up the corporate ladder. With a 30 year career at a company called central maintenance which is used to maintain schools, hospitals and office buildings. Sally started her career as an office secretary but with an excellent work ethic and a mind for impeccable organization she has risen to the second most senior position in the regional offices, personal assistant to the operations manager. Sally loves her job, organizing, filing, making sure everyone is in the right place, with the correct tools, at the allotted time. About 5 years ago when Amazon Global subsidiary company amz-hydro power started installing all the hydro sub stations on

Manhattan Island which power everything from homes to businesses, Sally's company which is based in Harlem was taken over, rebranded and is now called hydro substation maintenance. Sally's sole job is to make sure all the sub stations are fully operational at all times.

It was 5.30 on a Friday morning and Sally's alarm is sounding. Quickly opening her eyes, its Friday she thought, it my long weekend off. All employees who work for Amazon Global in whatever capacity are given a long weekend off once a month and this weekend was Sally's. Into the shower, cleaned her teeth, now stood in her bedroom deciding what to wear? Sally was an odd woman, she always felt that she didn't fit in. People saw Sally as a strange quirky spinster, she also had her own sense of style. With her jet black bobbed sixties hairstyle and her thick black rimmed glasses, she dressed more like an old fashioned head teacher. With no family to speak of and not really any friends, just work colleagues to speak to but Sally was happy, happy with her job, happy in her little cosy apartment and happy with life generally. After getting herself dressed and putting on her suede flat moccasins it was off to the kitchen for a nice hot cup of coffee. Sipping her hot drink, Sally's mind slowly drifts away, sitting there smiling thinking about all the erotic, naughty, sexual things that she has planned for this coming Saturday evening party. Putting her empty coffee cup into the sink it was time to head off to work, luckily work was only a 15 minute stroll away. Sally normal worked long hours, sometimes she would also work a Saturday or a Sunday shift if they were short.

But Sally didn't mind because she really enjoyed her job and second, she had no one to go home to. It was 6.55am and Sally was walking through her works reception," morning chip how was the night shift?" "Yes, good Sally nothing to report all quite out there last night." "That's the way I like it chip, no problems for me to sort out, especially as it is my long weekend off starting today and I will be out of here by 12 o'clock on the dot." The day ran very smoothly and before Sally had chance to blink it was 12 o'clock, mmmm no work until 7am on Monday. After saying goodbye to everyone on her way out Sally's thoughts turn to her special meal that evening.

Sally normally eats rubbish food all week, sandwiches, Chinese, hotdogs, bagels etc., lots of sugary, salty, fatty foods that are not really good for you but amazingly Sally still had a well-toned body. After collecting her obligatory bottle of white wine, Sally then called to all her favourite little shops. She now had enough ingredients to make her late mother's show stopper!! Chicken and bacon lasagne, with homemade chapati garlic bread and a crisp green salad. Feeling very pleased with herself and eagerly looking forward to her scrumptious evening meal Sally heads home. As Sally reaches the steps to her apartment block one of the residents is slowly struggling to descend down them. It was Britney, she was being helped down the steps by her mother Rose. Rose had Britney in one hand and a large bag in the other. Looking up Sally smiles," hi Britney," "hi Rose off anywhere nice." Speaking in a very anxious voice Rose explains to Sally that Britney has been having some contractions and they were off to the hospital next door. "Gosh you're looking a lot bigger since the last time I saw you Britney," gasps Sally," I know, I am only 8 months gone but I feel like a big fat heifer and I'm not ready to drop yet." Sally lets them pass and wishes them the best of luck. God I am so very glad that I have never been pregnant, Britney is a lovely young girl with a beautiful African American complexion, but she looks ready to explode. Smiling Sally climbs the steps, enters the lobby and stands holding her wonderful evening feast waiting for the elevator to decent.

After a few moments the door opens and in she steps, pressing number 15 on the control panel, mmmmmm nearly home, a whole weekend off and I can't wait for my illicit rendezvous on Saturday night. As the elevator doors slowly, close Sally was away with the fairies, smiling, dribbling, fantasizing about her monthly get together. When suddenly an arm protrudes through the almost closed elevator door." Hold the lift," it was Brad, he is a lovely 64 year old man who lives directly above Sally's apartment. "Oh, Brad, you startled me, I was miles away," "that's ok Sally how have you been keeping." "Yes, I'm good, same old! How about you Bradley," "Bradley, who's Bradley, you know I like to be called Brad" raising up his shoulders, straightening his back, a cheeky smirk on his face," my name is Brad ... after Brad Pitt Sally, it is a shame he is no longer with us" "I know Brad, I was only teasing, how is the wife these days, still driving you mad is she." "Driving me mad!! This is the fourth time I have been out today," "what has she got you picking up this time Brad?" ... Raising his arm, waiving a little white and blue box around ..." bloody haemorrhoid cream." Both laughing, the lift arrives at Sally's floor." You take care Brad and don't forget to say hello to Gene for me when you get home," "ok Sally will do, you have a good day." Still chuckling when Sally reaches her door, ah Brad and Gene are a lovely couple, they are both only about 5 foot 1, they look so sweet together and Bradley is always smartly dressed in his dark grey three piece suit. I bet Gene is always driving him mad, but I think he worships the ground she walks on.

Opening her door, then quickly inside, closing it gently behind her. mmmm my long weekend starts now she thought, let's go and unpack all my wonderful delights. Walking into her open plan kitchen, putting her bags onto the kitchen table she delves deep inside, one cooked chicken, smoked bacon, onions, pasta sheets, my late mother's secret ingredients?? And of course, my lovely bottle of wine. Sally put the wine straight into the fridge, right she said, Sally often spoke out loud to herself, she had lived on her own for basically, forever and was used to just talking, talking out loud. Putting all the ingredients neatly on the kitchen table Sally makes a start. While she chops the onions Sally then plans the rest of her Friday. It's 12.50pm now, it will take me about 25 minutes to prepare the lasagne, then I'll have a spot of lunch. I need to tidy the apartment and then have a lovely long soak in the bath with plenty of bubbles, plus shave all my hairy wobbly bits. Before long Sallys beautiful lasagne was ready with lashings of soft yellow cheese scattered on the top. I must say myself, that looks absolutely scrummy, putting it in the fridge to be cooked later. Putting the kettle on and making herself a light lunch, Sally then sits at the little kitchen table, staring out of her large window, watching all the doctors and nurses scurrying around in the hospital opposite. Eating her food and sipping on her cup of coffee, Sally drifted away dreaming about tomorrow night's salacious activities.

Meanwhile ....

In the apartment directly above Sally, Brad and his wonderful nagging wife Gene were just finishing their lunch. Brad and Gene had met 46 years ago. Gene was working in a newspaper stand, she was only a slip of a girl, a shy 18 year old trying to make a living. Brad, Bradley back then, worked as a trainee mechanic, also 18 and full of beans. Walking to work one day he spotted Gene in her newspaper stand happily chatting away to her customers, my god he thought, I wouldn't mind a bit of that, she is absolutely gorgeous. With her flaming red hair and her hour glass sumptuous body, our young impetuous Bradley was hooked. So, every day Bradley would go and buy a newspaper, hoping Gene would notice him. Bradley never read the papers, he just used to put them in the garage office for customers to look at. After 3 weeks of buying unnecessary newspapers, Bradley finally summoned up the courage to speak to her."

Hello my name is Bradley, can I ask your name?" "I'm Gene" she giggled, tossing her long flaming hair from side to side, from that moment on they were inseparable. Getting married a year later, now 45 years on, they only have one child a little girl called Ruby, not so little now she is 30 and works as a news reporter in New York city. They are both retired, and they have never left one another's side. Brad is washing up the lunch dishes like he always did, Gene is in the living room watching her usual afternoon program on television," BRADLEY ... BRADLEY don't leave any Marks on those plates," "I won't dear, do I ever," a few minutes later, "BRADLEY... BRADLEY don't forget to put the trash out," "I've already done it my sweet." 5 minutes later BRADLEY ... BRADLEY .... BRADLEY," yes dear, ""don't forget I'm having my hair done tomorrow morning so you can tidy up while I'm out." Drying his hands as he walked into the living room," don't worry about anything Gene it will all be spick and span by the time you get home." Sitting down next to his beautiful wife Brad and Gene sit on the sofa watching TV together, there is nowhere else in the world they would rather be, than sat side by side together.

Meanwhile ....

At the hospital Britney has been seen by the doctor, the baby isn't coming yet but as a precaution they have asked Britney to stay in overnight." Mom, I don't want to stay here on my own, I'm only 16 and I've never been away from you before, I'm scared." "Listen here Britney, the doctor has said that you and the baby are ok, they want to keep you in overnight so they can monitor the baby's progress. You have got your bag, you will be fine Britney, your 16 now and you need to stand on your own two feet a bit more and stop relying on me." "But mom I'm frightened, is it going to hurt when I give birth." "You should of thought of that before you dropped your knickers my girl, for 16 years I have fed and looked after you and this is the thanks I get. Anyway, Britney I can't be doing with this, I have got bingo tonight so I will leave you in peace." "Mom don't go please, please mom" ..." No Britney, I will phone the hospital in the morning to see what time they are letting you out and I will see you then." As her mother leaves the porters arrive to take Britney to the ward," will I only be staying here for one night" asks a teary Britney," I don't know "replies the porter," you will have to ask the doctor in the morning. Let's just get you settled in." Arriving at the ward Britney is greeted by three other ladies all lying flat on their backs, with all manner of machines binging and bonging. "Hello" asked one," what is your name?" Sniffling and still a little scared," I'm Britney," "you will be ok girl, we are all one big happy family here." As a calmer Britney settles into the ward, the other woman makes her feel at home.

Meanwhile ....

Across the bay In Brooklyn there are three extremely excited young girls, Madison who is 18, twins Lily and Grace both 13. They are going to see Ed Sheeran at the George Floyd stadium in the morning. The twins were only allowed to go without their dad if their big sister Madison takes them. Their dad Eric is very strict, no talking to strangers, make sure you all stay together, straight home afterwards. Eric wanted to take his girls in the car to the stadium, but Madison had convinced him that they would all be safe and could they go on the train. As a compromise Eric said" yes but I will drop and pick you up from the station." Lily and Grace had been on line all week telling all their young friends that they are going to see Ed Sheeran. Eric always worries about his three little precious girls, their mother had died when the twins were only two, in a hit and run and ever since then Eric has been obsessed with keeping them all safe. This will be the first time ever that all three girls will be out without their dad to protect them, and Eric is duly concerned. "Girls dinner is ready" ... dad, dad, dad," calm down girls I know your excited," "yes dad we've been telling all our friends about tomorrow and we can't wait." "Well girls dinners on the table, let's sit and have a nice meal and don't forget it will be an early night tonight, we are all up at 8am so we can get ready." Sitting around the table was Eric's favourite time, him and his wonderful three little girls.

Meanwhile ....

Back at Sally's apartment it was almost 5.30pm and nearly time for Sally's long hot bubbly soak but first she had to go into the bedroom and sort out her costume for tomorrow night's event. Standing staring at all the different outfits in her closet, what shall I wear, who will I become!!! Sally had lots of strange and wonderful things to wear at these ... so called parties but who shall I be this week. Ah I know, I'll be Lady Scarlet. On her knees digging through her bulging naughty closet, as she called it, Sally selects all the items that makes up Lady Scarlet persona, folding them neatly and putting everything on the chair in the corner of the bedroom. Smiling and contented Sally strolls into the bathroom, putting loads of lovely bubble bath into the tub she turns the hot water tap on full blast. Leaving the bath to fill Sally turns her attention to her scrumptious dinner. Turning the oven on to warm, Laying the table and then she thinks .... wine, it's got to be time for wine!! Taking the now chilled bottle out of the fridge Sally pours herself a well-deserved glass, mmmm that's nice. Setting the ovens time for 40 minutes Sally pops in her heavenly lasagne. Taking her crisp cold glass of wine with her to the now full bathtub, adding a little cold water, Sally strips off and slides beneath the bubbles. Lying there slowly sipping her lovely glass of wine she says, right Sally you have got 40 minutes before the oven pings, wash, shave, soak, you can do it Sally. Smiling to herself, I think I will have a nice soak first ahhhh.

Meanwhile ....

At the Kirks it is Friday early evening, and everyone is home, Shona is over the sink, again, washing up all the pots after the family's meal and Richard is having a lovely hot shower after a long week away. Ryan is in his bedroom talking on the phone to one of his mates and Charley in the corner of the kitchen nagging her mother for some ice cream." Come on mom I need some ice cream I'm starving," "you're not starving Charley you have only just had your dinner." "But mom I'm a growing girl and I need more food," "ok then there are biscuits in the cupboard," "no mom not that kind of food, ice cream food." "Just wait, let me get these dishes done and then we'll see." "Dad would let me," "your dads in the shower and I'm in charge of the kitchen, so you will have to wait." Just then with his hair still wet Richard walks into the kitchen," dad, dad mom said I can have some ice cream." "No, I didn't Charley, stop winding your dad up, just go and watch some telly for a bit, I need to talk to your dad." "Ok mom but I'll still need ice cream later," "ok darling we'll see, just let me speak to your father." Shona washes the last of the dishes, while Richard walks up behind her putting his arms around her waist," how are you my little honey bun?" As he slides his hands up under her top and caresses both breasts at once." Are you feeling horny, I am my little Shonie, I've had a long hard week." "Let us sort the kids out first, then we'll see." "No Shona that is what you say to the kids, we'll see!! Come on, I haven't see you all week. Ok, is that ok we will or ok we'll, see?" "Richard it's ok we will, let's just decide about telling Charley about her special day out at the cinema." Smiling Richard spins Shona around getting soap suds everywhere, pulling her in close and giving her a long sumptuous kiss." Richard, I think we should tell Charley about the cinema in the morning, she will be too excited to sleep if we tell her tonight." "Ok Shona, if you think that's best .... but I really wanted to tell her tonight, I'm excited too and I can't wait to see the look on her little face." "No, I think the morning will be best." "Please I've been away all week, I just want to tell my little darling girl ... please ... sad face .... very sad face ... please my little Shonie." "Ok then you can tell her" ... shouting... "Charley, Ryan I need to see you in the kitchen, come on Charley, where is Ryan!!" Ryan and Charley enter the kitchen," let us all sit around the kitchen table. "Ryan comes sloping over, slumps down on the chair, folds his arms and has this nonchalant look on his face. I know what's coming he thinks, a family day out at the cinema watching a kiddies film, how very exciting!!

Charley on the other hand comes bouncing over to her seat, a little apprehensive and slightly intrigued to what her dad wants them all for." What have I done this time dad," Charley asks! "Nothing my darling girl." All four of them gathered around the kitchen table waiting intently, impatiently for dad to start one of his lectures." Right my lovely children, your mother and I have organized a family day out tomorrow" ... with that Charley's sits up in her chair, leaning forward and putting her arms onto the table."

A day out dad," inquires Charley grinning like a Cheshire cat, Richard then leans forward himself and puts his arms onto the table, looking directly into the slightly excited eyes of his very impatient daughter ..." we are all going to the .... museum tomorrow!!!" SILENCE........ Shona trying her best not to laugh or grin too much and Ryan sat there rolling his eyes, looking up to the heavens. "The museum dad" her little face starting to crumple, her voice croaky and disappointed. "The museum are you being serious, oh dad that sounds rubbish, you know I hate going to places like that, it's boring." "Come on Charley it will be brilliant, theirs paintings !! umm .... sculptures !! umm loads of things to do and look at. You will really enjoy it. "By now Charley's whole body is bitterly disappointed, her shoulders are slumped, her arms are dangling down towards the floor, her face ... her little face looks sooooo sad." Come on Richard stop messing around and put the poor girl out of her misery!!!" "Ok Shona" ... smiling looking intently into his daughter's distraught face, "Charley .... I'm joking, we are not going to the museum!!!!"

Sitting up once more, the smile starting to re-emerge onto Charley's sad little face," seriously dad, no museum !!" "Yes, Charley we are not going to the museum. We are going to the ....!!!!! Before I tell you I just want to change the subject for a minute," "oh dad I hate it when you always do this, just tell me." "In a minute Charley, your mother" ... Charley is sat with her arms folded, with half a pitiful smile on her dumbfounded face ... still waiting for her dad to stop going on and on and get to the point ... "your mom was telling me that there is a new movie coming out soon in the cinemas that you wanted to see !!! something about fluffy purple burps or something." Charley starts rolling with laughter, putting her little hands over her mouth," oh dad you make me laugh so much, a movie about fluffy BURPS!!!" Composing herself ...." yes, dad it's a movie about" ... Charley had totally changed now, sat on the edge of the chair, smiling, being very animated, waiving her little arms about, all excited about this new movie that she wants to go and see ... little furry creatures called the Zooodons , "they look amazing dad, all assorted colours, little like me with little wobbly arms and little wobbly legs and the main character is called Zaaarow and he's got a wife and two cuddly ... oh dad, adorable tiny little children called Zaaanin and Zaaabin ..... and when the Zooodons laugh big purple bubbles explode from their mouths." Still laughing," not fluffy purple burps dad, you make me laugh so much dad."

After Charley calms down she leans forward once more putting her hands back onto the table, with an inquisitive look on her face !!" right dad can you get to the point." Poor old Ryan is still sat there with his arms tightly crossed thinking ... come on dad just tell her and stop winding Charley up like you normally do, God I wish I were 18. Shona pipe's up, "come on Richard put the poor girl out of her misery!! Tel her where we are going tomorrow??" With an enormous grin on his face Richard looks deep into his daughter's bemused eyes .... "Right Charley where we are going Tomorrow ... mmmm .. ok Charley you know the Zooodons" !!!" Yeeees dad "......." we are all going to the cinema tomorrow to watch THEM!!!!!!!!." Charley is still learning forward, with her hands resting on the table, her eyes slightly squinted and her mouth half open." Are you being serious dad!!" "Yes, Charley I am, seriously!! Yes, Charley I'm being serious." "Mom is dad being serious this time," "yes, my darling girl, your dad is being serious" ....!!!!! "The Zooodons, the Zooodons," leaping out of her chair Charley starts running around the kitchen shouting the Zooodons, the Zooodons , running around to her mom, Charley gives her a giant monster hug, while kissing her on the cheek, whispering," mom is dad being serious!!" "Yes, Charley he is." "Yippee, yippee we are all going to the cinema" while spinning around and around and still around. Ryan then stands up," can I go now!!" And off he went. After Charley's stopped spinning, she runs and jumped onto her dad's lap," thank you dad."

After planting a big sloppy kiss on her dad's lips Charley walks slowly towards the kitchen door. "I can't wait to tell all my friends that I'm going to see the Zooodons tomorrow" .... suddenly Charley stops and burst out laughing and laughing, tears rolling down her little happy face, holding her sides leaning backwards and forwards. Shona and Richard looked at each other, shrugging their shoulders!!! Trying to speak through the laughter," dad now that you are taking me to see the Zooodons, you know that you'll have to buy me all the Zooodon goodies." Looking a little puzzled ..." what Zooodon goodies?" "You know dad, Zooodon lunchbox, water bottle, rucksack, pencil case, you know dad Zooodon stuff but don't forget the most important things .... The Zooodon stuffed toys, lots of them all different colours !!!" Charley continued laughing as she skips out of the kitchen. Richard turns to Shona and this time he had a serious look on HIS face!!!!" You never said anything about merchandising," laughing she said," that will teach you for teasing poor little Charley." Slowly the Kirk's all disperse to all four corners of the house enjoying the rest of the evening.

Meanwhile ....

Sally has finally washed and shaved all of her womanly crevices apart from a little tuft of hair just above her clitoris, which she likes to play with when she is having her womanly private time. Sally is having her last relaxing soak while sipping the last of her lovely refreshing glass of wine. Pinga ling .... Pinga ling .... Pinga ling oh well, time to get out, that's the alarm on the oven sounding, that was a quick 40 minutes Sally thought. No time to waist, by now Sally was absolutely starving and the smell wafting through the apartment was divine. Out of the bath she jumped, then rapping a white fluffy towel around herself, slipping on some comfy white slippers it was off to the kitchen to take out her beautiful lasagne. Putting the hot lasagne onto a wooden chopping board Sally then turns the oven up and pops in her home made garlic bread. Right, she said, 10 minute's and everything will be ready mmmm I can't wait. I just have time to dry and powder myself, PJs on then dinner. As Sally exits her bedroom feeling all clean, fresh and cosy in her PJs her doorbell rings.

Who could this be!!! I never get visitors. Putting her pink and white dressing gown on as she walks to the door wondering who it could be. Peeping through the peep hole, Sally sees a young woman stood there, who is that she thought!! Putting the chain across the door, Sally opens it slightly," hello can I help you?" "Hello sorry to bother you, I am Simone, I have just moved in across the hall from you." With a smile, Sally closes the door, taking the chain off and opens it fully. "Hello Simone my name is Sally, would you like to come in." "Oh yes please," closing the door behind them Simone enters the apartment," oh Sally your home is lovely, and something smells beautiful." Before Sally had chance to answer .... Pinga ling .... Pinga ling." Excuse me a second Simone, that's my oven timer going off, please take a seat." After taking the home made garlic bread out and turning off the oven, Sally then joins Simone on the sofa. "So, Simone what brings you to my door tonight?" "To be honest Sally, yours was the first door I knocked, I am after a screwdriver if you have got one? I am trying to put a chest of drawers together." "Yes, Simone I have got some tools, I'll just go and dig them out for you."

Handing her new neighbour, a small bag, Sally explains," there is a couple of screwdrivers, a hammer and some bits and Bob's in here, just use what you need and then give them back to me when you have finished." "Thank you so much Sally, these will come in very handy, I won't keep them long." "Simone keep them for as long as you need them. Anyway, Simone what brings you to our humble neighbourhood," smiling and feeling more at ease." Well Sally I only moved in this morning, and this is a new start for me. I was actually born here in Harlem, but my parents moved away when I was only three. I have been training to become a veterinary nurse, I have already done over two years at college, but an opening became available at the animal sanctuary here in the new Harlem village, so I jumped at the chance. I can still do my studying and I also get hands on experience. What do you do Sally?" "I work for Amazon hydro power, making sure all the sub stations are fully serviced and running efficiently." "I work for Amazon too Sally !!" "I don't know if you are aware Simone, but Amazon owns most of this new complex." "I didn't Sally, but I feel I have taken too much of your time up, it has been very nice to meet you Sally and I'll get your tools back as soon as I can." "That's ok Simone," Sally thinks, I don't get many visitors, especially ones as nice as Simone.

Simone is a lovely sweet young lady, her family originate from Egypt, if you ever wondered what Cleopatra looked like, you only have to look into Simone's beautiful little face to imagine it. With her long dark black flowing hair and her sumptuous, mesmerizing smile, Simone is a truly beautiful young girl ... "Simone have you eaten today?" "No not really Sally, I've been unpacking boxes most of the day." "Right then Simone you can stay and have dinner with me, I always cook too much anyway, and you are more than welcome to join me. I know that we have only just met one another Simon but I feel that I have known you for years not minutes, I'm so comfortable around you, plus we can finish off our chat and I can tell you more about our new village." "Yes, Sally I feel exactly the same, it's uncanny. I would love to stay and have dinner with you Sally, I am a little hungry." "Ok then, take a seat at the table by the window and I will dish up." As Sally dishes the food ..." How old are Simone?" "I'm 23 Sally, I am not asking how old you are Sally, not until I've had my dinner anyway!!!" "No Simone don't ask, I haven't got enough candles anymore."

Sally and Simone both laugh, putting the lasagne, garlic bread and crisp green salad on the table, Sally sits down and joins Simone. "Thank you, Sally this looks and smells absolutely amazing, can I ask what it is?" "Of course, you can, it is my late mother's famous chicken and bacon lasagne." "I have never heard of a chicken and bacon lasagne before, but I can't wait to tuck in ... Mmmm Sally this is heavenly, and the garlic bread is lovely too." "Your very welcome Simone, I'm glad you like it." "I didn't realise Sally that your kitchen window was directly opposite the hospital, from here you can see everything." "Yes, I sometimes sit with a coffee and just watch all the nurses and doctors scurrying around, I find it relaxing. The hospital is called The Royal Archie Memorial, named after prince Harry's son Archie. Have you heard of prince Harry of England Simone?" "Only a little Sally," "well going back many years ago, a young prince Harry married an American actor called Megan, they had two beautiful children, a boy called Archie and a lovely little girl called Lilibet. Harry fell out with his Royal family and moved his family to America, he then lost some of his Royal titles. Some people said that he was more interested in making money, rather than being a royal, especially with the privileged education and upbringing he had been given but most people around the world thought he was a good man just looking after his family. Anyway about 7 years ago Archie was rushed into hospital with a life threatening illness, for weeks Harry sat by his son's bedside terrified that he was going to die. There was a rumour that one night Harry held his sons hand and prayed to God ... please God, please save my son and I will be a better man. A few days later, Archie became well again and Harry, now back to being prince Harry. As promised, he had turned into a nicer man, made up with his estranged family. His brother Prince William, now his Royal highness King William of England has bestowed all of his former titles back upon his brother. Prince Harry over these later years has created some wonderful things, helping millions of people all around the world and this hospital in Harlem in conjunction with Amazon Global is just one of those amazing things that he has accomplished. Prince Harry and his wonderful family raise millions of dollars each year, all to make ordinary people's lives better, I have always loved the British Royal family, most Americans do."

"Sally that was one of the best homemade meals I have ever had, people don't normally cook these days, it's all take out, fast food." "I know Simone, I eat rubbish food all the time but once a month on my long weekend off I always cook myself a fresh homemade meal. Do you fancy a glass of wine Simone," "thank you Sally that would be lovely." Sally pours two glasses of wine while they talk more about the village." Yes, Simone I think you'll enjoy working and living here, there is so much right on our doorstep, restaurants, lots of wine bars, shops, bowling, cinemas and the people here are so friendly. Have you seen the new George Floyd stadium yet?" "Only from the ground floor Sally, it looks enormous." "Simone you are in for a real treat, come into my bedroom." Sally and Simone walk into the bedroom, "oh Sally your bedroom is lovely, I hope mine is half as nice as this once I've opened all the boxes scattered about the place." "Right Simone come and stand by the window and close your eyes, come on you can trust me, it will be worth it I promise. The stadium was named after George Floyd, the man who died by the hands of the police all of them years ago." "Yes, I know Sally we were taught about George Floyd in school, I am so glad that people are more equal today" .... Swishing back the curtains," you can open now!!!" "Wow I see what you mean Sally, you can see right into the stadium from up here, it looks amazing, it's so big and all those lights WOW!! and you have a balcony too, I am so jealous." "Sometimes Simone I sit on my balcony with a coffee, or a glass of wine and I just watch and listen, it's like I'm in the stadium. Do you know that Ed Sheeran is playing two gigs in there tomorrow." "Yes, Sally I have heard but I'll be working all day tomorrow, let's just hope my boss has got the radio on."

As they are about to leave the bedroom Simone notices something peculiar on a chair in the corner of the room, "Sally I hate to be nosey but what are those!!" pointing at the neatly folded garments on the chair. Getting a little flustered and going slightly red in the face, "ah mmm they are my dressing up clothes Simone." Sally has never had to explain her erotic outfits to anyone before, she feels a little uneasy and to be honest a little TURNED on too. "Well Simone I like to dress up, I have lots of different personas to choose from and that there is my Lady Scarlet outfit." "I'm intrigued !!! go on Sally put them on for me," "no Simone I couldn't, I only ever wear them when I am at a party." "A party" says Simone," what kind of party? Please Sally I know we have only just met each other but I feel that I've known you for ever, we seem to get on so well." Sally has never ever worn any of her sexy, daring, salacious outfits in front of anyone outside a party environment before, especially a total stranger!!! But the thought of it was truly turning Sally on," ok Simone, I'll do it. Go and pour me a large glass of wine and I will be out in few minutes .... Are you ready Simone," "yes Sally I'm ready, come on I can't wait to see what you look like." The bedroom door slowly opens and out steps Sally wearing deep red knee high boots, with 6 inch heels and black glossy laces that fasten zigzagged up the front, deep red Crotch less knickers, a deep red shimmering hooded Cape just long enough to cover her modesty with the opening of the cape running down the middle of her luscious body revealing her ample cleavage, a flaming red long curly wig and a deep red jewel studded masquerade mask. Strutting slowly around the living room putting her hands on her hips ... "hello Simone I'm Lady Scarlet nice to meet you." "Oh my god!!! Lady Scarlet, you look absolutely fabulous, I wouldn't have the guts to wear something that sexy, but you look positively gorgeous."

After a short strut around the living room Sally quickly returns to the bedroom. Within a few moments Sally re-emerges from her bedroom back in her comfy PJs. Flopping onto the sofa next to Simone the two girls laugh and laugh, still giggling." I can't believe I've just done that Simone, no one outside of the group as ever seen me as Lady Scarlet, or any other persona come to that." "Sally, I don't mean to pry but you keep mentioning the party, the group, can I ask what exactly you do as Lady Scarlet." Taking a very large gulp of wine Sally explains." Well Simone, you might not think it to look at me but ... I'll just say it as it is ... Once a month on my long weekend off I like to dress up and go to this luxury mansion, members only mind and I get well and truly fucked by lots of different men." Simone's mouth falls open, her eyes wide with amazement," Sally ...... Sally, I don't know what to say, you have totally shocked me. You mean you let strange men have sex with you !!" "No Simone it's not as seedy as that, all the men and us women are vetted first, and nothing happens unless it is consensual. Then and only then are we free to fuck, the faster and the harder the better." Smiling," I know people might judge me Simone, I love having sex, but I hate the thought of having any kind of boyfriend, God forbid a bloody husband." Falling around laughing the two women were having a great night." I really enjoy your company Simone, I am so very glad that you've moved in, I think we will be good friends." "Yes, Sally I feel the same, I feel like I have known you for ages." "More wine Simone?" "Yes, please Sally, I'm glad I knocked on your door, I'm having a great night ... better than opening bloody boxes!!" As Sally and Simone settled back putting the world to rights, their evening was ticking along nicely.

Meanwhile ....

Upstairs directly above Sally Brad was in the kitchen making himself and Gene, a nice hot mug of coco." BRADLEY .... BRADLEY Don't forget the biscuits, you know the ones with the cream in the middle." "Yes, dear I have already taken them out and yes before you shout, I've put them on a plate." I don't know why she moans about the crumbs, she doesn't even do the bloody hoovering. Placing the tray with the biscuits and mugs of hot coco on the living room table," here you are dear, be careful the coco is hot." "Thank you, Bradley, you do look after me," "yes dear let's just sit back and enjoy our coco and biscuits," he thinks to himself, in bloody peace. Sat there watching TV drinking coco, eating biscuits quite content in each other's company." BRADLEY" ..." There is no need to shout Gene I'm only sat here, what is it." "I'm having my hair done in the morning and I have forgotten what time it is, could you go and check." "Ok dear," Brad goes back into the kitchen and looks at the appointment card that is pinned to the cork notice board. After grabbing a few more cheeky biscuits out of the packet he returns to his seat." Your hair appointment is at 10.45, I will make sure that you are up and ready for then, ok dear," "thank you Bradley." Just then Brad's phone rings," who's that calling you at this time of night." "Give me a chance Gene and I'll go and have a look. Its Ruby" Brad shouts over," hello darling how are you?" "I'm good dad, I thought I would call just to see how you both are?" "Yes, Ruby we are fine" ...." BRADLEY .... BRADLEY pass me the phone" ...." I can hear mom is her normal self-dad," "yes, she is Ruby, I'll just pass you over to her, love you," "love you dad." "Hello Ruby love its mom, how are you keeping?" "Yes, mom I'm fine, how is that leg of yours, is it still playing you up?" "It's not too bad Ruby love, I don't complain!! Anyway, how is your young man, what's his name again?" "Oh, you mean Edward, yes Edward is fine, it's still early days yet mom. I don't get to see him very often at the moment, he is always flying around in that little helicopter of his reporting on the weather, but we are getting on ok. Right mom I have to go, I will catch up with you and dad next week, give my love to dad." "Ok Ruby stay safe, love you," "yes and

I love you to mom." Brad and Gene cosy up on the sofa and enjoy the rest of the evening with one another.

Meanwhile ....

At the hospital young Britney is settling into the ward, she feels a little scared and alone, but the three older women are trying to keep her spirits up. They are all lying flat on their backs with wires and tubes sticking out everywhere, machines binging and bonging all over the place. Britney is the only one who is there just for overnight observation, the others have different types of operations planned. The three women take turns SHOUTING advice, so Britney doesn't feel so alone......" Britney your first baby is always the hardest!!" "No, it's not, my 3rd was a nightmare!!" "You've only had 3," "I've pushed 4 of those horrible buggers out!! Your bodies is never the same again!!" "I know, stretch marks everywhere!!" Someone says stretch marks," my stomach is like the surface of the moon!! And don't forget your tits, painful and oozing with milk, it's like being in a permanent wet t-shirt competition!!" "I know, there was a time when I couldn't hold a pencil under my breasts but now, I can hold the entire bloody pencil case!!" Lots of cackling going on and lots and lots of laughing. The more the women shout out, the more Britney sinks into her pillow, even more scared than she was before ... "And don't mention the stitches, it feels like someone has cut you open from hole to hole with a rusty old power saw!!" "And did I mention my flaps" ... Britney shouts out," what are flaps?" ... "you know dear, my flaps, my fanny flaps, looking down there you would of thought that Donald duck was poking his bloody beak out of my fanny!! Quack Quack." The whole room bursts out laughing and laughing "and the worst part is ladies, you have just had your baby and then you get to go home ... You have your stretch marks, your enormous leaky tits, stitches from hell, the piles poking out of your arse, Donald duck peeping out of your bloody fanny and then as soon as you walk in the door your fella is at you, come on darling I haven't had it in ages ...... he can just fuck off!!!!" The three women are howling with laughter and poor little Britney is hiding under the covers feeling far worse than when she first came in. The next thing the nurse comes marching in, "come on ladies you are making too much noise, come on calm down, it's time to sleep, the doctor will be around early tomorrow morning." They all agree to settle down and get some rest.

Meanwhile ....

Back at the Kirk's, Richard and Shona are sat on the sofa enjoying some quiet time." Shona do you think Ryan was a little quiet tonight, is there something up with him?" "No Richard I don't think there is anything wrong with Ryan he's just a 16 year old boy going through 16 year old things. Your son is slowly turning into a young man, and he just needs to find his feet. You were evil to Charley earlier, keeping her hanging on like that." "I know I was Shonie, but I can't help myself, it's the only pleasure I have in life, winding my little Charley up, she loves it really and she always gets me back. Right Shona, I think it time to go up the wooden hill, you get yourself ready for bed and I will go and check on the kids." "Ok Richard, I will see you up there." Richard pops his head quietly around Ryan bedroom door ... ah good fast asleep. Richard then slowly and quietly opens Charley's door, but she is not asleep, she is lying there with her little tiered eyes wide open. Richard sits on the bed next to her," come on Charley it's time for sleep." "I can't dad, I am tried but I'm tooooo excited." "I know you are my darling girl, but you need to get to sleep. Come here Charley and give your old dad a big hug" .... squeezing very tightly," Charley you give the best hugs in the world," "no dad you give the best hugs in the world, and you are the best dad in the world too." "Come on then my little girl, give your best dad in the world a big kiss and then it's off to sleep with you." Tucking her in, big hug, big kiss," night night my darling girl, see you in the morning, love you," "love you too dad." "Come on sleep, I'm closing the door now, but I will be back soon to check that you are fast asleep." Yawning," I will dad, see you in the morning, love you."

Meanwhile ....

Sally and Simone had polished off two bottles of wine and they were both a little tiddly." Have you seen the time Sally, its gone 11 o'clock and I've got work in the morning." "I haven't got work in the morning" giggled Sally," I'm having a well-deserved lye in, mmmmm I can't wait." "I tell you what Sally, this has been the best evening in, I have had in my entire life, thank you for making me feel at home." "Your welcome Simone, I have really enjoyed your company and I think we will become good friends," "yes me too Sally." "Come on then Simone let's get you home," opening the front door and giving each other a hug," oh look Sally," pointing her wobbly finger," I only live there "... both giggling, "so you do Simone!!" Sally closes the door after saying good night to her new friend Simone. I think it's off to bed for me. So, Sally gets herself into her cosy, comfy bed and drifted off to sleep.

THE AWAKENING

As the residents of Manhattan Island slept, they were blissfully unaware of the unimaginable horrors that were stirring, awakening right below their feet. When poor terrified Tina was taken to the hospital on that fateful night, the black ...

ugly ... spider had never left her side. For the two weeks after her gruesome attack, the spider had watched and waited in the shadows, following Tina's every move, never a stone's throw away from her tiny black ugly babies growing deep inside of her. Even when Poor Tina was taken to hospital, the black ... ugly ... spider followed. Attaching itself to the underside of the ambulance stretcher as Tina lay on top, screaming in agony. Then scuttling beneath Tina's bed in the hospital itself, eagerly awaiting the emerge of its offspring. Waiting, listening, sensing the arrival of its evil black spawn. As thousands upon thousands of tiny black babies streamed down the blood soaked bed onto the floor, the black ... ugly ... spider, now mommy, was waiting, waiting to whisk her babies away to safety deep underground, until they themselves were fully grown and ready to re-emerge as adults to wreak havoc upon the world. It has been four weeks since Tina's untimely death and it takes four weeks for the tiny black babies to develop into fully fledged terrifying ADULTS!!!!!!!!!!!!!!!!!!!!!!!! JUST LIKE MOMMY.

Saturday 8.10 am

Lily and Grace are in the kitchen eating their breakfast, dad is in the shower and Madison is still in bed." Oh, Grace I can't wait to see Ed Sheeran on that big stage, can you believe we will be right there watching Ed, actually there, not watching him on the TV." "Yes, Lily it's amazing, it won't be long before we are all on the train."

8.22 am

"Morning girls," "morning dad," "where's Madison?" "She is still in bed dad." "Ok girls finish your breakfast, and I will go and wake her. Come on Madison it's time to get up," "sorry dad I'll be right there." The family spend the rest of the morning excitedly getting ready for their fabulous day out.

8.46 am

In the hospital Britney is sat up in bed having her breakfast." How are you feeling today?" one of the other women asks," a little tiered, it was hard to sleep with all the binging and bonging from all those machines, but I feel ok today and there are no more contractions,

I think." "That's good Britney, you will be out of here before you know it. The doctors normally do their rounds by about 9.30 so you should know more then."

8.58 am

Brad and Gene are up, washed and dressed and have already had their breakfast." Right Gene I'm off, I will be about half an hour picking these bits up from the superstore but don't worry love I will be back in plenty of time to walk you down to your hair appointment." "Ok Bradley be safe, and I will see you soon."

9.10 am

The Kirk's are all up and getting themselves ready to go to the cinema." Morning Ryan how are you feeling today?" "I'm ok mom, do I really need to go the cinema today?" "Come on Ryan we all need to go and support your sister, you know that she has been going through a lot recently." "" ok mom." Shona and Ryan then go into the living room and join Charley who is playing on her phone. "Morning mom, morning grumpy Ryan," "Charley stop teasing your brother, he doesn't have to go to the cinema with you today, but he is coming just for you Charley." "Ok mom, sorry grumpy !!" dad enters the room," morning and how is everyone today? Ryan!" "Yes, I'm fine dad." "Charley, are you ok darling? I bet you are all excited" ... Charley doesn't respond," Charley ... Charley," "yes dad." "What is so important on your phone?" "Come here dad let me show you. I have downloaded the new app," "what new app Charley?" "The new Zooodons app dad and its brilliant." Richard looks over towards Shona," and how much did that cost?" Charley pipes up," nothing dad, it's free, for now !! come on dad let me show you what you have to do."

Richard sits and puts his arm around Charley's shoulders, "ok darling I'm watching." "You can play the game on your own but it's better when your friends all link up and play together. Are you watching dad?" "Yes darling," "right dad, basically you have to make the Zooodons laugh, the more they laugh the more the big purple bubbles come out of their wobbly mouths and turn the sky purple. It's great fun dad." "Yes, Charley that does look fun. Right, everyone we all need to be ready by 10.15am because that's what time the taxi is coming to pick us all up." "Why so early Richard?" "Because my darling Shona, for one, there will be loads of traffic going to the stadium to see Ed Sheeran and for two we need to call to the candy shop on the way so we can buy some candy, soda and some popcorn." "RICHARD!!! Stop being so tight, we are not calling at the candy shop, it's Charley's Day and she can have candy from the CINEMA," "whatever her little heart desires but my darling Shona, the cost!!" "Don't my darling me Richard, in fact we can have, whatever all our hearts desire ... because you're paying." "But ..." "but, no Richard, and that's an end to it. Any way you can call this payback for teasing your daughter last night." "Ok Shona, you win, come on the Kirk's, we will all have a great day out." under his breath," no matter the bloody cost."

9.27 am

Sally was slowly stirring, rolling over, Yawning, stretching. Ah my head is splitting, how much wine did I have to drink last night? Lying there gradually coming round her thoughts turn to

Simone. I had a fabulous night last night, Simone is a lovely young girl. She was interesting and fun mmm I think that we will become good friends. Oh, bloody hell … I've just remembered!!! I was prancing around the living room as Lady Scarlet, cheekily grinning, in front of Simone, what was I thinking. The more she thought about it, the more turned on Sally got. Closing her eyes and remembering Lady Scarlet seductively swooning around half naked in front a total stranger!!! God I'm wet, I feel really horny. Sliding her hand down under the covers, her fingers slowly massaging her trim belly. Then down further, placing her hand onto her soft womanly mound while stroking her little spiky tuft. My fanny is soaking …. Stop that Sally, she says out loud, you have tonight to look forward to, so come on let's get the day started. So, Sally dragged her hungover tiered body out of her nice warm bed and staggers straight into the bathroom, a quick shower and I will be right as rain.

9.48 am

Sally is up but still in her PJs sat at her kitchen table drinking a nice hot black mug of coffee.

Ahhhh This will wake me up, looking across at the hospital watching all the people milling around. Sipping her delicious coffee, contemplating all the things that she has to do today!!!

THE BEGINNING OF THE END

The black ugly baby spiders have been hiding away deep in the darkness below, waiting, feeding, growing .... growing big, growing strong. They are fast, they are very intelligent, they are eager to ascend from the depths of the darkness below to destroy our world. Up they come, crawling ever nearer, hundreds of thousands of unstoppable black killing machines. Now fully grown with tiny babies eggs of their own ready to implant into the hapless citizens above!!!!!!! THEY ARE NEARLY HERE.

9.58 am

Back at the hospital Britney has seen the doctor and she has been given the all clear to return home. Sat on her bed with her bag already packed, she sits patiently, waiting for her wonderful, loving mother !! to help her home whenever she can be bothered to turn up. The other women in Britney's room try to reassure her that everything will be alright, having overheard Britney's mothers nasty outburst yesterday. "Don't worry Britney you will be back home before you know it and forget the silly things that we were all prattling on about last night, it was just girl talk." With half a smile Britney nods, she has sat a lifetime waiting for her caring mother to show up.

10.10 am

At the Kirk's everyone is all dressed and ready, waiting for their taxi to arrive. Charley is bouncing up and down," I'm so excited dad, I can't wait to get there." Ryan is stood with his hands nonchalantly in his pockets just going with the flow. Shona is doing her mother hen, making sure everyone is together and happy and Richard is stood there thinking, how much is this little lot going to cost me!! "Come on" Shona shouts," the taxis here." "Yippee" Charley is the first one in," mom, dad, Ryan come on." They all pile in and it's off they go.

10.26 am

The three girls arrive by subway beneath the enormous stadium." Come on Lily and Grace, stay close there are thousands of people here trying to get into the stadium," "yes Madison we will." Joining the hundreds of excited fans up the escalators from the deep subway station beneath the huge stadium to the turnstiles above. After presenting their tickets, they enter the gigantic arena. Wow ... the three of them look around in amazement, this place is spectacular, there are thousands of people everywhere. After fighting their way through the hordes of expecting fans they find their seats. "We are here" they shout," we can't wait" they scream, the excitement building as 87 thousand men, women and children eagerly wait for the man himself, Mr Ed Sheeran to enter the stage.

10.35 am

"Come on then Gene are you ready for your hair appointment." "Yes, Bradley I'm already, please take it nice and easy, my hip is playing me up today," "ok dear I will." Taking Gene gently but firmly by the arm, Bradley guides her into the elevator and onto the street below." Come on dear we will just take a gentle stroll and I will get you there in plenty of time." Walking arm in arm down the busy boulevard Bradley and Gene had spent their entire adult lives together. Inseparable when they first met and still inseparable today, the old couple that were happiest just being together." Right Gene we have arrived, in we go. Just sit here dear and I will tell the lady that you are here." Grabbing Bradley's hand Gene looks up," thank you Bradley, I don't always tell you but thank you." Smiling giving Gene's hand a little squeeze," that's ok dear." Bradley returns from the stylist," Gene the lady says you'll be done by 12 noon, I will come back and pick you up then, ok dear." "Yes, ok Bradley, I will see you then." Smiling at one another Bradley leaves and heads back home.

10.52 am

Sally had spent the entire morning still in her PJs nursing a sore head, two paracetamol and three mugs of strong steaming hot coffee and she's back to her normal self. Sally has washed a few dishes and tidied up a little but nothing too strenuous. Sally is really looking forward to her steamy liaison later on tonight. The one thing that Sally can't get over is how turned on she was, prancing around in front of Simone as Lady Scarlet. She has thought about it all morning and the more she thought about it the wetter she got. Right, come on Sally, let's get those thoughts out of your head, let's do something to take your mind off it. I know it's my long weekend off .... but shall I have a sneaky look at some work emails?? Walking into the bedroom, grabbing her laptop and sitting on the bed, Sally opens it up. Right their staring Sally straight in the face, in the corner of the screen is her favourite porn site. Rocking back and forth, rubbing her interlocked fingers together. Mmm it won't hurt she thought, just a little mess ... The next thing Sally had clicked onto the link, PJs thrown to the floor, then she jumped naked under the covers. Kicking the website into action Sally gazed longingly into the screen. Slipping her eager hands below the covers, Sally started gently rubbing her aroused hard nipples. One nipple in each hand rubbing around and around, then trapping each sensitive nipple between her soft fingers, tightly gripping, pulling outwards, releasing and repeating. Slowly as if by magic, her excited trembling legs started to drift apart all on their own. Moving one of her hands slowly down Sally started playfully caressing her toned, tense belly ......

THE SPIDER'S ARE HERE!!!

The black ugly hairy deadly creatures have finally ascended from the blackness below. Hundreds and thousands are slowly and deliberately infesting every school, hospital, police station, apartment block, every building in a three mile radius of the Royal Archie Memorial. Creeping and crawling under floorboards, up the insides of the walls, every nook and cranny, every tiny little space that they can fit their black terrifying bodies through and still these hideous murderous beings still are out of sight. They are strong, fast, intelligent and highly organised, fanning out, hiding, waiting, pulsating with anticipation. Only attacking when they are all in position, this unstoppable, uncompromising black wave of death and destruction is almost ready to unleash itself upon the good people of Manhattan.

11.22 am

The stadium is rocking, 87 thousand people on their feet, singing, dancing, clapping. Madison, Lily and Grace are having the best time of their little young lives!!!!

11.25 am

Poor Britney is still sat on her hospital bed waiting for her lovely mother to collect her!!!!

11.27 am

The cinema is packed with two hundred men, women but mostly children crying with laughter enjoying the Zooodons !!!!

11.30 am

Bradley has quickly cleaned the apartment ready for when he goes to collect Gene from the salon but first, he needs a poo, I'd better have one now so the smell can go before she gets home!!!!

11.33 am

Sally is in full flow now, transfixed looking at the screen, watching big hard cocks going in and out of bold wet fannies, loads of moaning and groaning. Sally's hands have reached her inner thighs, rubbing, scratching, softly caressing. Moving her right hand up slowly, then with two fingers tweaking her little bristly tuft up and down. Her breathing has quickened, her fanny is absolutely soaking, her skin is so very sensitive. Bringing her legs all the way up and tucking the heels of her feet under her throbbing bottom. Moving her right hand ever so slowly forward Sally parts her quivering luscious lips with the tip of her dainty middle finger. Pushing it slowly and gently ever deeper while moving her hand up and down. Then in ... her finger is deep inside her, moaning, groaning, panting, arching her back, her finger penetrating deep inside her aching wet fanny, thrusting her groin forward as she finger fucks herself, faster and faster. Her left hand fondling her left ample breast. Then

Sally's finger stops, withdrawing softly from the wetness until only the tip of her dainty finger remains. Moving slightly upwards until her finger reaches her sticky, sensitive pulsating clitoris. Moving her finger ever so gently around and around, adding slightly more tentative pressure on each rotation. Lifting her bum off the bed, then with two strong stiff fingers Sally firmly strokes her quivering little bean from top to bottom and back again. Harder, faster, deeper, her skin sweating, her breathing short and sallow, faster and faster, harder and harder, her groin gyrating forward against Sally's formidable magic fingers. Moaning ... groaning ... panting ... Sally's shallow breathing quickens, her sopping fanny leaking juices down the crack of her sweaty bum hole, her wet sticky fingers moving quicker and firmer, faster and faster, harder and harder .... then boom .... *** .... Sally erupts, her whole quivering body shuddering and shaking, thrusting her bum high into the air, quickly ramming her two stiff wet fingers deep inside her aching eruption Sally can feel her soaking wet fanny contracting and pulsating, her inner walls constricting tighter and tighter around her sticky happy magic fingers …. after letting out a long satisfying ahhhh … Sally's contorted exhausted body flops back onto the bed, her legs are still upright and wide open. Mmmmm that was lovely Sally thought, her skin still tingling as she nestles her weary head back onto her soft white pillow. As Sally lay there all happy and contented the black ugly terrifying spiders had infiltrated her apartment block. They had crept silently through the inside of the building and are now lying in wait, very near to their victims for the onslaught to begin!!

11.51 am …!!!!!!!

All at once the hideous black creatures swarmed out of their confinement, their sharp black pointy fangs dripping with excitement. Sally's spider comes out from under her bed, runs up the strewn covers on the floor, then up onto the foot of the bed and then crawls straight towards Sally. Up on all of its eight black hairy spiny legs the spider marches purposeful until it reaches Sally feet which are still tucked under her bum. Sally is blissfully unaware, still lying there naked with her head on her soft white pillow, looking up at the ceiling, still quivering from her exertions. Out with its black long pointy fangs!! the spider rears itself up to full height and with one almighty pounce it plunges its razor sharp fangs into Sally's inviting ankle .... Sally let's out a piercing deafening scream ...... but there is no sound, she screams again ...... but still nothing, Sally can only hear the sound of the porn movie still playing on her laptop beside her. The pain is excruciating, Sally screams and screams but the sound is only in her head, instantly frozen solid and unable to move a muscle Sally is frantic, rolling her eyes around trying to see what has happened to her but she can only see the top of the walls and the ceiling. What the FUCK!! Something is starting to crawl onto her feet, its warm, its hairy, it's disgusting. Sally is running around in her own head at a thousand miles an hour, pulling the hair out at the roots, while hysterical screaming and screaming, what the fuck is it, the pain in her foot is agonising ... and still she can't move a muscle, but Sally can still hear and feel everything that is happening to her. The black hideous spider with its long bristly eight legs starts walking up Sally's left calf, stopping at the knee, then slowly the spider creeps down her inner thigh, its thick bristly hairs scratching as it descends lower and lower.

Sally is going crazy, shouting, screaming, what is it, where the fuck is it going ...... No!!! As the ugly creature reaches Sally's still wet pulsating fanny, it sticks one of its front hairy legs inside, moving it around, poking, probing. Then another black hairy leg gets shoved deep inside her. Then with its two front bristly legs the spider starts to open Sally's sticky lips, wriggling forward, now four legs are inside of her. Sally is hysterical, lying there unable to move, naked, helpless, she can't even shout for help. All Sally can do is hope that it will be over soon, whatever is happening to her... Crawling forward using all of its bristly legs the spider's entire black hairy body slips into Sally's virgina. Sally can feel something horrible wriggling up inside her stomach, the pain is excruciating, it's like someone or something is ripping your insides out piece by piece. Higher and higher it goes, wriggling, twisting, scratching, then it stops ...!! Nothing, no movement, no pain .... Sally is just lying there waiting, wondering, is it over .... her hysteria has lessened, her screaming has evaporated, all Sally feels now is trepidation, the waiting seems like an eternity .... is it over!!! Then suddenly the spinning and the wriggling start up again, this time moving downwards, downwards towards Sally's female opening. Down it comes, quicker this time. Wriggling, crawling until one black hairy leg sticks out, then another, and another, then with a big sticky PLOP the spider is out of Sally's violated, naked body, quickly scurrying away back into the depths below. ... before Sally has time to think, her eyes start to close, her legs become heavy and start to drop, her whole body relaxes inside and out and then .... Sally falls into a deep haunted sleep.

11.49 am

Bradley has been sat on the toilet for a short while, his gentleman parts hanging down between his legs as he leans slightly forward enjoying his poo .... hiding under the rim of the toilet seat just below where Bradley was sitting was a black hairy deadly spider, quietly waiting.

11.50 am

Bradley has now finished and is cleaning himself up, thinking I'd best be quick, I'm picking gene up in a few minutes ...

11.51 am ......!!!!!!!!

The black ugly spider leaps from under the toilet seat and wraps its eight bristly spiny legs tightly around Bradley's ball sack. Shocked and surprised Bradley quickly looks down but as he does the spider sinks his black razor sharp fangs deep into Bradley's balls. FUCK ...!! The pain ... The excruciating pain was unbearable, Bradley screams out in absolute agony but once again ... no sound could be heard, Bradley was also frozen solid, his eyes and mouth wide open, still looking down in horror at the terrifying spider gripped around his bollocks. I can't move, I can't shout but the agonising pain, it feels like someone had ripped his balls off with their teeth. The black hideous spider then spins around and crawls straight towards Bradley's bum hole, first inserting one bristly spiny leg, then another. Ripping Bradley's arse open and climbing in one leg at a time, until its entire black gruesome body was up Inside Bradley's battered bum hole. Up it went, crawling, scurrying, squirming, Bradley could feel the spider wriggling around deep inside him, but he was numb, his brain couldn't comprehend what was going on. The unbelievable pain, the spider, up inside me, poor old Bradley's mind was scrambled, he was in total shock. Before Bradley had time to think the spider was worming his way downwards, pulling and tugging at Bradley's poo pipe as it crawled downwards, then with one big squeeze the black hairy ugly spider emerged from Bradley's violated bum hole. Scurrying up and over Bradley's legs, the black terrifying spider vanishes from sight. Bradley sat there calm and serene, still in shock, his balls throbbing in agonising pain but slowly his eyes begin to droop, his violated body relaxes, and Bradley still sat upright on the toilet falls into a deep restless sleep.

11.48 am

Young Britney is pacing up and down waiting for her lovely caring mother to show up. The doctors have given Britney the all clear for now, so she is ready to go home. The three other women on the ward are giving Britney words of encouragement and wishing her all the very best with the rest of her pregnancy.

11.51 am ......!!!!!!!!

Screaming and shouting can be heard coming from down the hospital corridor, Britney pops her head out of the ward. People are running in all different directions, doctors, nurses, patients screaming spiders ... spiders." What's going on Britney," the three women shout. As Britney re-enters the ward, she is just about to tell the women what she had seen but it was too late .... evil, ugly, black spiders invade their room. Leaping onto the three women's beds, everyone including Britney is screaming, yelling," spiders, spiders." As quick as a flash the black terrifying spiders sink their sharp pointy dripping fangs into the three ladies, their eyes and mouths fixed wide open with terror, their bodies stiff and rigid, unable to move. Britney is screaming hysterically in the corner of the room, a spider drops from the ceiling right onto her head, runs down Britney's terrified face and sinks its black hideous dripping fangs into her cheek. Then the black dirty hairy spiders descend down the open mouths of all four of the women. Wriggling, crawling, squeezing through their wind pipes, gagging, choking, the pain, the anguish, the unbelievable terror etched across all of their traumatised faces. The black terrifying creatures sweep through the entire hospital, biting, infecting, terrorising everyone in their path .... and then they are gone, leaving only mass hysteria behind them as all the terrified souls fall slowly into a haunted terrifying sleep.

11.50 am

The concert is in full flow, Ed Sheeran is on the stage giving the performance of a lifetime. The crowd is up on their feet, singing, dancing, waving their arms around to the music. Madison, Lily and Grace are having a fabulous time, the young 13 year olds had never been away without their dad before and they were making the most of it.

11.51 am ......!!!!!!!

Shouting, yelling, screaming coming from the corner of the stadium. Shouting, yelling, screaming coming from the other side of the stadium. The three girls who were stood in the front centre of the arena stop singing," Madison what's going on, what are they shouting about?" "I don't know girls, but the people are running our way, quick let's get onto the stage." Ed had stopped singing and was asking for calm but lots of frightened and confused people, including the three girls were invading the stage to avoid the oncoming screaming crowd. Then they saw it, a black terrifying wave headed straight towards them!! It was Like a black shiny carpet engulfing the entire crowd, hysterical people screaming, shouting, crying, running for their lives ... SPIDERS black evil killing machines thousands of them, sinking their black dripping pointy fangs into confused terrified people, then descending down into their traumatised throats, laying thousands of eggs ready for the next generation of monsters to be born. The spiders overran the stage, even Ed Sheeran lay stiff and rigid like all the other poor souls who had paid to watch him perform that day. Then as quickly as this terrifying vicious onslaught started, it was over. The black ugly evil creatures vanished, thousands of them gone in a blink of an eye. You wouldn't of thought that they had ever been there ... apart from the tens of thousands of terrified, mutilated, screaming people that were left in the spiders terrifying wake.

11.45 am

The cinema was packed, two hundred, men, women but mostly children were crammed into their seats, laughing, crying, tears of joy, watching the Zooodons having a wonderful time. Charley was obviously sat next to her dad. Whispering, "do you like the film dad, its brilliant isn't it, Zaaarows little fury kids are my favourite, they are so cuddly and cute." "Yes, Charley the film is really funny and yes Zaaarows kids are adorable."" Dad, dad," tugging at his sleeve," when the toys come out next week which of Zaaarows kids can I have, Zaaabin or Zaaanin?" Richard leans closer to Charley talking very quietly," Charley don't tell your brother, but you can have both." "Yippee, thanks dad ... I love you."

11.48 am

While everyone is having a fabulous time watching the Zooodons, the black terrifying spiders have infiltrated the cinema. Slowly creeping from behind the cinema screen and down onto the dark flickering floor. Up through the floor boards, squeezing their hairy hideous bodies through any crack that they can find. Slowly and methodically crawling along the dimly lit walkways and sneaking under everyone's seats, creeping and crawling in-between children's feet and up onto the backs of the reclining chairs, surrounding the joyous room in a black evil shroud, pulsating waiting until the terrifying attack can begin.

11.50 am

Little Tommy and his loyal Jack Russell Benji have arrived on the Planet Zoooton, trying to make all the Zooodons laugh. Everyone at the cinema is rolling around in their seats, laughing, crying and really enjoying themselves, even Ryan is having a good time.

11.51 am ...... !!!!!!!

Then they came, those black terrifying ugly spiders poured out of their hiding places, black hideous creatures their hairy bodies glistening against the flickering light of the cinema screen. The whole cinema screamed at once, two hundred men women and children screaming hysterical at the top of their terrified voices. The agonising sound vibrating around the dark panic stricken room, the sound was deafening. Up on all Eight spiny bristly legs the deadly spiders run, engulfing everyone. Richard lifts his screaming little Charley up into his strong arms, but it was too late, the evil spiders had surrounded Richard and were crawling up his trembling legs, up and up the spiders crawled all over Richard and Charley. Looking down he could see a spider wiggling down his beloved Shona's throat, her eyes fixed and wide open, her face hideously contorted as the terrifying spider descend below. Charley is shouting, kicking and screaming "dad, dad spiders, spiders" but Richard is still. His eyes wide open, his body frozen in time where he stood, his strong loving arms still tightly gripped around his screaming terrified daughter's waist. Charley had to watch in horror as the black hideous spider crawled up onto her dads stricken rigid face, then wriggling and twisting the black ugly creature dived deep into her dads gagging, gasping throat. "Dad wake up, dad ... dad," hysterically screaming Charley started slapping and kicking her comatose dad to try and wake him before the spider came back.

Still kicking and hysterical screaming the spiders that had covered Charley's terrified little body had crawled back down her dads stiff legs too the flickering cinema floor and had disappeared, none of the spiders had bitten her not one. Looking around the dimly lit room, Charley could still hear the Zooodons laughing and blowing big purple bubbles into the air on the big screen in front of her but there were no more spiders. Charley could see loads of adults frozen in all sorts of positions and lots and lots of traumatised children screaming, shaking and crying but no spiders .... Then suddenly a big horrible lump appeared in her dads throat, Richard started gagging and gasping for air as the hideous beast started to re-emerge from his gaping wide open mouth. All the terrified children started screaming once more, including Charley as all the black ugly spiders started coming out of their parents wide open contorted mouths. Out they came, their pointy black fangs still dripping, their hairy black wet bodies still glistening, scuttling down to the dimly lit cinema floor and then they were gone. Everyone who had been attacked started to slowly close their traumatised eyes, their wide open mouths starting to fall, their violated twisted bodies and their terrified confused minds fell into a deep haunted sleep.

The hysterical children were still screaming, looking down Charley could see her mother and brother soundly asleep next to her upright dad. Right, she thought ... what would my dad do!!!! Shouting at the top of her little trembling voice ...." someone help me?? Some body get me down." Two little boys about 10 year old, still shaking and weeping came over to Charley, looking up at her," grab my feet" she shouts. The two little scared boys reached up, took hold of Charley's dangling feet and started to pull," pull" Charley shouts," pull." Then all of a sudden Charley's exhausted little body came crashing to the cinema floor. Most of the terrified children hadn't been attacked, the black ugly spiders engulfed the whole room but left the screaming young children alone. All the traumatised children sat huddled together watching their families sleep, crying, weeping, holding each other's hands too afraid to leave.

12.04 pm

The black hideous monsters had risen from the depths below, they had swept through Harlem unopposed, biting, terrifying, violating anyone in their path. Strong, intelligent, ruthless black killing machines Laying millions upon millions of their black evil eggs deep inside their violated victims, then disappearing back into the blackness, waiting patiently for their new babies to be violently born out of the blood and guts of the unexpected people above.

The stadium was full of thousands upon thousands of unconscious souls locked into a restless haunted sleep. Their children physically untouched sat waiting for their family and friends to wake, too afraid and too scared to leave their sides. Lily and Grace were sat holding hands, praying for Madison to open her eyes once more.

It's been nearly an hour since the horrific attack and Sally who is still lying naked on her bed is starting to stir. Moving her arms and her legs, slowly opening her eyes …. Up like a shot, out of bed Sally's running around her bedroom screaming, shouting, tears streaming down her bemused face. Tearing at her battered and torn virgina with her fingers, scouring the room looking for the hideous hairy thing that violated her in the most unspeakable way. Panting, crying, scared and confused Sally doesn't know what to do with herself. Phone the police!! The phones are not working, the internet is off, what the fuck! Getting some clothes on, still panicking, Sally is pacing up and down in her apartment working out what to do!!! There are screams coming from the hallway, someone is crying their eyes out. Tentatively Sally sneaks over to the front door, peeping through the peep hole Sally spots Simone on her knees whaling like a baby. Still frightened and very apprehensive Sally slowly unchained the door, turns the lock and steps out into the hallway. "Oh Sally," fighting back the tears, "it's you … I've … I've been attacked by a horrible black spider." Sally kneels down in front of Simone, the two girls crying, hugging sharing each other's pain." What do we do now Sally?" "I don't know what to do. I don't know Simone, the phone and the internet are not working." The girls sit in the hallway for a while, crying, shaking, comforting each other." I'm too scared to go back into my apartment Sally," "yes me too Simone, I think it was a spider that attacked me to ... come on Simone let's grab our coats and go and find someone to help us, we can't stay here they might come back."

Together they put their shoes and coats on and went outside. It was a bright and sunny Saturday afternoon, Sally and Simone were shuffling down the street arm in arm looking for someone to help them ... No cars, no buses, no taxis whizzing up and down, just people, lots of frightened lonely people wondering aimlessly up and down the street. Everyone looking lost and confused, with bloodied bite marks on their legs, their arms and some with fang marks on their terrified faces. Office workers, medical staff, fire and police officers, everyday people just shuffling around, scared, lost, confused, crying, sobbing, all looking for someone to help them.

As Sally and Simone wondered slowly down the street, they meet Gene coming from the other direction. Breathing heavy and very distraught." Hello Sally, I was having my hair done and we were all attacked by these hideous looking spiders. I've only just woke up, but I need to get home to my Bradley," gripping Sally's hand," I would be lost without him." "Yes, Gene we were all attacked by the spiders," "oh my goodness I'd better hurry, God bless you, Sally." Gene finally reaches her front door, tentatively she inserts her key not knowing what she will find inside." Bradley ... Bradley dear," shaking and still in shock Gene scours the apartment. On reaching the bathroom Bradley is still sat on the toilet with his trousers around his ankle sound asleep. Gene rushes over, putting her soft hands around his shoulders," oh Bradley ..." Bradley wakes with a start, "oh my balls" he shouts," my balls they are on fire." Gene and Bradley sink to the cold bathroom floor, hugging, crying holding each other tightly." I'm so glad that you are alright Bradley I would be lost without you," giving his Gene a peck on the cheek," yes dear I'd be lost without you too." Still sat on the bathroom floor Holding hands, staring into each other's eyes, the both of them in total shock just happy to be back together again.

The scared children were still sat huddled on the cinema floor hoping and praying that a grown up would come and rescue them or their families would wake up from their deep slumber ... Ryan is moving, slowly opening his frightened eyes. Charley goes running over, flinging her little frightened arms around her brothers neck." Ryan, Ryan you are, ok?" Ryan stands up pushing poor Charley to the floor, "spiders, spiders" as he starts pulling at his open mouth. Scared and confused young Ryan was in a panic, shouting, crying, spiders, spiders. Charley jumps up from the floor," no Ryan they have all gone, the spiders have gone." Giving her brother a big squeeze," it's ok Ryan I'm here." People slowly start waking up, scared, terrified but mostly in shock, their relieved children hugging and crying." Ryan, mommy's waking up." Shona slowly opens her eyes, then up she gets frantically looking around the room tugging at her sore aching throat, spider, panic and confusion written all over her poor terrified face, but she is so relieved to see her two beautiful children standing before her, Shona bends down and scoops them both up into her weary arms." My babies are you alright?" "Yes mom, the spiders didn't bite me, they were all over me, but they didn't bite me." "Oh, Charley" giving her an enormous hug the tears still streaming down Shona's frightened face "my darling girl, I love you," "I love you too mom." Drawing her attention to Ryan," how about you son?" Ryan's face crumples, tears welling up in the corner of his distraught face." Mom," he mumbles, "the spiders attacked me too." Falling into each other's arms mother and son hug and cry," it will be ok my darling boy, moms here with you now." Charley squeezes in and the three of them comfort each other ..." Mom, Ryan, dads moving,"

Charley jumps up and starts tugging at her dads frozen arms, "dad, dad," jumping up and down tears of joy in her poor little face," dad wake up." Richard opens his eyes, his body stiff and aching, Charley's crying, tears of joy rolling down her little screwed up face, tightly gripped around her dads waist," your awake dad, your awake," Shona and Ryan smiling up at him. Richard looks around the room, in shock and a little disorientated, spiders putting his hands around his throat, the terror still written on his face, trying to be brave in front of his tearful little daughter, tears rolling down his battered face." My family" he mutters," my family," bending his stiff hurting body, Richard opens up his arms and they all embrace, crying, weeping, sniffling. Everyone in the cinema is awake, hugging, crying, still terrified but relieved to be all back together. "Shona are you ok my darling" giving her a big kiss on the lips, "are the spiders gone," "yes Richard the spiders have gone. Ryan was attacked just like us, but they didn't touch Charley." "Oh, Ryan my boy, we will all get through this my son," "yes we will dad." "Yes, dad those horrible spiders didn't bite me, they were all over me and I was scared, I was crying for you to wake up." "You are my brave little girl Charley" giving her a massive loving hug. Everyone gathers their bemused and traumatised families together and wonders out into the daylight looking for someone to help them. People are just walking around, totally confused, scared that the black hideous creatures may return at any moment. The phones and the internet are not working, police, fire and ambulance staff walk aimlessly around in circles, lost and alone, dazed, not knowing where to go, along with all the other residents of the Harlem district.

"Richard there are men in white body suits coming towards us, there are soldiers too, with rifles and they are all wearing respirators." Scared terrified people are swamping the soldiers and the men in white overalls." Please help us, the phones are not working, and we don't know what to do, we have been attacked by enormous black spiders." The sacred people swamp the men in white overalls thinking they are here to help them, time will tell. But how wrong they all are!! Richard and his frightened family are swept along with all the other distraught and displaced people, herded like cattle towards the inside of the shopping mall by the soldiers and the men in white overalls.

Corralled inside, kept away from the outside world but for what purpose??

Back at the stadium everyone was awake, scared terrified people milling around not knowing what to do, or who to speak to. Madison, Lily and Grace were huddled together, hugging, crying still petrified at what had happened ... "Come on girls" said Madison" we need to find help, we need to get home, dad will be worried." Picking the tearful girls up off the floor, Madison grips their hands tightly and pushes their way through the hordes of desperate people. Down they go deep below the stadium towards the underground train station. There are hundreds of stranded people waiting for the trains to arrive but there are no trains, they have all been cancelled." Madison where are all the trains?" "I don't know Grace, there will be one coming along soon" ... After waiting for a short time Madison decides to take the girls up onto the street above to see what they can do about getting home." Come on girls quick, there's a man over there getting into a car, let's go and see if he can help us get home. Sir, please help us we need to get home, the trains have stopped, my little sisters" ...." get out of here, get out of my way," as he tries to put his wife and daughter into his car." Please sir, please my sister's need to get home," Lily and Grace start crying, holding tightly onto their big sister's arm.

The man's wife steps out of the car, "come on Jim we need to help them" "but Mary the spiders might comeback" .... "No buts Jim they need our help, look at those little girls." Looking inside his car at his own sobbing daughter Jim agrees to help them. "Ok get in, where do you live?" "Thank you so much sir, we live in Queens." "That's not far from us Jim, we can drop them off on the way." Off the two family's go driving through streets packed with thousands of lost, disorientated people milling around with nowhere to go." Do your phones work girls?" "No sir our phones are not working." "Yes, just like mine, the radio in the car is off too." "Jim there are soldiers coming from over there, there are people in white suits too." The people milling around on the street surge towards the soldiers, hundreds of them blocking their way." Jim the road is crammed with people how are we going to get out?" "it's ok Mary I'll go around, I'll use the back roads, we need to get home, we need to get out of here." Setting off around the side streets, dodging wondering confused people as they go, heading for third Avenue bridge so they can get off the island ... "The bridge is closed Jim, we can't get through, they have put up barbed wire and concrete bollards across the road, we can't get over the bridge." The girls are crying, there are people everywhere trying to get off the island but there are hundreds of armed soldiers in their way. Scared People shouting and waving their arms in the air at the soldiers to let them get across.

THE MILITARY INTERVENTION

"Colonel the crowd is getting out of hand sir, they have swamped the bridge, hundreds of them." "Captain tell your men to hold their ground, you have your orders ... no one gets out of the quarantine zone. A full briefing will be held in due course but for now you have my orders captain, I'll be in the command post if you need me." Colonel Stuart enters the command post," lieutenant Saunders is everything ready for when the president arrives later tonight." "Yes, sir all arrangements have been made, professor Charles Henderson is on route and will arrive here from England by 21 hundred hours. The chief medical officer Mr Hocker from the CDC and Mr Robert Winters from homeland security have both been collected and will arrive by 20 hundred hours tonight sir." "Very good lieutenant, keep me posted. "

21.15 pm

"Colonel sir, the president has arrived," "very well lieutenant show him to the central command post, I will be along shortly." Colonel Stuart is a military man down to his very core, just like his father and his father's father. If he was to bleed, it would be red, white and blue. With his chiselled rugged features and a toughened body to match. At 59 years old, Colonel Stuart has well and truly earned his rank. After a few minutes colonel Stuart enters the command post," sorry Mr president for my delay, I had some last minute details to attend to." "Right Colonel Stuart give me an update, where are we right now on the ground? What threat are we facing and what are we doing to stop it." "Yes, Mr president but before I update you on what's happening right now, we have got new people in the room and not everyone is up to speed on developments." The command centre is packed, everyone is eagerly awaiting Colonel Stuart's briefing, not everyone knows what exactly is going on." Good evening, everyone, it is you people in this room today, right now, who will solve this catastrophe spreading across Manhattan Island and possibly around the world. So, let's get to it, I will introduce everyone so we can get the ball rolling. Mr president, we have Mr Robert Winters, joint chief of staff for homeland security. Admiral George Hoffman, head of naval operations. Mrs Janet Hocker, chief medical officer for the CDC. General Rogers army Corp and Professor Charles Henderson world's leading expert on arachnids. Professor Charles Henderson of England has been involved in this dire situation from day one, his expertise in arachnids will be invaluable."

With his steel rimmed octagonal glasses, a well-manicured goatee and patches on the elbows of his tatty tweed jacket he looks the epitome of a typical college professor. There are lots of other people in the room, all departments have also brought their own personal with them." My name is colonel Stuart I've been appointed by the Pentagon to take charge of this operation. This all started four weeks ago when we were contacted by the CDC (Centre for Disease Control) relating to the death of a young woman called Tina Smith. Initial reports suggested that Tina Smith had been infested with hundreds of thousands of spider eggs laid deep inside her. The baby spiders then burst out of her body killing her and then they all mysteriously disappeared. Lieutenant, hand out the dossiers so everyone can follow and have the video screen ready for the autopsy results," "yes sir colonel." "As you can see from the screen above and your dossiers before you, at least 250 thousand eggs had been laid inside poor Tina's body. The remnants of the egg shells still attached to the inside of her abdomen. The statements from Tina's partner Sam and the medical staff on duty is testimony to what happened on that fateful day. The autopsy report lays out in detail the circumstances of Tina's untimely death. We quickly closed down any and all internet traffic relating to any kind of spider attack. Since then, we have been in constant contact with professor Charles Henderson in London, keeping him fully updated on any further developments and putting a plan of action in place. On his recommendation we started operation quarantine, covertly building a ring of steel, made from army personnel, wire and concrete ready to erected at a moment's notice to quarantine any further outbreak. Professor Henderson could you please take over," "certainly colonel. Mr president after reading the first reports on Tina's death and the interim report from the CDC, I concluded that the threat to life was real. The CDC had sent their team into the hospital and interviewed all of Tina's colleagues. Only one, her best friend nurse Roberts recalled a conversation between herself and Tina two weeks prior to her death. She remembers Tina telling her being attacked by a horrific black spider that went down her throat, but Tina dismissed the attack and said it must of been a horrible dream, it was far to horrific to be real. So, Mr president my only conclusion is ... the spiders are real, the threat to life is real. Working closely with colonel Stuart we devised a plan. We were almost positive that this spider scenario was real and not a hoax. We only had Tina's body and autopsy, sketchy traumatised statements from her dead boyfriend Sam and testimony from the medical staff on duty that day. So, gentlemen and ladies this is what we know today, Young Tina was infected, two weeks to the day the baby spiders were born, four weeks after that the babies became adults and attacked everyone this morning but not the children, we don't know why at this moment, we don't have enough information. Colonel, do you want to conclude, ""thank you professor. Mr president after the baby spiders mysteriously disappeared from the hospital, we knew that they would be back, but we didn't know when or where. In secret and out of sight we constructed our quarantine ring of steel, ready to be deployed at a moment's notice. At precisely 11.51 am this morning the spider's attacked and by 12.10 pm not one spider remained. By 13 hundred we had deployed the army and quarantined the whole area, stretching from Washington Heights down to the upper east side. Every possible exit point closed, a double ring of army and navy encircling the whole area. All phones and internet disconnected, all communications severed. Special forces along with our medical teams are in the quarantined area guiding the infected people to holding areas, sports halls, shopping malls, large office blocks, anywhere that we can find to keep the people safe and calm. "

The president stands up and paces the room, at 39 president Collins is America's youngest ever president, he was elected with a huge majority, a mandate for change, endorsed by the American people. Most top ranking officials thought he was too young, to inexperienced, to naive, to run the country, he has only been in office for 95 days. "Right people this is what we know, so what are we going to do about it? We are not leaving this room until we have a concrete plan on the table, anyone … please speak freely." Rising her hand slightly," Mr president, Janet Hocker CDC, this is what I think we need to do right now. We need human subjects, to see if we can somehow remove the eggs from inside of them. Second, I don't know how but I need at least two living spiders so we can get them into the laboratory and find out how to kill them. If I can't find a way to destroy these hideous creatures, then basically Mr president I think we are all screwed. We need more information, so I recommend we send a team back into the "yes professor," "sir I'm a psychologist behaviourist my team and I predict that we have between 7 to 10 days before the quarantine area gets overran." "Explain professor," "yes Mr president, at the moment we have our medical and armed military personnel in the quarantine area in respirators and protective clothing trying to keep everyone calm in our secure holding areas, shopping malls, hospitals, schools etc. They think that we are there to help them sir, but we are not" …

"Wait a minute professor, you're telling me that we are not in there to help these poor American citizens, we must be doing everything possible to help these poor souls." "Mr president these people are already dead, we have at least 250 thousand infected people in there with no way at the moment to treat them. At this time, we have very little information, we can't be 100% sure who is infected and who is not. Mr president we need to be real about this catastrophic situation, there is no sugar coating this situation ... These are facts on the table right now sir, if one spider can produce 250 thousand new spiders, Mr president in 14 day's time there will be millions upon millions of new spiders spewing out of the citizens of Manhattan and we have no way of stopping them ... the clock is TICKING !!!" "My god professor," the president puts his head in his hands." My god, so what is the predicted time line for the next 14 days?" "At the moment our teams inside the quarantined zone are keeping everyone contained, we have beds, food but most of all reassurance. Keeping the people calm and all together but at some point, they will want to go home. They don't know that they have thousands of tiny spider eggs deep inside of them waiting to explode out of their bodies. There are thousands of people inside the zone who have not been infected and they will get extremely restless being contained for no particular reason. So, Mr president we think we can keep the quarantine in place for about 7 to 10 days but then it will fall apart, people will be desperate to get out and they will use any means necessary. So, I recommend we have a second command post ready across the water in Brooklyn, for when that time comes" … "Mr president," "yes professor Henderson," "I have been involved in this situation from day one, having had many conversations with all the different heads of departments trying to draw up a strategy to defend against the oncoming onslaught. Spiders are my forte, I have studied them all my professional working life, but these deadly spiders are unlike anything that I have come across before. They are fast, strong but surprisingly very intelligent. They are animals driven purely by instinct, there is no reasoning with these hideous creatures and when they attack, we have no possible way of stopping them. So, Mr president in the dossier before you I have drawn up a contingency plan. Lieutenant the screen please, on the screen in front of you we have a map of Manhattan Island. All the bridges and tunnels that connect the island to the mainland are marked. When the quarantine zone fails in about 7 days, we will pull back to command post bravo in the old naval yard in Brooklyn at this point we will need to quarantine the whole of Manhattan Island itself, erecting an impenetrable ring steel around the entire island. Blowing up all bridges, flooding every subway and underground tunnel, severing the island completely from the mainland" ....

"Just one minute professor Henderson," "yes Mr president," "you expect me to authorise the destruction of billions of dollar's worth of infrastructure on your say so." "Let me be totally Frank with you Mr president, if you do not follow my recommendation and you allow millions upon millions of these blood thirsty creatures to escape this island, they will rip through America killing every man, woman and child in a matter of months and furthermore Mr president when Manhattan Island is under full lockdown no one can be allowed to leave the island. Every soldier guarding the perimeter must be under strict instructions to shoot on sight anyone who tries to leave." "Colonel

Stuart stands up, "one minute professor Henderson, let me stop you right there. Are you telling me to order my men to open fire on unarmed men, women and children." "Yes colonel, be under no illusions Colonel, if only one of these black ugly spider gets onto the mainland its game over. So yes, colonel I am TELLING you to order your men to kill anyone who tries to escape." "You are one heartless mother fucking English man!! I can't order my men to shoot civilians essentially children." "Right calm down, colonel sit down," "yes Mr president." "Right, everyone calm down just give me a few minutes," the president rises from his chair, he starts pacing the room for a few moments.

.... "I have read through all of the reports, weighed up all of the options. Colonel Stuart!! prepare to have all the bridges and tunnels ready for detonation but only preparations for now. Secondly: have all the plans in place to secure the entire island but we need to do this out of sight and not to frighten people. Third: send teams back into the hospital and to Tina's old apartment to see what, if any further new evidence that they can gather. Fourth: we need human and arachnid specimens so we can try and start to find a way out of this unbelievable situation and fifth: ...... we need all this done yesterday people, I know it's very late and a lots of you are exhausted but we have, all of us, just 14 days and counting to come up with a solution. The lives of all Americans are in our hands and maybe the entire world, so come on people let's get our heads in the game. Colonel I am giving full presidential authority to use any and all means at your disposal to get the job done, keep me briefed on everyone's progress," "yes Mr president" everyone stands up around the table, "we will do our duty Mr president," the president leaves the room.

Colonel Stuart gathers everyone back around the table." Lieutenant Jackson," "yes colonel," "I need Captain Reece, captain Brown and major McCarthy from special forces here asap," "yes sir." "Janet is your CDC laboratory ready to receive human and spider subjects." "Yes, colonel the lab is fully operational, my team are ready and standing by." "Professor Henderson," "yes colonel," "your task is to work out a way of securely obtaining at least two live specimens and transporting them safely to the CDC for examination. Lieutenant Jackson," "yes colonel," "I am now reassigning you to aid professor Henderson in this vital task. Provide him with whatever he needs, men, machinery anything, this operation is paramount to the success or failure of this mission. If we cannot capture our two arachnid specimens to examine, we will not have the ability to destroy them." "Yes, colonel I will provide professor Henderson with anything that he requires Colonel, captain Reese and captain Brown are here," "captains," "yes colonel," "select a small team using CDC and homeland security personnel, I need you to go on a fact finding mission. Captain Brown, once assembled, take your team and go to the Royal Archie Memorial hospital, quietly and covertly try and gather as much information about a deceased subject called Tina Smith as you can. All relevant information about the subject is in your folders," "yes sir, I will get right to it." "Captain Reese, your mission is the same as captain Brown's, but I need you to go to Miss Smith's last known address. The area is mostly deserted but try and gather as much evidence as you can. These missions are vital, keep me posted," "yes colonel," "dismissed."

Sunday 4.30 am

People in the quarantined zone have been told that a plague of spiders randomly attacked everyone, the military have found their nest killing them with poisonous gas. They are being kept isolated for their own safety because the spiders may have been carrying a deadly virus which only manifests itself in 14 days after infection. They are oblivious to the fact that they are incubators for the next terrifying wave of black hideous spiders to be born into the world.

The president is in crisis talks with the joint chiefs of staff over the outbreak. The CDC are busy in their laboratory getting prepared for the arrival of human and arachnid specimens. Homeland security in conjunction with the military are making sure the quarantine zone is totally secure. Professor Henderson has amassed a large team of experts and are busy trying to work out how to retrieve live specimens from deep underground. Colonel Stuart has sent out teams on fact finding missions, he is also overseeing preparations to detonate and destroy all links to the mainland plus organising the ring of steel that will encompass the whole of Manhattan Island once the inner quarantine zone has collapsed.

Sunday 7.45 am 13 days and counting!!

After just a couple of hours of sleep professor Henderson and his devoted team are hard back at work. They are all sat around a makeshift table in one of the back offices in the command post brainstorming about what the next step should be. Around the table are four leading academics in their field, mostly bug and creepy Crawley professionals. When these geeky insect professors talk, they talk at each other, bouncing ideas around the room until they find a solution .... "Spiders. how do we catch a spider?" "We need a container. " "yes, something impregnable. with holds in, so they can breathe. ""what about the fangs? according to Tina's autopsy ... very sharp." "Yes, very pointy. we need a suit." "Yes, good idea but what kind of suit?" "Impervious to sharp pointy fangs. mmm something ... impervious. Tin." "No, can't move your arms. thick rubber." "No, not tough enough. How will the soldiers breath.?" "Some form of oxygen tanks." "What's on his head?" "A strong mask. A divers mask. " mmmm putting their chins onto their fists "something strong enough ... something bendy enough ... something breathable ...... !! what about a stab vest." "Yes, that can stop a sharp blade." "What if we double the thickness." "Yes, that could work. ""stop gentlemen please, I think you have all come up with the perfect solution. A doubled layered stab vest material, a divers helmet and slim oxygen tanks inside the suit. "

"Professor Henderson. I've been going around the departments checking on their progress, how is yours going here?" "Yes, very good colonel, I think we have a possible solution to capturing a spider." "That's very good professor don't forget the clock is ticking, your task is absolutely vital to the success or failure of this entire operation, let me know when you have a workable prototype on the table." "Yes colonel, hopeful very soon" .... "Listen up everyone, I have just told colonel Stuart that we will have a working prototype on this table very soon ... but we only have 13 days left to go and we haven't even started yet. This is what needs to happen ... right now, to be honest we haven't got a minute to lose." "Yes, professor we are all right behind you," "this is what I need ... a suit made out of a double thickness stab vest material ... slim oxygen tanks to fit under the suit ... a deep sea divers helmet... a strong impervious box with tiny breathing holes to safely contain the spider. So, everyone, go out to where you need to go, see whoever you need to see, we have presidential authority to do whatever we need to do to get the job done. I will see you all back here in 24 hours' time, I can't stress enough how urgently we need all these elements completed and back here, good luck everybody."

Sunday 14.30 pm

Back in the command post," colonel ... Major McCarthy is here from special forces to see you sir," "very good captain show him in. Major

McCarthy I have an impossible mission for you, have you been briefed on your way over." "Yes, sir I am fully up to date, but Colonel can I be candid," "yes Major of course." "Colonel, this can't be real, can it." "Yes, Major I'm afraid to say … it is. No one outside the command post is fully aware of the perilous situation we all find ourselves, if one of these hideous beasts gets out of containment and onto the mainland its game over. Your task and this comes directly from the president himself, is to select three of your bravest, best men, they have to be volunteers, because this could very well be a suicide mission. They will decent into the depths below, search out the spiders nest and bring back at least two live specimens. All this with no weapons and strapped inside an experimental suit that may or may not work." The major's mouth drops open, his face pale and grey," yes colonel" …" Major, I need them to report directly to me by 21 hundred this evening, make sure that they are fully briefed and are totally prepared and willing to do their duty in the eyes of God and the American people." "Yes, sir colonel, my men will do their duty sir," "Very good Major, dismissed."

Sunday 15.05 pm

In the laboratory of the CDC human subjects are being led in, blindfolded. Two men, two women and two young children, a boy and a girl. Segregated, put in isolation so the testing can begin.

It's been a full 24 hours since the spider's vanished, leaving the poor terrified people of Harlem confined inside a ring of impenetrable wire … steel … and solitude. Isolated, pocked and prodded, kept away from their families and friends. Being lied to about the evil spiders agenda and their impending gruesome … horrific … agonising death.

Sunday 16.14

Over in the news desk in New York city Ruby was frantically trying to get hold of her parents, Bradley and Gene. "Edward it's been 24 hours now and I haven't been able to contact them. The government are saying that the area is in lockdown because of a new strain of bird flu but it just doesn't sound plausible." "I know Ruby they have also imposed a no fly zone over

Harlem and the lockdown measures are totally draconian. The place is lockdown that tight not even information is leaking out. No radio, no television reports, not even social media can penetrate the quarantine zone." "So, Edward what are we going to do? I'm frantic, I need to know if my parents are ok." "I know Ruby, we both work in the media industry so we will have to keep digging until we get some answers." "Yes, Edward but its unprecedented for somewhere ordinary like Harlem to be cut off from the outside world, no one aloud in or out, no news, no internet, nothing, it doesn't feel right." Holding Ruby's hand and looking into her distraught face," Ruby ... everything will be ok, we will get to the bottom of this." Ruby has been a news reporter for many years now, with her short cropped mousey hair and her thick rimmed glasses Ruby has a dogged personality to match, she will find out the truth.

Sunday 17.10 pm

Back at the command post. Lieutenant Morgan and his team have just arrived back from the quarantine zone with footage from inside one of the shopping malls, showing the spiders attack. Lieutenant Morgan," yes colonel," "I have gathered all the department heads here to listen to your progress report, what are the conditions like inside the quarantine zone at the moment?" "Colonel, the situation at the moment is good. Initially the people were terrified, confused, in shock, wondering around like lost souls not knowing what to do, finding it hard to come to terms with the horrendous violation that they had suffered. But now over 24 hours later we have tried to reassure the residents in the lockdown area, the attacked and non-attacked that we are there to help them all collectively to combat this new virus from spreading around the world. The spiders have been eliminated deep in their nest so there is no possible chance of any further attacks." "Very good lieutenant, you have footage to show us." "Yes colonel, part of my team retrieved this footage from the shopping mall showing ... I must say colonel, gruesome, awful pictures of the spider onslaught. We have sharpened up the imagery and spliced together the footage to give you the best possible view of events as they happened."

"Very good lieutenant, play the video." All the department heads and many other people are sat and stood around the room waited eagerly to see what had transpired that fateful Saturday morning. NO ...!! GOD ...!! FUCK ...!!

The room watched in horror as the black hideous monsters leapt out of their hiding places engulfing the hapless shoppers in a black carpet of pure evil. Sinking their razor sharp dripping fangs into the screaming adult population as they ran for their lives. The black ugly spiders immobilising, freezing the terrified People where they stood, then crawling, twisting, descending down their wide open gagging throats, the agonising pain and anguish written on their distorted faces. The children screaming, spiders crawling all over their tiny little hysterical bodies, their parents frozen solid in time, but the children stay untouched frantically running around screaming uncontrollably trying to get away from the black hideous creatures. We don't know as yet why the children have been speared this horrendous ordeal, but we have human subjects entering the CDCs laboratory and hopefully we will find out more. The watching, transfixed people in the command centre are in shock, some holding their shaking hands up to their wincing faces, some being sick in the corner of the room. Everyone in no doubt that what they were watching was real, the horrendous black spiders are real, the enormity of the situation sinking in, like a dagger being thrust deep into their aching hearts.

The command centre is deadly silent apart from the sound of whimpering disbelief emanating off the cold white walls, spreading around the horrified room ...." Colonel Stuart," "yes professor Henderson," "we can be in no doubt that this terrible ... terrible situation is far worse than we could of ever imagined. Seeing those horrendous images, the spiders attacking without remorse, without any form of compassion, driven on by purely evil animal instinct. Relentless, unstoppably killing machines now waiting patiently deep below us, waiting for millions upon millions of their blood thirsty offspring to explode out of the unsuspecting innocent people in less than 13 day's time. Its predicted that within this time the quarantine zone will fail, thousands of scared, frightened people will overrun the quarantine area and even invade this very command post. So, Colonel I recommend that we relocate to command post bravo as soon as possible, moving everything across the water and by the end of this week evacuating all of our personnel out of the danger zone, simultaneously putting the whole of Manhattan Island in total absolute quarantine. No one in, no one out, soldiers with machine guns and flame throwers, every two feet guarding the entire perimeter. As I said earlier Colonel, we can't afford for even one of these infected souls to escape this island, so I need to illiterate ... no one can leave ... no one. People will try, men, women and children will try to escape this god forsaken island, so Colonel you will have to order your soldiers to shoot on sight and incinerate anyone who tries. Furthermore Colonel, I implore you, you must get every single soldier involved in this operation, especially the soldiers on the front line, to watch this harrowing, terrifying video. They must be under no illusions that if they fail in their duty, that unrelenting evil ... on this screen, in front of them ... is what will happen to their family's back home. "Colonel Stuart stands up, slowly pacing the room, his face sullen and heavy with the burden of command." Professor Henderson I called you a heartless motherfucking Englishman before. I was right, you are ... but unfortunately, you are 100% right about what needs to be done here today .... Lieutenant, start all preparations to move the entire command post across the water," "yes Colonel." "As from this moment I am declaring a state of emergency, all military personnel's leave is cancelled, everyone is to return to their bases and await further instructions. Operation containment is to be accelerate putting the whole of Manhattan Island in total lockdown. All bridges, tunnels and any other form of escape closed and guarded before the end of this week. I will now go and update the president on the events we have witnessed here today."

Sunday 10 am earlier in the day

"Captain Reese," "yes sergeant," "our team has scoured every inch of Tina Smith's old apartment, we can't find any evidence of any kind, relating to the dossier we have been given.

The apartment block itself is deserted, all the other occupants are being detained in the isolation areas. We have sent personal to speak to them" … "excuse me captain," "yes corporal," "we have found a doorway hidden beneath Tina's apartment block, it was hidden behind a load of trash, cleverly concealed with heavy duty chains and padlocks, we can't gain entry sir." "Sergeant," "yes captain," "get on the radio and get some heavy duty cutting machinery down here asap," "yes captain," "corporal lead the way," "yes captain, this way." Leading the captain down behind the building, through some thorny bushes, over piles of rotting trash arriving at a black fortified steel door. Thick metal chains with heavy duty padlocks barred their way. Soon the sergeant was back with cutting machinery to prise open the door. Angle grinders doing their job, heavy duty chains crashing to the floor, the big fortified metal door slowly swings open. Sunlight starting to stream in, revealing a large dark dusty, damp old laboratory. Equipment smashed and strewn all over the place, an empty sturdy metal barred cage at one end of the room and upended stainless steel tables at the other." Sergeant," "yes captain," "secure this room, I'm going to find out who owns this laboratory, no one in or out," "yes sir."

Sunday 19.10 pm

Captain Reese returns sometime later with a bearded, dirty, thin, slightly bloodied young man. "Sergeant this is Jerry Holloway he is the owner of this underground cellar. We found him hiding in his parents attic. He is going to tell us EXACTLY what he was up to in here, aren't you Jerry, or do you want me to be more persuasive this time." "No sir, no, I will tell you everything. ???"

Back at the CDC the Male adult subject had been anaesthetised and is on the operating table awaiting the surgeon's knife." Doctor, having seen the scans, do you think it's feasible to remove the spider eggs from our subjects?" "I don't know Mrs Hocker, the tiny eggs are buried deep inside the abdomen, clustered around many vital organs. We will know more when my team and I cut him open." "Ok doctor,

I will be in the viewing platform above." Many doctors gather around the Male subject, the lead surgeon opens his microphone, looking up," can you all hear me ok up there," thumbs up and nodding heads the surgeon begins. Microscopic goggles on his head, a razor sharp scalpel in his right hand, the surgeon slices the subject straight down the middle, from chest bone to belly button. Sucking the excess blood out of the way, they splay open his chest and abdomen revealing the bloody inner workings of the human body. Carefully probing and poking deeper and deeper until they reach the cluster of thousands of tiny translucent spider eggs buried deep within. The anaesthetist carefully checking the patient's vital signs as they go." As you good people can see in the gallery above, I have surgically opened the subject's torso, splayed open his flesh and exposed the tiny eggs to the daylight. I am now attempting to remove one of the eggs" ... As soon as the surgeon's knife touches one of the eggs a clear liquid is released, the patient starts shaking, violently unconsciously thrashing around the operating table, his vitals going off the chart.

"Stop, stop," the anaesthetist shouts," doctor the patient is going into shock, his body is on the verge of a cardiac arrest." The surgeon stops, withdraws the razor sharp scalpel and backs away, letting the medical doctors rush in to try and save the young man's life. Looking up once more," I'm sorry Mrs Hocker we don't know what happened, we had to stop the operation, the patient body was going into distress. For now, this operation is over. We will know more once we have run some tests to find out what happened. Mrs Hocker I will bring my full report to you as soon as I have it."

Sunday 21.55 pm

"Colonel sir, Major McCarthy from special forces is here to see you." "Sorry lieutenant something very important is happening, inform all the department heads to meet me in the operations centre as soon as possible," "yes sir. Sorry Major the colonel has been delayed, he will be with you shortly" .... As all the department heads take their seats, Colonel Stewart stands up. "Everyone ... captain Reese is back from Tina Smith's apartment block, he will very shortly be bringing us proof of how this horrific attack started ... Professor Henderson," "yes colonel," "how advanced is your team at the moment, how close are we to constructing a protective suit." "Two days colonel, we anticipated having a fully working prototype on the table ...in two days." "Colonel, captain Reese is ready for you now sir, please follow me." Leading everyone into a separate room where captain Reese has laid out the entire contents of the cellar." Captain," "yes colonel," "can you tell everyone here what they are looking at," "certainly colonel. At approximately 10 am this morning, we discovered a basement directly below Tina Smith's apartment. After gaining entry, we discovered that the basement had been used as some form of laboratory. I tracked down the owner of the basement, this man standing here before you, Mr Jerry Holloway. The contents of his laboratory laid out in front of you, for your examination. I think it would be better for Mr Holloway to tell you, in his own words what happened. Come on Mr Holloway it's your turn now to tell everyone here the truth." Taking half a step forward and a big intake of breath

Mr Holloway, Jerry, nervously begins his story .... "Approximately 7 weeks ago my dear friend Steven Jackson and I were working on a cure for Alzheimer's disease. We mixed various DNAs together from lots of different animals and injected our subjects with the mixture, we then analysed the results. We fully documented our progress, on paper and with CCTV mounted on the basement walls. Our last test subject was George, and the captain has got our footage to show you ... As you can see, George our friendly ape was strapped onto the table. We injected him with the latest batch, the DNA combinations written on the paperwork before you. Instantly George becomes erratic, knocking the syringe out my hand and smashing it onto the basement floor below. His eyes spinning wildly inside his head, his behaviour becoming more aggressive. Wrenching the thick leather straps away from the table, then thrashing around the laboratory smashing everything like a mad man. Our colleague then rushed into the room shooting him with a tranquilliser dart, putting George to sleep."

"Stop, stop, go back a little Captain, I saw something buzzing around the ape's head, yes

Professor Henderson, keep going, a little further back, nearly, stop. There, what is that, can you zoom in captain ... Stop right there, that's a fly buzzing around George's head. Captain, can you play the footage at a slower speed. There it goes, follow it ...... wait its diving down towards the basement floor. Its landed by the syringe ... it's off, look at it, the fly is going crazy, spinning around and around and around ... just like George did, the fly is infected !! look at it, its flying around at a million miles an hour ...... it's gone!! Its disappeared, somewhere up into the corner of the dark ceiling .... That must be when the spider got infected, it must of devoured the infected fly. The infected spider then crawled up into Tina's apartment above, starting this catastrophic disaster we now face today ... What happened next Mr Holloway." "We managed to put George's unconscious body back into his cage, we then cleaned up the basement the best we could. George has destroyed a lot of our equipment, so I sent out our researchers to try and acquire some replacements. Steve and I remained in the basement trying to analyse what had happened.

About two hours later while Steve and I were dissecting the DNA profiles George began to wake. Once again, his eyes were rolling around in his head, up on his feet, growling and snarling trying to smash his way out of his cage. We had never seen old gentle George like this before, he was normally a quiet contented ape, gentle and kind with a lovable personality. The next thing we knew, George had ripped open the thick metal bars of his cage and he was out ... Spinning around on the spot, his ape like fingers clawing away at the back of his head. Moaning, snarling, bearing his impressive sharp pointy teeth. George was obviously in a lot of pain, thrashing around. My best friend Steven then stepped forward to try and calm George down, but poor old George was in so much pain he accidentally knocked Steven to the floor killing him with one single blow. George's behaviour became even more erratic, writhing in agony clutching at his chest, his ape like screams echoing off the dirty basement walls. Then he suddenly stopped, falling to the floor with a hefty thud, George was dead."

"Not knowing what to do, my best friend was dead, George was dead, the laboratory virtually destroyed ... I rang my father. He helped me cover everything up, my best friend Steven died of a heart attack, George's body was cremated and scattered in secret. We did do an autopsy on poor old George before we burned him, his heart ... it had exploded inside his chest killing him instantly." Jerry sinks back into his chair, his hands covering his face, tears trickling through his fingers, "what have I done, what have I done."

Sunday 23.45 pm

"Lieutenant," "yes Colonel," "escort Mr Holloway to the holding area, make sure he has food and water and is fully rested, we will continue his interrogation at zero 7 hundred hours, also inform Major McCarthy that I will see him at zero 6 hundred in the morning," "yes sir." Colonel Stuart stands up, "right people it's late, it's been a long hard day for everyone, I suggest we get some well needed sleep and reconvene back in the command centre at zero 6 hundred hours. We can't get the job done if we are all dead on our feet, dismissed."

Monday 06.00 am .... 12 days to go

"Colonel Stuart and all the department heads are back in the command centre," analysing, discussing, picking over the bones of the last two days developments." Colonel sir, Major McCarthy is here with three men to see you, Major McCarthy from the green berets has returned with three of his bravest men, they will be the ones who have volunteered to descend down into the depths to try and retrieve our live arachnid specimens for testing. All this with no weapons and strapped inside an experimental suit that may or may not work." "Very good lieutenant, show them in." Standing up, saluting ... "Morning Major," "morning Colonel." "Colonel, may I introduce from the green berets special forces, sergeants Robert Samuel and Brandon Rogers," saluting," morning Colonel." Their commanding officer second lieutenant Mitchell Lewinsky, "morning Colonel. At ease men," "thank you Major, you are dismissed. Would you like some coffee gentlemen," "yes thank you Colonel." "Morning everyone, morning colonel, these brave men before you have volunteered to go down into the depths and retrieve the deadly specimens we require, please make room for them" … "Gentlemen, the Major has briefed you on the importance of your mission," "yes Colonel" … "Professor Henderson," "yes Colonel," "could you inform the room on your current progress."

"Morning everyone, my team and I think we have a workable solution, a breathable, manoeuvrable suit that is impervious to the spider's extremely vicious bite. We should have a working prototype here tomorrow, if testing shows the suit is viable, we will hopefully have the green light to start 'operation retrieval' on Wednesday morning. Colonel if the men could follow me at the end of this briefing so we can start the measuring process," "yes, thank you Professor. Mrs Hocker, have you fully analysed what went wrong yesterday with the CDCs attempt to remove the spider eggs from your male subject." "Unfortunately, Colonel the male subject died earlier this morning. When our chief surgeon tried to detach just one of the spider eggs, the eggs secreted a clear liquid, a powerful toxin that shuts down most of the subject's vital organs, resulting in his death. Primarily reports show, trying to remove the eggs is virtually impossible without killing the host. So, I conclude Colonel, this evasive medical procedure is not viable, and we are unfortunately back to square one." "What about the children Mrs Hocker, are we any closer to finding out why they were not viciously attacked," "initially reports show Colonel, the children we have obtained are physically ok, no bite Marks, no eggs but at this time we do not understanding why the children were left unharmed." "Thank you, Mrs Hocker, keep me informed on any further developments" ... "Mr winters Homeland security," "yes Colonel" "how are the preparations going to totally secure the whole of Manhattan Island." "Well Colonel we have covertly hidden explosives on most of the bridges, from Henry Hudson to Third Avenue and down as far as Williamsburg bridge. All the Subterranean tunnels are primed and ready for flooding. We will have everything in place by 21 hundred hours on Wednesday Colonel."

"Very good, don't forget it is imperative that everything is in place, by Wednesday as we are moving this entire command post over the

Brooklyn bridge and relocating at Brooklyn's old naval yard. Everyone on the island outside the quarantined zone has no idea that on Friday we will be putting the whole of Manhattan Island into quarantine. No one in and definitely no one out" ...." But Colonel why can't we evacuate everyone off the island apart from the contaminated people in the quarantined zone." "NO!! The interim reports from our psychology, behavioural committee concludes, people won't just leave. We have over 12 million people living in New York city alone, trying to get them all out in an orderly fashion is impossible. The quarantine zone is holding, the general population thinks that we have an infestation of human bird flu, imagine the panic, the unadulterated chaos that black terrifying spiders are attacking people. The media, the internet would have a field day, we will lose our control, we will lose our advantage, we will lose our country. Over 280 million Americans devoured by this unstoppable black army of death and destruction. I say NO!! We have a chance, a very slim chance to defeat our enemy here and now, they are trapped on this island, what we do today safeguards our nation's future, we have a small window of opportunity so let's give the CDC a chance of defeating this black army of death ... Right people, please keep me informed on your progress, I have to keep the president updated hourly. Good luck and God speed."

Monday 8.15 am

Ruby has been at her news desk frantically trying to find a way of talking to her parents. Not one shred of information has passed over the quarantined walls, not knowing if her beloved parents Bradley and Gene are dead or alive. Human bird flu, that's all they have been told but that doesn't explain the total news blackout, the not knowing is driving our poor Ruby mad.

Monday 9.10 am

It is coming up to nearly two days now and the hapless people in the quarantined zone are still isolated, confined to their beds, not knowing what is really happening to them. Segregated, frightened and alone, kept away from their families by the men in white coats and the many soldiers with guns. How long before the occupants in their tiny little cubicles become restless, angry, frustrated at the men who they think are there to help them. The clock is ticking.

The black terrifying spiders lay in wait deep below the hospital, in the cold blackness cocooned in their nest waiting patiently for their evil black babies to be born into this world. What terrors await the men, women and especially the children far above, totally oblivious to what the black hideous ungodly creatures have in store for them once more.

Monday 12.30 pm

At the CDCs laboratory more hooded human subjects are being led in, scared, confused people, children crying, no one telling them exactly why they are there. Separated from their family and friends, poked, prodded, drink this, another blood test. No one to talk to, no counselling for the physical, mental trauma and suffering they have endured. The talk of spiders long forgotten the words virus and diseases in their place. The men in white coats tending to their needs but still, they are alone, they are scared, they are terrified the black hideous beasts will come back for them.

The phone rings ..." Mrs Hocker, Colonel Stuart here." "Yes Colonel," "our engineers were Laying explosive charges in the Lincoln tunnels beneath the Hudson River where they found hundreds, possibly thousands of strange little cocoons about the size of your fist. I have ordered my men to take samples and deliver them straight to your laboratory so you can determine what they are. Please let me know asap on your findings," "yes certainly Colonel."

Monday 15.45 pm
The phone rings ..." Colonel, Mrs Hocker here, we have analysed those strange little cocoons you sent over earlier. Please recall all the department heads, I will be at the command centre by 16 hundred with my analysis."

Monday 16.00 pm

Colonel Stuart and all the department heads were eagerly sat waiting for Mrs Hocker to arrive ... Mrs Janet Hocker is a truly dedicated scientist, at 62 years old she spent her whole working life devoted to her cause. With no children she has spent her entire adult life protecting others. The only constant in her life has been her husband John, they have been married for over 40 years." Good afternoon gentlemen ... Colonel Stuart sent me some strange looking little cocoons over earlier, they had been found scattered around inside the Lincoln tunnels, reports indicate there were hundreds possibly thousands of these strange looking things everywhere. I have brought some for you to examine. As you can see, they are slightly smaller than your fist, the outer casing is actually made from spiders Webb. I have prepared some footage for you to see. Looking at the screen you can see the little cocoons are quite firm, no give in them at all. After cutting them open we discovered a dead rat inside, shrunk to under half its normal size, not a single drop of blood was left in its tiny little body. Toxicology reports show these were not just baby rats, but they were adolescent, pre puberty, rats that had not yet reached puberty. Putting the remains through our x-ray microscope we found hundreds of tiny pinholes in the cocoon casing and the same corresponding holes in the rat's carcass. There is only one conclusion that we can draw from this. The original black ugly MOMMY spider was catching rats, wrapping them up into a cocoon for her newly born blood thirsty babies to feed on. Hence the hundreds of pin holes and the fact that the young rat were sucked bone dry. There are millions of rats beneath our feet, so as the baby spiders grew, they had lots of food around them" ...

Colonel Stuart is looking slightly confused ..." Mrs Hocker," "yes Colonel," "so why didn't the baby spiders eat the adult rats?" "We don't know yet Colonel but" ......" Stop there, stop right there!!!" "Yes, Professor Henderson" ....." Colonel ... I can't even speak the words" ... "what is it professor" ....." the baby spiders sucked the adolescent rats bone dry .. because they like the taste of nice .. fresh .. young blood!!" ......" PEOPLE .. in under 12 day's time millions upon millions of new HUNGRY evil baby spiders will be .. exploding .. bursting .. spewing onto our streets .... And our adolescent untouched

CHILDREN will be their FOOD!!!" The room fell silent .... The enormity of Professor Henderson's omission echoing around the room, bouncing off the crisp white walls into the disbelieving ears of the open mouthed, shocked people listening ......!! The room erupts ..... everyone talking at once .. No .. We must get the children out .. Are you sure professor .. We can't let this happen .. My god .. get the children out .. That's insane .... "Everyone ... everyone calm down. Professor Henderson," "yes Colonel .. are you seriously telling me that our children will be devoured by those hideous black beasts in only 12 day's time !!!" "Yes Colonel .. Yes everyone, in my opinion our sweet innocent little children will be FOOD for the millions of black .. blood thirsty hordes erupting onto our streets in only 12 short day's time." All the department heads along with dozens of support staff scattered around the room are in total disbelief, their hands up to their totally dumbfounded faces, their minds trying to make sense of what they have just heard. "Colonel Stuart ... Colonel Stuart" raising her hand above the melee," yes, you are?" "Colonel my name is Doctor Catalina

Mendes, I work with Mrs Hocker in the CDC. Colonel, I think I speak for everyone here .. We can't let our innocent little children be fodder for these black hideous creatures, Colonel, we must get them all out." Colonel Stuart raises from his chair, his bereft face searching for answers among the distraught, shocked people before him. Pacing the room finding himself lost and with no direct plan of action ahead of him for the first time in his 41 years of military service ...!!

"Ok people settle down ... The Pentagon put me in charge of this entire operation, but it is you good people sat here right now who will solve this horrific situation that we find ourselves in. My team and I scoured the globe in preparation for this impending catastrophe. We knew from the first moment of poor Tina Smith's awful, gruesome death that something horrifying was on its way. We didn't know what and we didn't exactly know when, but we knew it was something ungodly. Something truly unspeakable, an unstoppable army of pure black evil, emerging, crawling from deep beneath our feet, descending on us like a black hideous tsunami, washing humanity into the blackness below .... So, people I am just a soldier, I am a man used to the horrors of war, but this is beyond me." Look around," it's you people in this room who will defeat this unstoppable black army from decimating our society. You are the best at what you do, the best and the brightest from all around the world, it's you good people right now who will solve this thing. So ... please go away, do what you do best but I need a full and detailed report Laying out your solutions for the children on my desk by 22 hundred this evening so I can keep the president appraised of these new developments." The department heads along with their dedicated personnel retreat back into their respective departments trying to hatch a plan to evacuate all of the doomed children off Manhattan Island.

Tuesday 06.00 am .... 11 days to go.

After a long restless night everyone is back in the command centre for the morning's briefing." Thank you everyone, take your seats. I have submitted all of your detailed reports to the president and the joint chiefs of staff last night.

He has assured me that after his advisers have dissected all of your reports, he will have a plan of action on the table with respect of the children." "But Colonel we need the children out now," "I hear what you're saying, that decision is down to the president alone, he has assured me personally that the children are his top priority," "ok Colonel." "Right then who wants to kick things off this morning" ... "Colonel," "yes" "Mr Winters homeland security, as I reported earlier everything will be in place by 21 hundred tomorrow night. All bridges, tunnels, subways, every possible Avenue of escape off that island will be ready to be severed on your command sir. Furthermore, I have requested 100 thousand more military personnel and equipment to strengthen our outer perimeter. We have sent engineers into the inner perimeter checking that all possible routes are closed off" ....

"Colonel, I am professor Armstrong leading entomologist at Columbia university, Professor Henderson and I have been going over Mr Winters secondary quarantine plan. All bridges and Subterranean exits will be blocked but what about the water" ... "The water professor?" "Yes,

Colonel the Harlem and Hudson rivers. We have concluded that all manmade avenues have been dealt with but not the water itself. When the spiders re-emerge, there is nothing stopping them from floating across the rivers and onto the mainland. We don't know if these intelligent, fast, strong creatures can simply float, several species of arachnids can run on water, we just don't know" …" So, Colonel we propose putting a ring of fire around the entire stricken island, sailing oil tankers around the island with their oil valves fully open leaving a thick black oily trail behind them, encapsulating the whole area ready to be engulfed in flames stopping anything from leaving." "Yes, professor I think you have spotted a flaw in our operation … Mr Winters," "yes Colonel," "has this contingency been considered," "no Colonel the rivers have been totally overlooked, we were concentrating on bridges and subways, not the water itself". "Professor Armstrong," "yes Colonel," "I want you to work very closely with homeland security to eradicate all water exit points, extradite any and all measures you deem fit to protect the mainland," "yes Colonel I will get straight onto it."

"Mrs Hocker CDC, have you anything new to report?" "No Colonel nothing new to report this morning. We are still running lots of different tests and procedures on our human subjects, trying to medically dislodge the spider eggs but I'm sad to say, nothing is working at the moment. Our containment protocols are all in place ready for live spider specimens so we can determine how to kill them." "Very good Mrs Hocker … Professor Henderson," "yes Colonel," "where are we on the developments on the protective suit?" "I am assured by my team on the ground that we will have a workable prototype here in the command centre by Wednesday evening the latest. We will then run the protective suit hastily through our safety checks and if everything goes to plan, we will construct the remaining suits overnight and have them ready for deployment first thing on Thursday morning." "How are the volunteers shaping up professor?" "As you can imagine Colonel the men are terrified, but they are professionals, their work ethic is beyond reproach. Their dedication and professionalism to the job in hand amazes me, they are putting their lives in my hands. One wrong move, one missed calculation and they are dead. Yes, Colonel the volunteers are ready." "Very good professor. Right people we have only 11 days left … so let's get this show on the road."

Tuesday 7.45 am

Outside the quarantined zone for the last three days life has continued on as normal, or as normal as can be with a very large section of Manhattan Island in a stricken lockdown. People are duly concerned, human bird flu, they are worried that the infection will seep out of containment and affect all their lives. Covid 19 is still circumventing the globe but with the new and improved vaccine people are learning to live with it. At the news desk in New York city Ruby is still waiting for news on her beloved parents. She has contacted all of her media colleagues but to no avail, not one shred of information has leaked out of the quarantined zone. Edward Ruby's boyfriend returns to the news centre. "Edward, have you got any news?" "No Ruby, I have been out and spoken to everyone I know but there is nothing, no news of any kind. I have even spoken to my military contacts but all they keep telling me is … human bird flu." "I'm starting to get worried now Edward, its agonising not knowing if my frail old parents are alive or dead." Wrapping her arms around her boyfriend's neck Ruby has a little cry, she is normally a very strong and driven woman but not today. Wiping away the tears," Edward have you spoken to your boss about us using your weather helicopter yet?" "No Ruby not yet but if she says no, I will try and convince the pilot to take us, his sister is in the quarantined area too." "Ok Edward please try your best, I know the quarantine area is a no fly zone but I just need some news."

Tuesday 9.10 am

Three days of isolation is having its toll on the inhabitants confined to their little cubicles of solitude. Doctors constantly walking in and out, armed soldiers making sure everyone follows the rules. The Kirk family are oblivious to the fact that they are all within touching distance of each other. Richard, Shona, Ryan and Charley segregated, forcibly confined against their will by the very men and women who they think are there to help them. No counselling, no kind words, no close human contact to try and heal the deep psychical and mental scars they have all suffered. The people are getting restless, angry, rebellious, starting to question those who they think are there to protect them. The quarantine zone is starting to shudder, thousands of scared frightened people wanting answers to questions no one is prepared to give.

Tuesday 14.35 pm

"Come on Ruby I have sorted out the helicopter, my boss has given a definite NO, but I have convinced the pilot to take us as close as we dare." Descending down onto the streets of New York Edward and Ruby are amazed how people's lives are continuing on as normal. The sidewalks packed with sightseers, the highway full of bustling tooting traffic, people out enjoying the bright summer sunshine without a care in the world. Hailing a taxi, climbed in .. "New York central weather station please." All the drivers can talk about is the weather, celebrity this, celebrity that, how busy the roads are, not once has he mentioned the quarantined zone. The American people have been Indoctrinated, conditioned to believe if spun the right way, believe everything that the government's says, believing their lies, believing their rhetoric. Arriving at the central weather station Edward and Ruby ascend to the roof where the weather helicopter is fuelled and waiting. Taking their seats, strapping in, headphones on, "this is John the pilot," "nice to meet you John I'm Ruby," "nice to meet you Ruby, I will try and get us as close as we can but as you know we can't fly to close to the quarantined area." Up they go leaving New York city far behind them, no flight plan, no permission but on they go. Passing the empire state building, over central park ...." there it is. Edward, it looks more like a concentration camp", watchtowers, barb wire, snarling guard dogs patrolling around the perimeter. "That doesn't look like a quarantine zone it looks more like a prison to me."

As they circle slowly around the quarantined zone, they can see people being taken from one place to another. The men in white coats leading the way, followed by hospital gowned hooded patients with armed soldiers taking up the rear. SUDDENLY an Apache attack helicopter appears above the horizon, its automatic machine guns trained onto the unauthorised craft, its speakers bellowing out deadly commands." Weather helicopter 259 you are in a restricted no fly zone, follow me or we Will open fire." "Shit, fuck, I'm sorry Ruby but I have no choice but to follow. Weather helicopter 259 roger that," "follow us to the command post." Following the Apache away from the quarantined zone our three heroes realise the seriousness of their actions … "Edward," "yes John," "there is no point us all getting caught, you see that tall building up ahead," "yes, I see it John, do you see it, Ruby?" "Yes, I do John." "As we pass, I will suddenly descend to about 20 feet away from the top of the building, I need you to slide open the door, firmly grab onto Ruby's hands and jump onto the roof." "No Edward, I can't do it" … holding Ruby firmly by the hand, looking deep into her eyes .." Ruby yes you can, we need to be free to help your parents, you can do this". Down the little helicopter goes, doors open and out they go landing safely onto the roof below. The little helicopter quickly backs up following as if nothing had happened. Edward and Ruby quickly leave the rooftop and join the hapless people on the streets below." What will happen to John?" "I don't know Ruby but with no flight plan, no manifest and no authorisation I don't expect to see John for quite some time. Come on Ruby we better get back to the news room, let's hope you haven't been missed."

Tuesday 18.30 pm

Colonel Stuart had assembled just the department heads in the command centre." Everyone as you are all aware we will be moving overnight this entire command post over the water to Brooklyn's old naval yard. Mrs Hocker your new CDC laboratory will be up and running by 20 hundred hours this evening on Roosevelt Island," Roosevelt Island is a small island situated on the Harlem River, only a stone's throw from Manhattan Island itself." All connections have been severed from Manhattan Island and the mainland making sure your facility is totally isolated. The navy has a ship standing by to ferry yourselves and all of your equipment over to the small secure island. please make sure everyone in your teams knows their new location and everything is packed away, boxed up ready for shipment. I will be out most of the night personally checking on how the new quarantine area is progressing. So, unless we have any other business to attend too, I will bid you all a good night. I will see you all at the new command centre at 09.30 tomorrow." All the department heads filter back to their departments knowing full well that they have an extremely long night ahead moving their entire operation.

No one can be in any doubt, not the president, not the Colonel, not anyone who has attended the command centre, how much of an enormous undertaking this is, the terrible weight they all carry upon their shoulders. One bad mistake, one lapse in concentration, one error of judgement and the game is over. The game in question is life, not life for the poor souls in the quarantined zone as they are already dead but life outside. The lives of over 280 million ordinary Americans are in their hands, they don't know it and possibly they never will but these men and women here today fighting this savage monstrous black army is their only hope of survival. Only pulling together and doing the things that most normal people would be horrified at, is sometimes the only way to win. But who will win, the spiders or mankind ...... only time will tell!!!

Wednesday 9.30 am .... 10 days to go.

"Morning everyone," "morning Colonel." "I know it has been a very long night for everybody, most of us are absolutely knackered, it has been a monumental move, but we are here. I hope you have everything you need at your disposal, the president has immobilized all our armed forces to help us defeat this monstrous black army. If there is anything you need or anything that you can think of, please ask. A state of emergency has been privately declared and we are all in this thing together ... Professor Henderson," "yes Colonel." "Are we still on track with the protective suit," "yes Colonel the prototype should be arriving sometime this afternoon." "How do you rate its chances professor," "well

Colonel I have personally been overseeing the suits construction, it won't be until we get the fully assembled suit back here that I will I know if it's up to the job." "I can't stress enough professor, the success or failure of this entire operation rests in your hands. No spiders to dissect, no possible way of knowing how to destroy them. Your task is that vital the president himself will be here to oversee the retrieval of the live specimens … Mrs Hocker how are your new facilities on Roosevelt Island," "yes Colonel they are excellent, my team and I are eagerly awaiting the spiders arrival. I have an impeccable team of toxicologists standing by with every possible poison, nerve gas, chemical weapons at their disposal to see if we can kill these hideous beasts" … "Colonel," raising her hand, "doctor Mendes CDC. Has the president decided how he is getting the children out, the clock is ticking, and we don't have a lot of time left." "Doctor Mendes the president has reassured me that every possible Avenue is being pursued in relation to evacuating the children, I am hoping that when he arrives later tonight, I can present a plan to you all on how he wants the operation to be done. Right, everyone back to it, please don't hesitate to contact me if you have any further developments or you need anything. Carry on."

Everybody in the new command post is busy scurrying around getting everything shipshape and Bristol fashion. There are many more people to accommodate now, and the stakes could not be higher. The president will be arriving later this evening so everything must be up to scratch.

Wednesday 15.35 pm

An armoured convoy turns up at the gate," it's the suit." Professor Henderson and his eager team waste no time getting the precious package carefully unwrapped and into the lab for testing to begin. They must make sure that the suit is impervious to the spiders sharp pointy fangs, if the suit is compromised in any way what so ever, its game over. They need to get live specimens back to the CDC so the experts can start dissecting, analysing, finding a way of killing these black terrifying monsters. The toughened Perspex container that will house the vicious black beast is located on the belly of the suit, with microscopic holes so that the creatures can breathe.

Wednesday 18.00 pm

Professor Henderson and his team are sufficiently agreed that the hastily assembled protective suit will give maximum protection for a very limited time. They are still unsure of the severity of the spiders vicious bite, the spiders are strong, they are fast and there are hundreds of thousands of those hideous creatures waiting for our brave volunteers in the darkness below.

Professor Henderson gives the green light so the other two protective suits can be quickly assembled so our three brave volunteers can begin their perilous journey deep below, with no guns, no weapons of any kind to protect them, just this stab proof layer to stop them being devoured by these evil black terrifying monsters.

Wednesday 21.20 pm

The president and the joint chiefs of staff with their many advisers arrive at the new command post. "Colonel sir the president has arrived," "very good lieutenant please show him to the command centre and inform all department heads to attend," "yes Colonel" ... The command centre is full to capacity, professionals from all walks of life, the military, doctors, professors, scientists from all over the world are here with one common goal ... to insure the survival of the human species.

"Colonel," "yes Mr president," "please give everyone here an update on where we are right now on the ground," "yes Mr president." Composing himself and taking a large intake of breath the Colonel begins ... "Mr president, everyone, we anticipated that we have approximately 9 and a half DAYS before millions upon millions of new baby spiders are born into the world. We have two things in our favour today, one .. we have total containment .. two, we have the spiders trapped on an island. The quarantine zone is holding, the people being held there are being subdued with lies, we have told these terrified traumatised people that the spiders came, went and have been destroyed, possibly leaving behind a deadly pathogen in its wake. They have all been quarantined to stop a deadly virus being unleashed into society, they think we are there to help them but as you know, we are not. We are there to keep them calm and segregated from the main population. Mrs Hocker and her extensive team at the CDC have been working tirelessly to find a way of safety extracting the spider eggs buried deep inside our infected subjects but I'm sorry to say, to date with no avail. Our first test subject died on the operating table, poisoned by a secreted substance released as a defence mechanism by the tiny spider eggs. All further attempts at removal have failed, we cannot detach the thousands of eggs without killing the host. All testing on the children has come back negative, apart from the mental trauma that the children have suffered they do not seem physically affected by the spiders attack."

The Colonel continued "After reading the psychology behavioural committees extensive report we concluded that the inner quarantine zone will fail within 7 to 10 days of implementation. So, it was decided to move the entire command infrastructure across the water to safety.

All preparations are in place to encompass the whole of Manhattan Island in an impenetrable ring of men, concrete and steel to prevent this ungodly black army from reaching the mainland. Professor Henderson and his team have carried out extensive testing on the new protective suit and have authorised the remaining two suites to be quickly assembled, to be delivered here by midnight tonight. If we cannot retrieve the live specimens we require, then we have no possible way of determining how to destroy these unconscionable, unstoppable black terrifying creatures from engulfing our great nation. So, Mr president this is where we are right now, we have tried to think of all eventualities but if we fail sir, we have no plan B."

The many faces around the room are silent, trying to digest the enormity of the dire consequences of failure, the unfathomable and unspeakable terrors that will befall every man, woman and child if they fail to stop this black army of death right here, right now.

The president, our commander-in-chief, the man entrusted with the fate of this entire nation resting on his heavy shoulders, slowly stands up ... His eyes scanning the room at the expecting faces of his flock, they are eagerly awaiting their elected representative to miraculously save the day ..." Thank you, Colonel" ... Everyone, the president slightly bows his head in recognition of all the dedicated people in the room." I would firstly like to personally thank everyone here for their tieless and unwavering support in this time of need. We find ourselves in an impossible situation, a terrifying unspeakable black army of creatures have descended upon us, and we have no conventional defence against them. My many advisers and I have been working night and day feverishly reading every report that you good people submit, trying desperately to devise a comprehensive, iron clad plan of action. We have allowed the citizens of New York and most of Manhattan Island to carry on as normal, keeping the quarantined zone totally isolated, detached from the general population, no information in or out. By doing this we keep control, being in control is key, keeping the masses ignorant, calm and oblivious to what is going on around them. For over four days now we have kept our great nation and the rest of the world blinded by the events unfolding in front of our own eyes. We must stay the course, the unconscionable decisions that we MUST make in these terrible days to come will decide the future of humanity."

The President looked around the room and continued "Initially we had several lines of attack on the table .. round up the hundreds of thousands of infected people and burn them... but no, we couldn't explain our diabolical actions to the world. Plus, the black hideous adult creatures would still be hiding beneath our feet waiting to impregnate the terrified people once more ... Evacuate the entire island leaving the infected behind, then blowing it all to hell ... but we couldn't be absolutely confident in evacuating millions of people without a coherent excuse, a good enough reason in the time frame we had, or that we would inadvertently release just one of the infected souls onto the mainland ... so people we have just over 9 days to win this terrifying battle or ... I have deliberated long and hard, agonised over what HAS to be done

… so, people if we fail, if the quarantined zone is compromised, I have authorised, with a heavy heart, the total obliteration of the entire island of Manhattan by nuclear thermal devices. Which I'm sad to say would also kill us all and millions of unsuspecting Americans in the blast radius. This is the last case scenario, so Colonel I have decided to stay here in the command post with you all and let's hope God will prevail in our hour of need."

You could see the president had the whole of America on his shoulders, "So people we are all in this thing together, has anyone got anything else to add." Raising her hand," Mr president, Mrs Catherine Mendes CDC, what are we doing about getting the children out of there?" "Thank you, Mrs Mendes, we have extensively read Professor Henderson's report on what he thinks about the children. The Pentagon's scientific body believes that the children were not attacked and impregnated with thousands of spider eggs because their little metabolisms couldn't sustain the growth needed to bring the eggs to full term" …" But Mr president we can't in all good conscience leave the helpless children in there, we have 9 days, surely, we can do something" ...... "Mr president," "yes Professor Henderson," "I think your scientific reports are wrong, I have fully read through these reports, they are full of superstitions and conjecture, nothing of any substance just a baseless hypothesis why the children were not attacked. Mr president I strongly urge you to re-evaluate your position, after birthing these baby spiders will need sustenance. We have the cocooned bodies of the adolescent rats as evidence that our poor frightened children will be sucked bone dry by these hideous creatures when they spew upon the world." "Thank you, professor, I will take your comments under advisement but for now, the children stay ... Colonel Stuart," "yes Mr president," "it's getting late, I suggest we all retire to get some food and rest, we can then reconvene back here when professor Henderson's protective suits arrive," "yes Mr president."

Everyone in the command centre slowly disperses, tiered, worried people not knowing what the next frantic 9 days will hold.

Thursday 12.45 am

The final two protective suits arrive at the command centre." Lieutenant," "yes professor Henderson," "could you please inform sergeants Samuel and Rogers and second lieutenant Lewinsky that their protection body suits have arrived. Can you arrange for them to meet me in my laboratory in an hour so my team and I can finalise all checks and procedures before they head out on their crucial mission," "yes professor will do." Professor Henderson heads down to his laboratory to do final checks on all three experimental body suits before the brave volunteers arrive.

Thursday 05.00 am

Professor Henderson has had everyone awoken from their slumber and they are all, coffee in hand, sat waiting in the command centre for the professor and his brave volunteers to arrive ...." Morning Mr president, morning everyone, I'm sorry it is so early but time is of the essence. May I introduce our brave volunteers and explain the dynamics of their protective body suits. We have sergeant Robert Samuel, sergeant

Brandon Rogers and second lieutenant Mitchell Lewinsky all from the green berets special forces division. They have all bravely volunteered to go down into the blackness below to try and retrieve live specimens for our examination. Lieutenant Lewinsky," "yes professor," "can you please step forward. As you can see, we have had to construct a full body suit to protect these brave men from the spiders sharp pointy fangs. The whole suit is up to the neck area and is made out of a double layered black stab vest material, glued and treble stitched to give maximum protection. The protective gloves are sewn directly onto the sleeves giving limited dexterity. Lieutenant, can you please put your helmet on .. The helmet itself is a modified deep sea divers helmet, a toughened glass done for panoramic observation. The slimmed down air tanks are secreted under the stab vest on the lieutenant's back with rebreathing technology installed" ..... "Rebreathing technology professor ...??"

"Yes, when a person exhales a small amount of oxygen is expelled, this excess oxygen is reconstituted by the rebreather, it is then reabsorbed into the main air tanks to prolong the efficiency of the oxygen supply. Meaning our brave men will have more oxygen to breath. The moment they engage their air supply, they will have only 3 hours of oxygen in the slim air tanks to get in and out .. We also have a 12 centimetre squared thick Perspex box with microscopic air holes securely strapped to the lieutenant's abdomen for the retrieval of our arachnid specimens. We have installed lights inside the helmet and the lieutenant has got a high density video camera around his forehead with radio communications built in .. We have designed the suit to be very tough and strong, nothing on show, all wires, pipes anything that the spiders can sink their extremely sharp fangs into are hidden beneath the protective cover. They will have a hand held flashlight, mountaineering ropes and a motion sensor device to help them locate the spiders nest" ... "Very good professor." The president stands up and addresses our brave volunteers." May I once again shake the hands of our extremely brave men, sergeant Rogers" ... "Mr president" ..." sergeant Samuel "..."

Mr president" ... "and second lieutenant Lewinsky" ..." Mr president." "I wish you god speed on your perilous journey, let's pray that your dangerous mission is a success." Saluting ..." we will do our duty Mr president." The three brave soldiers exit the command centre and head out to the Archie Memorial hospital, the epicentre of the outbreak, ready to decent down into deep, dark, caverns below.

Thursday 07.51 am .... *9 days to go.*

Our three brave soldiers start their terrifying decent deep below the hospital .. !! The command centre is ready for action, the president and his entourage are sat with bated breath along with all the other occupants of the command centre. Colonel Stuart and his team sit headphones on in front of live action monitors, orchestrating every move our brave, intrepid volunteers make ..." Colonel Stuart," "yes Mr president," "how long before our men reach their goal?" "Well Mr president it's impossible to say, we have studied every walkway, subway, subterranean tunnel in the immediate area but we just don't know where the spiders are" …" Professor Henderson," "yes Mr president," "what are we expecting to encounter down there?" "Mr president the closer our brave souls get to the spiders nest the more in danger they are. These spiders are predatory and very territorial creatures, anything that threatens their nest is savagely attacked but Mr president we are counting on this" … "Explain professor" .. "The thick Perspex boxes strapped to our volunteers bellies have been impregnate with fly larvae. The spiders will hopefully perceive the soldiers as invaders and attack them, swarming all over their bodies trying to sink their blood thirsty fangs into their flesh. As our brave soldiers get closer to the nest, they will flip open the spring loaded front door of the box leaving the inners exposed. Then hopefully, fingers crossed Mr president!! as the black ugly spiders swarm all over our fearless volunteers at least one of the hideous spiders will venture inside the open larvae covered box. Then our brave soldiers … sweating, their heart rate going through the roof, scared out of their mind, hundreds of black terrifying monsters crawling all over his traumatised body trying to sink their sharp .. pointy .. hideous .. fangs into every crevice of their shaking bodies …. MUST, using the palm of their trembling hand, snap shut the front of the box ensuring a blood thirsty spider is trapped within" …" My god professor," "THIS is the best plan we have!!" it's all fingers crossed and no if, buts and maybes, those poor brave souls, God help them.

Thursday 11.05 am

Colonel Stuart and his team have been guiding our three brave soldiers deeper and deeper into the darkness below, wading through thousands of small cocoons the deeper they go. Everyone in the command centre is transfixed, their eyes wide open staring at the monitors in front of them, watching the brave soldiers flashlights illuminating the caverns below ….. "Colonel," "yes lieutenant Lewinsky" .." I think we have movement!! The motion detector needle is moving, I can't see a thing Colonel, but I can hear a faint dragging sounds coming from the north west …. wait the signal is getting stronger, the motion detector is going crazy sir" … "Colonel .. tell the men to put on their helmets and switch to oxygen," "yes professor. Alfa team, put your helmets on, switch to oxygen," "yes Colonel" … The command centre is totally silent, staring at the screens, peering into the darkness only the sound of heavy, nervous breathing combined with the thud thud ….. thud thud ….. thud thud of the heart monitors constantly checking the vitals of our three terrified, brave soldiers, edging slowly closer and closer in the pitch blackness towards the blood thirsty hordes crawling faster and faster towards them ……………. Then out of the darkness they came, black hideous creatures, swarming all over our brave souls, their bristly thorny legs clambering over their terrified bodies, their .. pointy .. razor sharp fangs jabbing, thrusting, dripping with venom trying to penetrate their protective body suits. Scurrying onto their domed glass helmets, the hapless brave volunteers watching in horror as the black hideous spiders just inches away, their long pointy fangs trying to smash the glass above their frantic faces. Screaming, shouting …

"Colonel, Colonel, spiders, spiders," terrified, their instinct is to run away but the three brave soldiers must stay and endure this horrendous onslaught. Waiting, praying their protective suit will hold, waiting, hoping a spider will enter the Perspex box ... Everyone in the command centre is glued to the screens, watching in horror as the black hideous monsters engulf the soldiers, the loud scrapping and endless tapping of pointy fangs hitting the glass helmets trying to smash it ...... The three soldiers holding their ground, shaking, terrified, feeling every sharp thrust of the spiders fangs trying to penetrate their suits, like a blunt daggers being driven into their very souls ..... Slam .. shut sergeant Rogers has snared a spider .... a second ... lieutenant Lewinsky slams the door on another .... The spiders are frantic .. "Colonel, we have two spiders safely locked up, but the spiders are going crazy," "ok lieutenant get your team out of there." Still covered in snarling, whirling spiders our three traumatised soldiers stagger ever so slowly upwards, their breathing erratic, their hearts beating out of their terrified chests but still the spiders attack. The three men encircled in a black hideous whirlwind spinning around and around them trying to penetrate their protective shield. The trapped spiders in the Perspex boxes bouncing around, smashing into the thick sides trying frantically to escape ..." Colonel ".... Out of breath, his speech becoming shallow, "oxygen running dangerously low, Colonel" ...." yes lieutenant Lewinsky, I can barely hear you." "Colonel we are not going to make it, the spiders ..... the spiders are relentless .... SERGEANT" his voice croaky, with tears in his bloodshot eyes, "sergeant Samuel NO ....!!! Colonel Stuart sergeant Samuel is gone, the spiders have penetrated his suit, the black hideous monsters are inside his helmet, hundreds of them ...... NOOOO" The command centre watches on in horror as sergeant Samuel's protective shield is compromised, the evil black spiders ripped open a tiny hole and pour in to devour our poor brave soul." Lieutenant .. lieutenant Lewinsky" ......" yes Colonel," "you and sergeant Rogers are nearly out of there, we have men with flamethrowers ahead .... keeping going lieutenant, your nearly home."

The two brave exhausted men battle on, the spiders still relentless in their pursuit. Closer and closer our brave volunteers edge upwards, upwards towards safety and out of this black hideous hellhole. "Lieutenant .... lieutenant, our men on the surface can see you, keep going lieutenant." Absolutely knackered and nearly out of oxygen our brave intrepid soldiers march on ...... Wooooshhh a blinding flash of extreme heat washes over our exhausted men, flamethrowers going off in all directions, the spiders scatter and run, back into their Hidie holes to fight another day. Our brave soldiers pulled to safety, battered, bruised and absolutely fucked!! Our two brave terrified volunteers are stretchered away, plucked from deaths clutches and returned to the safety of the command post.

The exhausted men are brought straight into the laboratory of the CDC, contained and isolated, the thick Perspex boxes carefully removed from around their waists, the spiders within spinning wildly, smashing into its thick plastic walls trying frantically to escape. The smouldering battered protective suits cut away from our traumatised volunteers pummelled bodies, exhausted and still in shock our two brave souls are carried away, their duty fulfilled, a job well done.

Thursday 18.00 pm

The two deadly spiders are carefully placed in their containment chambers, metal arms extend outwards releasing the angry creatures out of their Perspex confinement. Instantly the spiders start whirling around their 2 foot square metal isolation chambers, up on all of their spiny 8 black bristly legs running wildly from side to side smashing, crashing, using their long pointy, razor sharp fangs trying to find a way out. The isolation chambers are sat side by side, thick metal walls with reinforced glass viewing windows. The laboratory is totally secure, shatterproof double entry doors allowing only one person in, or one person out at any time. Mrs Hocker and her extensive team get straight to work, trying to find a way of killing these hideous beasts!!!

Thursday 18.45 pm

Back in the command centre everyone is relieved at the success of the mission but terribly sad for the horrific death of sergeant Samuel. The president and all the department heads have dispersed and gone back to their own departments ...." Colonel," "yes lieutenant," "we are getting reports in, that there is unrest in the quarantined zone. Angry people are leaving their isolation cubicles and are trying to escape the containment cordon." "Lieutenant, contact captain Rivers at quarantine HQ and tell him to deploy extra troops around the quarantined zone perimeter. I will be there in 30 minutes to take command personally, just remind the captain, deadly force has been authorised, no one and I mean no one is permitted to leave the quarantined area," "yes Colonel."

Friday 06.00 am .... 8 days to go.

Colonel Stuart has called an emergency meeting, the president and all the departments are in attendance. "Morning everyone, Mr president, I was called away from the command centre last night to deal with unrest in the quarantined zone. As predicted the quarantine area is starting to crumble, the people are no longer content with the excuses we have been giving them. They want answers, they want out. Thousands of scared frustrated people, men, women and children were unlawfully gathering

along the fence line, jeering, shouting, trying to escape the cordon. I ordered my men to shoot anyone who gets too close. Mr president I must report, during the early hours of this morning we have 41 dead, shot trying to escape. 35 men, 4 women and two small children sir. The tense situation was quickly resolved, the whole place is like a tinder box ready to explode. So, Mr president I recommend we implement quarantine zone bravo, the total lockdown of Manhattan Island. All preparations are in place Mr president, we just need your orders sir" ....."
Mr president, Mrs Mendes from the CDC again .. Mr president what is happening with the children, we can't in all good conscience leave those poor children in there. We have only 8 days before the new generation of spiders are born, if professor Henderson is right, our little children will be fodder for those hungry black monsters. So, Mr president I implore you, please let the children go" ......

"Mrs Mendes, everyone sat around this table watched that horrendous footage yesterday of those brave young men going down into the darkness, it's time to be Frank with you all today.

For over 7 weeks now the brightest minds in the world have been locked away in the Pentagon analysing, crunching the numbers and scenarios on all the possible outcomes. If we fail to destroy this hideous black army here today, we lose, humanity loses. These black demons are unstoppable, they are fast, strong and highly intelligent and at present we have no possible way of killing them" ..... "But Mr president we have had nearly 6 days already to evacuate as many people as possible from New York city and Manhattan Island, but we .. you Mr president have done nothing about it." "I understand your passion Mrs Mendes .... ok then let's put one of our scenarios on the table. Mrs Mendes in the aftermath of the spiders attacked we took control, creating a ring of steel around the affected area. No one in, no one out, with a total media blackout. As far as the world was concerned, we had an outbreak of human bird flu .... So, Mrs Mendes the table is yours, how are you going to, as you put it, get the children out, without starting panic that is" ...." Emm .... we could of taken all of the children out of quarantine" ..." But Mrs Mendes can you be

100% certain that the children haven't been affected in any way," "no Mr president." "Mrs Mendes, everyone, I am not a heartless president, I have children of my own. For days we have been trying to find a solution to this horrendous problem. People won't just hand their children over to you, they need a reason, fire, flood, earthquake, meteor, they would only leave when fire is actually raining down from the sky above but even then, some people would stay. We could of tried to evacuate everyone from New York city, what disaster could we dream up?? Trying to convince over 14 million people to leave their homes, their jobs, their way of live without causing a panic. It was believed by most to keep the people ignorant, oblivious, let them live their lives as normal. Control is our biggest weapon in this ungodly war, as I said earlier, we have over 280 fellow Americans to consider, hard choices have to be made."

"Professor Henderson," "yes Mr president," "in your professional opinion, will the spiders attack again, do we still have 8 days?" "Yes, Mr president in my opinion as long as the infected people stay on the island the adult spiders will stay concealed, keeping out of sight, protecting, waiting for their offspring to be born. If the current timeline prevails the baby spiders will burst into the streets of Manhattan sometime on Saturday morning, 8 days from now. I believe as the new babies are spewing into the world the adult spiders will re-emerge onto the streets attacking our little innocent children, wrapping their little frozen conscious bodies in their web ready to be drained while they are still alive by their hungry blood thirsty babies" ......" Mr president please ... after hearing what professor Henderson has just said, surely there is something we can do to save our poor defenceless children." "I am sorry Mrs Mendes, I truly am, but no ... the die is cast, we must stay the course... we must put our faith in the CDC, they will find the answers we crave."

THE LOCKDOWN

"Colonel Stuart," "yes Mr president," "I am giving you the order to remove all of our personnel off the island of Manhattan, abandoning the quarantine area and simultaneously putting the whole of the island into complete lockdown. An inner ring of steel comprising of men, barbed wire and concrete will be erected around the entire shoreline, all bridges, tunnels, subways to be taken control of. All explosives to be readied with an outer ring of steel facing the island, armed gunboats patrolling our waters, with fighter jets and Apache helicopter controlling the no fly zone. All military personnel on a strict 6 hourly rotation and with no exceptions. All military personnel will watch the horrific, harrowing video from the shopping mall, plus the footage our brave volunteers decent down into the depths. No one can be under any illusions about this black army of pure evil we face, every single person MUST do their duty. I must reiterate the use of armed deadly force is authorised, anyone .. man, woman or child trying to leave the quarantined zone will be shot on sight and their bodies to be incinerated where they stand" ....

"Colonel, the cover story is that the DEADLY human bird flu has leaked out of containment and infected most of Manhattans population. Anyone with the following symptoms must self-isolate immediately for 7 days, a sore throat, runny nose, a cough, feeling tired, aches and pains, a fever. With covid 19 still prevalent in the world most people are used to isolating, hopefully everyone will follow the guidance and stay at home. Once you have informed me Colonel that the quarantine zone is in place, I will make ready my broadcast, a presidential address to the nation explaining the dire situation we all find ourselves in. I will order everyone to stay home, all non-essentially businesses to be closed immediately, all aircrafts grounded, all subway and trains terminals closed. All transportation, driving or walking off the island to be suspended with immediate effect. For the next 7 days the island of Manhattan will be in full quarantine, everyone must listen to our quarantine Marshalls on the ground they are there to help. I will also announce that hundreds of people have already died in the old quarantine zone and the survivors experiencing horrific hallucinations. The talk of terrifying spiders quickly being dismissed as the babblings of a delirious sick person .... we need time Colonel, we will have the island completely contained. We don't need millions of scared people stampeding the border causing absolute chaos trying to leave .. one more thing Colonel.

"Yes, Mr president," "there are many rich and extremely powerful people in New York city, they will try and leave. They will use their power and influence to bribe, coerce or pay their way out, this must not happen Colonel, this cannot happen. I am entrusting you with the safety of over 280 million American citizens, don't let me down Colonel," saluting .... "I will do my duty Mr president, you can count on me sir." Colonel Stuart then departs the command centre to take personal charge of the redeployment of the new quarantine zone ... "Mrs Hocker," "yes Mr president," "how are things progressing with your arachnid specimens?" "Well Mr president professor Henderson and I have been working closely together trying to find out what makes these deadly remarkable creatures tick. On first inspection they look like any other house spider, they are slightly larger, but I must say Mr president they look a whole lot scarier than normal. Looking into their 8 hypnotic black soulless eyes it makes the hairs on the back of your neck stand on end, it also makes your skin feel clammy and prickly all over your body at the same time, making your whole body shudder from head to toe. They are definitely faster with the ability to jump high into the air, the muscles in their spiny long leg are much more advanced. Their deep black bristly hairs that cover its gruesome body shimmer making the spider appear wet. Its long pointy razor sharp fangs are at least twice as long as the average house spider, these spiders are formidable adversaries ... The two specimens are side by side securely locked in their metal confinement chambers but somehow, they can still communicate with each other. Walking upright on their spiny long hairy legs mirroring each other as they slowly stride around their isolation chambers looking for a way out. We think the spiders have a form of telekinesis that keeps them all connected somehow. They seem highly intelligent, almost problem solving as they slowly March around the chamber looking for weaknesses. Their bodies are as frail as any other animal on this planet, killing a single spider is easy, we can shoot it, we can squash it, we can drowned it but how do you kill millions of these terrifying monsters above and deep below ground at the same time, stopping them from leaving the island ... Mr president we only have 8 days left to try and find a poisonous solution to this catastrophic situation" ...

"Mrs Hocker," "yes Mr Winters," "why can't we just gas these monstrous creatures, surely we have some form of nerve gas that can kill them" ..." Yes, that is one possibility Mr Winters, we will be starting chemical and biological analyses straight away. We don't think killing these hideous spiders will be a problem, we must have the delivery mechanisms in place .... putting it simply Mr Winters how do we simultaneously gas millions upon millions of black evil spiders who have infiltrated every nook and cranny, form the tallest skyscraper in New York city to the deepest darkest caverns below ... Mr president and all you good people here, I promise you my dedicated team I will move heaven and earth to try and solve this monumental task, I will keep you informed of our progress."

Friday 8.32 am

In New York city Ruby and Edward were living a double life. On the surface they were doing their jobs as normal but behind the scenes they were trying their upmost to unravel the misery that surrounded the quarantined zone. No one knew that Ruby and Edward were on board the helicopter that got detained and confiscated on Tuesday afternoon, John who piloted the craft told the authorities he was alone trying to peer inside the lockdown area. Edward has gone to the mainland, a colleague of his, an old university pal, had agreed to take Edward up in his ultramodern news helicopter. So, they can zoom in and film with their high density cameras and try and see what was happening inside the lockdown zone, the telescopic cameras are that powerful they didn't need to go anywhere near the no fly zone. Almost everyone in the city had forgotten that the quarantined zone existed, bird flu they thought, nothing to do with me. Their lives were virtually unchanged, going to work, socialising, having a meal or drinks out with friends. The island is approximately 13 miles long and only 1 mile wide at its tip, extending to over 2 miles across at its base where New York city is situated. No one had really noticed thousands of military engineers, dressed in civvies with their high visibility jackets on putting the final pieces of the puzzle together, locking all the wire and cement in place around the entire perimeter of the stricken island ready for total isolation.

Friday 13.00 pm

In the laboratory of the CDC Mrs Hocker and her team have spent the entire morning carefully preparing the deadliest toxins, poisons and nerve agents known to man ready for their experiments to begin. It only takes a single drop of any of these most deadly substances to be exposed to the air and everyone in the CDC will die an agonising death. The experiments will be painstakingly slow, every safety measure being adhered to, all protocol followed.

Friday 17.15 pm

Colonel Stuart is back in the command centre personally briefing the president on the progress of the new quarantine zone. "Mr president," "yes Colonel," "I have spent the day going around the entire perimeter of the new cordon, making sure all equipment and military personnel are ready for deployment. Strict 6 hourly rotation will be in place on the front line, so all soldiers are fresh and alert at all times. As from this morning every member of this entire operation has been rotated into watching the two horrific videos. The gruesome attack on the shopping mall plus our three brave soldiers decent into the depths below, so every single person knows their duty. All commanding officers have been personally briefed by me on the severity of the dire situation we face. I have also informed them that every single man, woman and child on Manhattan Island inside the quarantined zone is infected with tiny baby spiders and that is why no ONE can leave that island alive. If just one person gets off that godforsaken island and onto the mainland the black hideous spiders will rampage through America killing all of their family and friends back home. I have reiterated to my officers that a presidential shoot to kill order is still in force and the president expects everyone to do their patriotic duty. I have ordered all military personnel to leave the inner quarantine zone at precisely 02.00 hundred hours tomorrow morning and pullback to the outer perimeter. Simultaneously closing all roads, train stations, subways, tunnels and ferry crossings and all aircraft will be grounded. Our naval forces will start their patrols taking charge of our waters, the air force is on high alert ready to enforce the no fly zone. I have done everything in my power to carry out your orders sir, in a short few hours I will be putting Manhattan Island under strict curfew, no one in and definitely no one out" …

"Can I speak freely Mr president," "yes of course you can Colonel Stuart" …. "Mr president you and the commanding chiefs have known about this terrifying threat for some weeks now, once the inner quarantine zone was established and all the affected were in isolation. Why didn't we evacuate everyone outside the quarantined area and get them onto the mainland and too safety. Also, Mr president as soon as you realised that the children inside the lockdown area were not infected, why didn't we swoop in and save them." "Colonel Stuart … once we realised that we couldn't neutralise this black gruesome army our only choice was containment and control, giving us crucial time to get a plan in place. We had many voices in the Pentagon that wanted to do just that, mobilise our armed forces and save as many people as possible. After reading the many reports and different scenarios it was thought ignorance was the best policy. The last thing we needed were millions of scared frightened people causing chaos and threatening the stability of the shroud of silence we had created. The only way to control the masses is to lie to them, to be honest Colonel the government has always lied to the American people, all governments do it. You have just done it ... you have just told all your subordinates that every man, woman and child on that stricken island has got tiny baby spiders growing inside of them. I will go on national television tomorrow telling everyone on Manhattan Island to isolated because human bird flu has infected most of the population there. Colonel the only chance we have of destroying these black evil creatures and stop them from wiping out mankind is to lie. This is the greatest threat our civilisation has ever faced, we need to kill those horrific things here and now while we have them contained. When you are in command Colonel, as you know, hard choices have to be made in the best interests of the entire nation. Radio through when the new quarantine zone is in place," "yes Mr president," "carry on, dismissed Colonel."

Friday 20.00 pm

Back in the CDC Mrs Hocker and her exhausted team have been working tirelessly trying to kill their two arachnid specimens. Injecting different extremely deadly compounds into each of the two containment chambers. As yet nothing seems to be killing these hideous monsters.

Saturday 01.45 am

After a couple of hours sleep Colonel Stuart is at the outer quarantine command post with his captains and lieutenants organising the withdrawal of all military personnel from the inner quarantine zone. "Men," "yes Colonel," "at 02 hundred hours precisely all personnel must quietly abandon the inner cordon and be safely located behind our outer ring of steel before 04 hundred. We will have until 05 hundred hours to completely seal off the entire island, let me assure you all, this will be no easy task. The president will not be making his address to the nation until 06 hundred hours later this morning, so we will have thousands of confused frightened people at the barbed wire trying to get on with their day not knowing exactly what is going on ... Containment gentlemen, that is the order of the day. All officers and sergeants at key exit points, bridges, subways, train stations, airports must keep order. The people waking up this morning will be totally unaware of the lockdown, we MUST keep the people calm. Radio and television announcements will commence from 06.15 hours with posts on all social media outlets instructing the people to stay home. People will be extremely angry giving many excuses why they need to leave the island immediately but commanders, this WILL not happen. Reassure the citizens that there is nothing to fear, the quarantine is a temporary measure stopping the bird flu from spreading into the wider population. Convince the people that help is on the way, and they must all go home and isolated for 7 days. Gentlemen, God speed with your endeavours, the safety of the United States of America is in your hands," saluting …" yes, Colonel we will all do our duty."

Saturday 02.00 am

All the people in the inner quarantine zone are sound asleep, isolated away in their little cubicles. Quietly and under the cover of darkness the many hundreds of military personnel that were there supposedly to help and reassure the infected souls slipped across Madison Avenue bridge to safety, the engineers barricading the crossing behind them. For days the military in high visibility jackets disguised as ordinary workers had closed roads, put up concrete barriers, suspended some bridge crossings all in the guise of essential road maintenance. Most of the infrastructure for the cordon hidden in plain sight, all the military had to do now was tightly fit it all together.

Saturday 04.45 am ……. TOTAL ISOLATION

The job is done, the island of Manhattan is in complete lockdown, every possible Avenue off the stricken island has been secured. Thousands of military personnel are inside the new quarantine zone waiting for the residents to wake. located at all major road intersections, subway and train terminals. Unarmed, with their boots highly polished, their camouflage uniforms clean and pressed. Wearing bright orange high visibility vests with the words here to help on the back and under quarantine written across the front. Clipboards in hand with surgical masks on their faces, giving the facade that they are here to help the islanders settle into a 7 day isolation period. Gently persuading everyone to go home for the good of the nation. The people who disregard their advice and still continue to the outer perimeter will be met with armed force, wire and concrete aggressively encouraging them to go home.

Saturday 06.00 am .... 7 days to go.
THE CLOCK IS TICKING

Young Ryan AWAKES, a load of booming voice is echoing out of his arm, the internet is working, his phone is back on. Rubbing his eyes, still half asleep Ryan stumbles out of bed. Trying to focus .. the president is ordering everyone to stay at home .. scared and confused Ryan notices that there are no armed guards walking up and down. Tentatively he peers through the flap of his isolation cubicle, nothing, empty, no soldiers, no men in white coats, not a soul anywhere. Voices can be heard, rumbling in the distance, getting louder, getting nearer as more isolated people begin to wake. Dazed, confused people stumbling out of their cubicles wondering why the soldiers have all gone. My FAMILY ... an excited but frightened Ryan joins the milling people in the corridor, his hospital gown flapping in the wind, "mom, dad, Charley" he shouts, sticking his head into cubicles as he goes. "MOM, DAD .... Richard and Shona Kirk, its Ryan can you hear me." Pushing his way through the swelling crowd of confused scared people shouting over and over the names of his family ... Then suddenly there he was, his dad, stumbling around the corridor with all the other lost souls. "DAD, DAD," they lock eyes across the melee of bewildered apprehensive people, half smiling with a sense of relief etched across their frantic faces. Pushing their way through the bustling crowd towards each other. They embrace like they have never embraced before, their arms tightly wrapped around one another, tears streaming down their joyous faces. "Ryan, are you ok my boy?" "Yes, dad I'm alright, I am so glad to see you," giving his dad I'm so very happy and relieved to see you HUG. "Dad the soldiers and men in white coats have gone," "yes, I know Ryan everyone is leaving their cubicles. Have you seen your mother or your sister Ryan," "no dad only you." "Right Ryan stay close, we will go and find them."

Hundreds of people are now out of their isolation cubicles frantically searching for their loved ones. A deafening wall of sound rings out as concerned people call out the names of the people they love, running around with their hospital gowns flapping in all different directions. Richard and Ryan keeping close together, they start searching and shouting, Shona ... Charley. There are scared people everywhere, running back and forth, shouting, calling. Some families finding each other, crying, hugging, so relieved to be back together. "Shona, Charley .... there is no sign of them dad, should we split up" ...." NO Ryan we will never separate again, we will find them both together." Then out of the confusion steps Shona, weeping, utter desperation written all over her face. Flinging her arms wide open, with an enormous smile spreading from ear to ear. Shona runs and jumps into both of their grateful arms. Crying, sobbing, tears of absolute joy rolling down their faces the three of them kiss and embrace so very happy to be back together once more .... Charley panic in her eyes," Charley, where is Charley Richard." Taking Shona firmly by the hand," Shona, we haven't found her yet ... in fact we haven't seen any children .. anywhere. Right Shona, where have you searched?" "I was over in that corner, she is not anywhere over there." "Ok, we've done all around here ... let's look over in that direction." The three of them head over that way, pushing, squeezing through the bustling crowd." There Richard there .. there are some open doors, let's go and have a look." Running down the passageways there are many rooms, cubicles in all directions. Charley ... Charley, the three of them running into different rooms frantically shouting. "Richard ... Ryan there are children over here, Charley, Charley, mommy's here." Shouting anxiously for her beloved little CHARLEY .... "Mom .. Mom is that you?" An excited smiling face appears through the sea of scared, frightened children. smiling wildly "It's you, it's my mommy." Running, Charley flings herself at her relieved mother, putting her little arms around her waist, squeezing her ever so tightly, her little feet dancing on the spot, "my mommy is here." At that very moment Ryan and Richard appear, "dad, dad," Charley's feet still dancing.

She can hardly contain her excitement as this little daddy's girl runs and leaps into her grateful dad's strong arms. Hugging him so tightly around his neck making his happy face turn purple, tears pouring down their faces, sobbing onto each other's shoulders. "Are you ok dad?" Richard mumbles through his happy tears, "yes, my darling girl, I'm ok, are you alright Charley?" "Yes, dad I'm all ok now." The pair embracing that closely together it was hard to see where one started and the other one finished ... All four of the Kirk family huddle together, so very relieved to be back together. "I even missed you

Ryan," "yes same here my little sis." More worried parents arrive, families being reunited after such a harrowing ordeal. Hugs and kisses being shared out left right and centre.

The Kirk family are stood there in a small circle holding one another's hands, amongst all the other grateful families are getting slowly back together. "Dad," "yes my little Charley," "look at everyone with their bums poking out, how are we supposed to go outside with no clothes on?" "Your right my dear girl, we better go and hunt for them." Firmly holding one another's hands, the Kirk's go in search for their clothes. There are many people still looking for their loved ones, crying people, happy people, hugging people, sad and lonely people but most of all, frightened people. Are the spiders coming back, are the men in white coats and soldiers coming back. All these poor lost souls were viciously, attacked, without provocation, molested in the most horrific way possible. Isolated, poked and prodded, without any compassion or explanation. Now what are they supposed to do now, no food, no water, no clothes, deserted left to fend for themselves by the very people who were here to help them.

"Mom look over there, people with clothes on," "quick Ryan go and ask them where they got them from?" The Kirk's step into a large store room, at the back, neatly packed into clear cellophane bags are everybody's clothes. All the garments had been careful tested to see if the spiders had left any form of residue behind, or any clues of any kind. Then itemised, neatly packed with the subject's name printed on the front and put alphabetically onto the shelves. Lots of people were already in the room searching for their clothing, the Kirk's went straight to K and the search began.

Saturday 08.00 am

All the department heads were back in the command centre giving the president an update on their progress, Colonel Stuart begins ... "morning everyone, Mr president, it has been a very long night, but this is where we are today. The inner quarantine zone was abandoned at 02 hundred this morning, all of our military personnel pulled back to the outer perimeter. Our new ring of steel encompassing the whole island was completed by 05 hundred, all roads, bridges, tunnels and subways closed, and all aircrafts grounded. There are lots of things behind the scenes you have not been privy to, the president has instructed me to give you all full disclosure. Weeks ago, we started many balls rolling, on the pretence of computer software security updates. We slowly and covertly moved this country's financial hub out of New York city, all trading and financing were switched to various locations around America including Paris and London. We instructed all food wholesalers to stockpile essential groceries, enough for at least 7 days. Telling them an oil crisis was on the way, so transportation would be affected. At various locations around the island, we have also stockpiled essentials. We know from bitter experience that total quarantine only works for a short period of time, so we had to come up with a way of making the citizens calm and obedient. When the people woke up this morning, their island was in lockdown, no one in and no one out. Simply having the president making demands was not enough, the people won't listen. We have armed soldiers guarding the perimeter to stop people leaving the island but if we send our armed forces onto the streets there will be anarchy, so a solution had to be found. We couldn't just lockdown the entire island and not give them any support. So, our solution was to send thousands of smartly dressed unarmed soldiers, holding a clipboard, with a medical face mask on but most importantly wearing a high visibility vest with the words HERE TO HELP written on the back. For some reason people seem to obey someone wearing high visibility clothing and holding a clipboard. Our quarantine marshals can calm the situation down, giving advice on how and where to obtain food and water, free if necessary. Telling the people that the quarantine is only for 7 days and please stay at home, with all other emergency services operating as normal. Yes, certain groups of people will try and leave the island, but these can be dealt with away from the major population. Keeping the people calm and in the quarantined zone is our priority.

We have only 7 days left to try and defeat this hideous army we face, having rioting and disorder on the streets will not help our cause" ...

"Colonel, what happens when the infected people get out of isolation, they will then join the population and start telling everyone about the black evil spiders." "That's a good question professor Williams CDC," "we have already announced that one of the side effects of having human bird flu is horrific nightmares. When the story's appear on social media and they will very soon, we will put it down to fake news and hallucinations. We have confiscated all video evidence of the attack but if anything materialises, we will close it down and say it was fake. It is all over social media, since my announcement that we imposed a lockdown. The world is watching, the world will be afraid, picking over the bones of what happens here. A break out of deadly human bird flu, the people will remember what happened in Wuhan. One case of coronavirus that soon spread around the world killing millions and we are still living with the effects today" ...." Colonel Stuart," "yes Mr president," "at present you seem to have the situation under control. Initially reports indicate that most of the people will follow the isolation protocol, wearing face coverings and staying indoors. There will be a minority who will try and escape the quarantined area, these people must be contained at all costs. We have just 7 days, we cannot let this situation decent into chaos .... Mrs Hocker, please tell me you have some good news."

"Sorry NO Mr president. As you can all imagine the work, we do is perilous, one slip, just one little mistake and everyone in the CDC is dead. These poisons, nerve gases, toxins and biological agents are the deadliest substances known to man. We have fully documented our painstaking progress so far. In the reports before you, you can see we have started with nerve agents as they dissipate into the atmosphere very quickly after use, the vapours can evaporate nearly as fast as water. After killing the black evil spiders, we need the gas to dissipate as quickly as possible, so we don't contaminate the soil any longer than we have to. If you look at the monitor on the wall in front of you, you can see our two arachnid specimens in their containment chambers. They are both constantly probing for weaknesses in their isolation pods, they seem to mirror each other's actions, we do believe that they are in constant communication with each other somehow. Simultaneously we saturated both chambers with cyanide gas, chamber B had a more aggressive version pumped in. Initially both of the specimens started spinning wildly around the chamber, bouncing off the walls in a frenzy. As the poisonous gas totally engulfed the compartment the spiders stopped in their tracks at the same time, curled up into a tight black hairy ball and didn't move a muscle. For 10 minutes there was nothing, no movement of any kind. At this point we all became a little excited, thinking we had done it, we had killed these hideous monsters. 20 minutes into the experiment we all agreed to disperse the gas out of the chamber to see if we had been successful. After the cyanide gas was expelled from the isolation pod the spiders were still motionless. Since we had no way of checking their vital signs, we could not be absolutely sure if they were dead!!"

"As you can see, we then decided to use one of the metal arms inside the chamber to determine if they were truly deceased. Poking and shoving them with the arm but still nothing, the spider is wrapped up as tight as ever, no signs of life at all. We had to be 100% positive that the black ugly creatures were dead. Opening the front of the chamber with only a flimsy hazmat suits on was not an option. If the spider was still alive, it would easily rip through the protective suit and kill our colleague using the metal arm ... Thermal imaging camera !!! that was the solution. In our haste to construct the isolation chambers we had no medical instruments in place to determine whether our specimens are dead or alive. After placing the thermal camera directly in front of the window of the isolation chamber we looked in and held our breath. No movement, no signs of life but ..... there was a tiny reddish dot in the centre of the thermal imaging camera, the spiders had shut down their metabolism down to a near death state ... they were still alive. We had to be sure, these highly intelligent creatures playing us for fools, ready to pounce at a moment's notice .. So, we sprayed hot steam into the chamber, at first nothing happened but then suddenly the spiders were up on their spiny long legs running around, smashing into the walls, trying to sink their sharp pointy fangs into the viewing window. They were very much alive, all we had done was totally piss them off. We then tried two different poisons but sadly with the same effect, killing these deadly creatures Mr president will be a lot harder than we first anticipated. We have just 7 days before all hell breaks loose on that island, so my team and I will be working around the clock to find a way of exterminating these black monsters. I assure you Mr president, we will find a way." All department heads return back to their stations and with 7 days remaining the fight goes on.

Saturday 07.35 am

The Kirk family along with hundreds of now dressed people are spilling onto the streets, shell-shocked people, angry people, kept confined for the last 7 days without any compassion, no dignity and still no answers, the government keeping them hidden away like a dirty secret. As yet most of these bewildered citizens are unaware that the whole island is in lockdown, soon they will be mingling with the general population. Will anyone believe them, the talk of spiders ridiculed, deadly human bird flu spoken in its place. These unfortunate souls oblivious to the fact that they are the hosts to the next generation of millions of hideous black beasts that will be unleashed into the world in only 7 day's time. Weary families keeping each other close trying to get home, no buses, no taxis, the roads mostly devoid of any motorised vehicles. 99% of the islanders obeying the stay at home rules, only the thousands of ex quarantined people, hungry and thirsty shuffling their way homewards.

What's this, more soldiers .. but this time no guns, smartly dressed with face masks on, a clipboard in hand and wearing a high visibility vest. Written on the back, HERE TO HELP, hundreds of confused and frustrated people swamp these so called quarantine marshals. We have been held against our will, black hideous spiders, we don't live on Manhattan Island, how do we get home. Men in white coats, we were attacked, I can't find my family. Many questions are being asked all at once, angry disconcerted people wanting answers. The marshals trying to explain, bird flu, face coverings, stay at home, the island is in total lockdown, stay calm, help is on the way. The overwhelming crowd getting bigger and angrier by the minute. The marshals on the radio calling for reinforcements, this scene being replicated all around the outskirts of the old quarantined zone as people fan out trying to get home. The bustling crowd knocking unarmed soldiers to the floor, fights breaking out as scared, lost people take their frustrations out on anyone in authority. Spiders they shout, why don't you believe us, we were viciously attacked … A military helicopter appears overhead, the downforce of its rotas pushing the crowd onto the floor as it hovers only 10 feet off the ground. A loud speaker booming out, you must disperse, go home, the entire island is under quarantine, the quarantine marshals are here to help you, disperse. The helicopter ascends, then flies off into the distance, by this time many more marshals have entered the area, picking wind swept people up off the ground, reassuring them that they are here to help. Anyone with no home to go to will be given temporary accommodation with free food and water, anyone with a home, please go home and self-isolate immediately. The angry crowd slowly starts to disperse, the quarantine marshals taking back control, ordering people to go home, aiding the others with the promise of free food, water and a place to sleep.

After being swept along with the crowd, Richard, Shona, Ryan and Charley decide to go home. After being cooped up in isolation for so long it will be nice to walk in the bright morning sun light, the family all back together once more. The talk of horrific black spiders suspended for now, trying to keep things as normal as possible for the sake of their little 9 year old daughter. The streets are busy, still filled with disillusioned people, families trying to find their way. The Kirk's only have a few short miles to walk home, telling the quarantine marshals as they go. The marshals are everywhere, keeping the peace, ordering everyone to go home, it will only be for 7 short days, lying, deceiving everyone they meet. Eager to get home the Kirk's link arms and push on, weaving through the lost souls on their way. Slipping her little hand into her dads,

Charley looks up at him and giggles, "what's up Charley, what is tickling you?" "Well dad .. there were 20 kids in our room and to pass the time we made up word games. One of them was ... if you had to lose an arm or a leg, which one would it be and why. Well dad my answer was, I would rather lose my leg than my arm, because, squeezing her dads hand really tightly, if I lost my arm, I couldn't hold your hand then dad could I." Smiling at one another, swinging their interlocked hands the pair have a father daughter moment ..." Mom, dad," "yes Ryan," "I have been looking at the internet since we were released. All the world is talking about is deadly human bird flu and Manhattan Island being in total isolation but mom, dad, there is no bird flu, it's a lie." "Yes, Ryan we know it's all a lie, but we don't know why they don't believe us. Do some digging Ryan and we can talk about it in private when we get home," "ok dad I will keep looking." The Kirk's are nearly home now, the streets are virtually empty apart from high visibility vests marching up and down.

In New York city Ruby had woken to the news that her parents quarantine zone has fallen, news reports showing all the scared, confused people spilling onto the empty streets. The internet reporting, human bird flu, the island of Manhattan in total lockdown. Hundreds of people dead ... Mom, dad she thinks, I need to get there to see if they are alright but how, we are in a strict quarantine. The president has ordered everyone to stay at home, all non-essential businesses to close immediately. Quarantine marshals on the streets making sure people follow the rules. Ring ... ring ... ring," hello Edward its Ruby, what have you heard about this lockdown, is there any news from the mainland?" "Morning Ruby, no the lockdown came as much as a surprise here as it did there, no one here in the news room knows anything. We were supposed to go up in the helicopter this morning, but the military has imposed a no fly zone over the entire island. Ruby this doesn't feel right, there is something very wrong here, the military have fenced off all of Manhattan in a matter of hours. No film crews, in fact no people allowed onto the streets to report what's going on at all, this feels like a white wash." "Yes, Edward this entire situation feels wrong, they closed everything down overnight, no one in and no one out. I will get my colleagues at this end to do some digging, can you do the same at your end Edward," "yes, I sure will Ruby." "I'm going up to Harlem to see if I can find my parents," "but Ruby, everywhere is locked down, how are you going to get there?" "I know everything is under quarantine, but I have to try Edward," "you be careful out there." "I will Edward, I know every back street and alleyway in this city. I need to get over to Harlem, with all these people dying, I need to know if my mom and dad are ok. Right Edward I'll be leaving shortly, please let me know if you find anything out." "I will Ruby, be safe my Hun."

The Kirk family are finally back home, exactly 7 days since they all excitedly left for the cinema. Charley has been sent for a bath, while Richard, Shona and Ryan sit at the kitchen with a strong coffee, with the door closed trying to get their heads around what has happened to them all. "Shona, we were attacked by hideous black spiders, no one believes us, everyone I spoke to coming out of isolation were attacked too. Hundreds of us, possibly thousands. Those supposedly quarantine marshals were not interested in what we had to say, there were hundreds of angry people shouting at them but all they could say was bloody bird flu and go home." "I know Richard, everyone I spoke too, told me the same. What did they do to you in isolation Ryan?" "It was awful mom. I spent the first few days just crying, every time I closed my eyes, I could see those hideous spiders clawing all over me. I can still feel the spider in my throat, I thought I was going to choke to death, it was impossible to breathe, I'm still having nightmares today." Rising from her chair mother and son have a little cry together and a well-deserved hug ...

"What was it like in there for you Richard?" "The same Shona, it was awful. Trying to come to terms with what had happened to you, with no help, no reassurance and no one to talk to about the total and utter violation I had gone through, we had all gone through. And you Shona?" "Yes, I feel the same, being kept in that tiny isolation cubicle not knowing if the rest of your family is ok, was torture. Armed soldiers taking you to the toilet, I felt totally alone and lost." "Ryan" "yes dad," "what is the internet saying about all of this?" "Well dad hundreds of posts have been posted, people showing faded puncture wounds and telling their horrific stories about being viciously attacked by black horrendous spiders. People saying that they were attacked but their children weren't. How people were put into isolation and how the men in white coats fobbed them off and would not let them leave ... but dad every time a post is submitted within a few minutes the post is taken down, thousands of people around the world are adding their own comments, it's fake, hallucinations, fake news, it's not real, you deserve to be bitten, you should all die, bloody new Yorkers, it's crazy dad, I've never seen it like this before and all the time bulletins keep popping up, deadly human bird flu, stay indoors, quarantine, isolate, only for 7 days. Mom!"

"Yes, my darling boy," "remember I told you about a story I read ages ago about a young woman being attacked by a spider, they published her autopsy online but then it got taken down. I think she died not long after that in hospital." "Yes, Ryan I do remember something

283

about that." "Well mom I will speak to my classmate Stephan, I guess he was attacked to, but he is a genius on the internet, if anyone can find out, he can. I'll go up to my room and message him, mom, dad if I find out anything I'll come straight down and tell you." "Ok son but not in front of your sister ... Richard what are we going to do about Ryan and Charley, this horrific nightmare has got to be playing on their young minds," "I don't know what to do for the best. I think for now we should take every day as it comes darling, no one believes us, we have no one to talk to about what happened. Ryan is busy doing his internet thing and I think we should keep things as normal as we can for little Charley." Hugging," I'm so relieved that we are all back under the same roof again Richard, it feels good to have my family back together again but I'm terrified to." "I feel the same Shona, we will get through this, I promise."

Saturday 15.00 pm

Back in the CDC Mrs Hocker, professor Henderson and the team are hard at work trying to kill these hideous monsters. The nerve agent they had prepared this time are, Sarin and VX the only synthetic compound known to man. Both arachnid specimens are still fit and healthy, angry hideous creatures, strutting around their isolation chambers waiting for their moment to escape. As the two deadly gasses are pumped into the chambers the spiders don't this time frantically run around like crazy. They just sit in the middle of the isolation pod and curl up into a tight black hairy ball. Their thermal image on the camera getting fainter and fainter, slowing their metabolism right down, as if they are dead …. the spiders are learning!! They had the ability to slow their metabolic rates down to almost zero, the deadly gases are having no effect on these ungodly creatures … Poisons .. that's what we will try next. After expelling the gas from the chambers, the spiders once again came back to life, up on all of its 8 spiny hairy legs, waiting, pulsating, its black hideous body quivering with anticipation, it was like they were taunting us, daring us to destroy them. The deadly poison was ready to be injected into the chambers, cyanide was slowly released into the isolation pods, once again the black evil creatures just sat in the middle of the chambers and curled up into a hairy black ball ... as the poison filled the chambers all we could do now was wait ....

Looking at the thermal camera to see if all signs of life are fading away. 30 minutes later a very faint red glow is still visible on the screen, the spiders life had not been snubbed out as we had hoped. All that was left was this minute warm glow of life emanating out of these hideous, vicious monsters that will not die. "Right professor Henderson we have tried nerve gas and poisons, but nothing seems to be killing these evil creatures. There is only one thing left to do, we must kill one of our specimens and dissect it, cut it up into lots of different pieces to see what makes this ugly thing tick." One of the lab technicians asks, "Mrs Hocker how are you going to kill one of them, we have been trying to destroy them for days now." "Mary as professor Henderson has already explained, these evil monsters are as fragile as any other creature on this planet. They are very easy to kill, if we had a big slipper, it would be dead by now, but we need to destroy millions of these ugly deadly things, they are hiding away in every nook and cranny of this vast city. They are extremely fast, very intelligent and at present nothing we have tried will kill them" …

Frustration and the lack of sleep takes control of Mrs Hocker. "Right, I will show you how to kill one of these hideous creatures." Entering through the glass double security doors and into the inner compartment, Mrs Hocker is now stood right in front of the chambers viewing window. Taking hold of the levers that control the inner metal arms inside the chamber, Mrs Hocker lifts up the Perspex box that still lays within and holds it way above the curled up spiders head …!!!! "MRS HOCKER … Janet, don't do this!!!" "But Charles we need to get inside one of these things, we need to analyse their genetic makeup and find a toxin that will destroy them." "Yes, Janet we do but not yet, we still have time. We know that these intelligent beings are telepathically linked somehow, if we kill one, we don't know what the consequences will be. Having two specimens gives us double the chance of finding a poison that will work effectively. We still have nearly 7 days to crack this thing, come on Janet put the box down and get out of there. You have been hard at this for over 48 hours straight and you need to get some sleep." She then pauses and looks over to the large viewing window at her colleges ..." Ok professor, we will give it a couple more days but if we can't find the answers we are looking for by then, I will have no alternative but to dissect one of these hideous monsters." Exiting the inner chamber a very tiered Mrs Hocker relents and goes for a short well deserved lie down, leaving her colleges carrying on the fight.

It's late Saturday afternoon now and most of the initial quarantine souls have found their way back home, Madison, Lily and Grace with many hundreds of other non-inhabitants of Manhattan Island are being housed in pop up shelters around the island. They have been given food and water and reassured that their accommodation is only temporary, the new quarantine should only last for 7 days. The three girls have phoned home and spoken to their frantic father Eric, they have told him about their horrendous ordeal "but dad, no one believes us." The girls are scared and want to go home, everyone is scared and apprehensive.

Are the terrible spiders coming back, is it true about the human bird flu, have hundreds of people already died as alleged by the government. Social media is awash with stories of black evil monsters going down people's throats but still they are not believed. There is no evidence to substantiate their claims, only the faded puncture wounds scattered around frightened people's abused bodies. All telephones and CCTV in the old quarantine zone have been wiped, the military have gone to great pains to destroy all video evidence.

Ruby has been out for hours now, driving through the alleyways and back roads of the city, trying desperately to reach her parents, the quarantine marshals thwarting her attempts at every turn. Long abandoned is her car, Ruby is making the long arduous journey on foot. The streets are mainly deserted apart from the people breaking the isolation rules and the wondering infected, lost and alone with nowhere else to go. The marshals are slowly rounding up all these individuals, sending them to temporary accommodation or ordering them home. Ruby has been telling the marshals for hours that she needs to get to her old frail parents, but they keep turning her back ... I don't know why I didn't think of this ages ago, Ruby thought. The next marshal I come across I will tell them that I have just been released out of the quarantined zone and I'm lost and confused and can't find my way home, but I will give my parents address as my own. Within minutes the next marshal appears, explaining her dire situation, putting on a bit of an act of course, Ruby is escorted through the quiet streets straight to the apartment block where her parents live.

Thanking the Marshall Ruby eagerly enters the lobby, into the elevator, then out onto her parents floor. Using her spare key Ruby tentatively opens the door, "mom, dad" she shouts, "are you here?" ... nothing, silence. After searching every room in the apartment there is no sign of them, dust had gathered on most of the surfaces, rubbing her panic stricken head Ruby is concerned for her frail parents welfare. What should I do, who do I call, where do I go?? Getting a little scared now ... after leaving a brief note, Ruby decides to go and see if Sally had seen them, they have been neighbours for years, perhaps she could help ... Knock, knock, Sally tentatively looks through her peep hole, its Ruby. Opening the door a grateful Sally flings her arms around a relieved Ruby, the two women hug, tears rolling down both their traumatised faces. "Have you seen my parents, Sally? they have been missing for over a week now." "No Ruby sorry I haven't, come in and I will tell you what's been going on." Ruby enters Sally's apartment and sits on the sofa. "Ruby this is Simone, she lives in the apartment down the hall." "I'm looking for my parents, their apartment is empty ... they ..." Sally puts her hand on Ruby's shoulder, "come on Ruby, I'll make you a strong cup of coffee." The three women sit at the kitchen table sipping on their drinks, "right Sally tell me what's been going on?" "Well Ruby where do I start" .... taking a big gulp of air, tears starting to well up in her eyes. "Last Saturday morning we were all attacked by hideous black spiders, I'm not going into the details of what those horrible things did to me, but the stories are true, everyone around here was savagely attacked by spiders. Look" .... showing Ruby her ankle, puncture marks.

"Oh my god Sally, all the awful stories are true" …" go on Simone tell Ruby what happened to you." A tearful and still traumatised young Simone tells Ruby about her attack and how the spider went down her throat while she was wide awake, "it was truly horrifying Ruby, I'm still having nightmares" … Ruby was having a hard time trying to get her head around what Sally and Simone were telling her, "that sounds horrendous, what happened next?"

"Well Sally after the attack Simone and I went out into the street looking for someone to help us, all we could see were people like us, hundreds of scared, terrified people wandering the streets. Police officers, bankers, plumbers, hundreds of hysterical lost souls, men, women and children, crying, sobbing just ambling around looking for anyone to help them but there wasn't anyone. Everyone we saw was just like us, bite marks on their hands, their arms, on their shocked bemused faces. They had all been viciously attacked by these black evil monsters, going deep down into their gagging throats while they were still wide awake. People were absolutely hysterical Ruby and then we saw the soldiers with guns, the men in white coats were amongst them, all suited up with respirators on. Everyone thought that they were here to help us. People swarmed around them looking for answers and all we got was isolation and more tests. Living in those horrible cubicles for 7 days was absolutely horrific, I could hear people screaming, shouting out in fear. We had to deal with our terrifying grief on our own, no compassion, no counselling and definitely no answers. I cried myself to sleep for days until I realised, I had to deal with this awful thing on my own. The pain and the unimaginable torment would either destroy me or make me stronger. I decided to be stronger, I will survive this agonising torment, I will beat my mental demons and come out the other side" ... "Sally, Simone, I have no words, we have all been lied to, the government has supressed and denied everything that you have both told me. Every story that appeared online is swiftly taken down and denounced. We were told, the world was told that human bird flu had broken out and that's why you were all in isolation. The world needs to know the truth, you need to know the truth. Ruby, Simone, please let me tell your stories so we can expose the government for the fraud that it is, then maybe, we can get some answers" ... Knock .. knock ...

"That might be my parents Sally, I will go and get the door. DAD ... !!!" putting her relieved arms around her dads neck, "oh Ruby love I have missed you," "I've been worried dad," giving her dad a really big squeeze, "are you ok, where is mom?" Sally and Simone come to the door, smiling, watching father and daughter reunited, "we are both ok Ruby love, your mother is upstairs, we have only just got home." "Come on dad let's go and see her, Sally, Simone, is it ok if I come and see you both tomorrow and take your statements?" Ruby the news women come to the fore, "yes Ruby, we need some answers." Taking her old dad by the hand the pair go to find Gene ..." MOM you're ok," they hug, tears streaming down both their faces. Taking her mother's hands, looking deep into her old frail face, "are you ok mom? I've been going crazy with worry." "Yes, my darling Ruby, I am fine, we got a little lost and these nice men in yellow jackets came to help us find our way home."

"Ruby love can you come into the kitchen and give me a hand with the tea," "ok dad, mom I'm just going into the kitchen with dad, I will be back in a minute." In the kitchen with the door closed, "Ruby your mother's memory has been playing her up lately." "Why didn't you tell me dad?" "I didn't want to worry you Ruby, she has an appointment booked for next month, I was going to tell you once we had seen the doctor" ... "What happened dad?" "I'm guessing Sally has told you already all about it, yes, your mother and I were attacked by black terrifying spiders, it was bloody awful Ruby, I'm not going into details ... but it's giving me nightmares. Your mother was attacked in the hair salon, she has forgotten about it, or erased it from her memory, either way luckily, she can't remember what happened."

"The government is telling us dad, that you and everyone else were in quarantine because of bird flu and now it has spread right across the entire island ... but dad we know this is rubbish." "What can we do Ruby, they kept us locked up in those cubicles for 7 days, all we had was a small plastic bag with a toothbrush, toothpaste, some soap and a towel and that bloody hospital underwear. We were taken by armed soldiers to the toilet and the food was awful" … "Dad, it's getting late now, let's go and have a nice evening with mom and then in the morning we can hatch a plan." Ruby and her mom and dad sit drinking tea and eating biscuits keeping the evening as normal as possible for poor old Gene.

Sunday 08.15 am …….. 6 days to go.

Colonel Stuart had spent most of the night going around the inner perimeter of the quarantine zone checking in with his commanders and making sure that the troops were in good spirits and that they all knew their duty. The quarantine marshals were doing a brilliant job, keeping most of the citizens at home and reassuring the people that the isolation period was only for 7 days. On the whole the entire island of Manhattan was quiet and calm, with the odd isolated incident at the wire and concrete fence that surrounded the island. The uninfected population had been fooled, they believed the governments propaganda, bird flu was rife and innocent people were dying. Wear a mask and stay indoors, it will only be for 7 days ... Hundreds of thousands of people had been savaged by the hideous black monsters, laying their eggs deep inside of them. As the attacked fled the old quarantine zone, fanning out over the city looking for a way home, the black ugly spiders had followed them, keeping their new offspring close. The black evil creatures had ascended from the depths below, keeping hidden in the shadows, waiting patiently for their new black terrifying baby's to spew out of the bodies of the unsuspecting innocent people above.

Sunday 09.00 am

At the CDC Colonel Stuart had arrived for an update, Mrs Hocker, professor Henderson and most of the team are assembled in their ready room as they called it. "Mrs Hocker the president is eager to see some results, have you got any good news for me today?" "Sorry no Colonel, you can tell the president that we are working 24/7, we have tried many different combinations of toxins, poisons and nerve agents but sadly to no avail. These spiders seem to be impervious to all our efforts, we still have many more deadly substances to try but professor Henderson and myself are in total agreement that if we don't get a breakthrough by Tuesday, we will have to kill one of our specimens so we can analyse its DND to determine what makes these evil creatures tick." "Why don't you just kill one today, Mrs Hocker, we only have 6 days left. The president and joint chiefs of staff have authorised the use of nuclear weapons if you fail in your task." "Colonel, we still have lots of different combinations to use, having two specimens gives us double the chance of finding one that works. Please tell the president that we are moving heaven and earth to get the job done."

Sunday 12.30 pm

Ruby has her news reporter head on this morning, the government is lying to us ... but why!! After getting up early, Ruby made sure her old mom was settled with her breakfast before grilling her dad on all the gory details of the past 7 days. Then down to see Sally and Simone getting a full account of what happened to them. Most of the residents in her parents block knew Ruby, so getting them to talk was quite easy, everybody needed answers, everyone was tiered of not being listened to. By 12.30 Ruby had amassed several eye witness accounts of exactly what had happened 8 days ago, videoing everyone's statements on her phone and after writing a comprehensive report, Ruby was ready. She had phoned Stewart and her editor earlier that morning, told them briefly what she had discovered and that with the help of the residents she would have her story completed by lunch time today ... "Afternoon Nick," her editor, "I have just sent through my story, it's more shocking than I first imagined, the scale of deception is unbelievable." "Thank you, Ruby, good work, we will splice and edit it all together for you, you will get full credit for this exclusive and it will be broadcasted as soon as we have finished the final cut." "Thank you, Nick, I'm going to spend some time here with my parents, they need me, if there is anything else you need, don't hesitate to call. All the devastated people I have spoken to can't wait until the lid is lifted on this terrible thing, the world needs to know what this government have been doing." "Ok Ruby, give my best to your parents, I will speak to you soon" ... Ring ... ring, "hello Edward, after speaking to you this morning I have gathered all the horrific evidence I needed. I have just spoken to Nick, and he is going to broadcast my exclusive as soon as it is ready." "That is good news Ruby, how are your parents holding up?" "It's absolutely shocking what's happened to them Edward, in fact it's totally horrific what's happened to everyone, and the government has covered it all up" ...

"Ruby, I have done some more digging after speaking to you this morning about all the horrendous things that you have uncovered. The scale of this thing is far bigger than we had previously thought, the government is controlling everything. A few days ago, the president announced privately, a state of emergency!! That means the government had special congressional powers, basically they can do whatever they want to do, with no questions asked. I have been down to our ultramodern weather station based in Queens, a colleague of mine called Chuck has been looking at the satellite imagery over Manhattan Island, Ruby its shocking. The whole island is surrounded, on the island itself there is an inner ring of concrete and barbed wire encircling the entire perimeter, with thousands of soldiers standing guard. It looks as if they are heavily armed, with watch towers every 100 feet. The same can be said for all the boroughs that boarder Manhattan Island, new Jersey, the Bronx, Queens and Brooklyn. They are all heavily fortified with barbed wire fences and concrete barriers and with thousands of soldiers on patrol. There is also something strange happening on Roosevelt Island on the east river. A brand new structure has been built and they have demolished one half of Ed Koch Queensbury bridge that crosses over onto Manhattan, cutting it off from the island ... Ruby there is way too much infrastructure and military personnel surrounding Manhattan Island for it to be just bird flu, it's like the government is getting ready for a war!!

"Yes, Edward there is something very wrong about all of this, bird flu my arse, this is all about spiders somehow. My editor will be broadcasting my story very shortly and we can blow the lid off the governments lies. Keep digging Edward, I'm going to check in with my parents, call me if you get any more information." "I will Ruby, you look after yourself in there and give my best to your mom and dad." Ruby returns to her parents apartment eagerly waiting for her explosive story to be released. "Hi dad, how are feeling you today?" "I'm ok Ruby love, your mother has gone for a lie down, she is feeling a little bit confused today and not her normal self." "Ok dad I'll pop into the bedroom and see her a little bit later. I'm just waiting for my editor to call me back, then I will go to the shops and get some food in, let me know later what you need" ......

Ring ... ring... "RUBY," "hello Nick" ... talking very quietly, "literally 15 minutes after you sent me your story, lots of men in black suits turned up waving all sorts of badgers and warrants around, they have seized your exclusive story .... Ruby" .... "Nick .... Nick are you there??" "What's wrong Ruby?" "I don't know dad, I was talking to my editor, then my phone went off .... wait dad ... there is a message coming through on my phone." Your phone has been deactivated dew to national security breaches, "my phone has frozen dad, it's not working at all, I've just got this message flashing on my screen. Can I use your mobile dad," "of course you can Ruby" ... Ring ... ring, "Nick my phone just cut off, what's going on?" Whispering, "the men in black are still here Ruby, they are going through everything, and they are asking lots of questions. They told me, that since the president declared a state of emergency, the government has new powers, in his words, to do whatever they want. Your message was received by the server which alerted the authorities, Ruby there is nothing we can do, your story is dead in the water." "I'm sorry Nick for getting you into trouble but the world needs to know the truth, my phone is frozen, I can't even post the truth about what happened here," "it's ok Ruby, we will find a way, you keep safe, I have to go!!"

"Are you ok Ruby?" ... "no dad the bloody government is covering everything up, I need to call Edward ... Hello Bradley, no its Ruby Edward, the government has turned off my phone, my story has been seized, the men in black are at my editor's office tearing it apart, Edward what are we going to do?" "I'm not surprised Ruby, my old friend Chuck was arrested earlier on today for looking through the satellite feeds, the government is determined to keep whatever is going on, a secret. Everyone here on the mainland seems to be in the dark, along with everyone else but I will keep on searching for the truth." "Ok Edward, I need time to think, my mom and dad need me here right now. Ring me on my dad's phone if you need me." "Ok Ruby, I will speak to you soon, take care."

As Sunday draws to a close the government seem to be winning, any mention of spiders is slowly being eradicated. The new quarantine zone seems to be holding, only the odd skirmish along the perimeter, most of the citizens are obeying the lockdown and staying at home.

Monday 09.00 am ONLY 5 DAYS TO GO.

Monday goes by in a flash, the CDC are working tirelessly trying every deadly compound under the sun, our two arachnid specimens are still alive and well, nothing at present seems to be touching them. If they don't get a breakthrough by tomorrow morning, then one of those hideous creatures will have to die!! Colonel Stuart is in constant contact with the president and the joint chiefs of staff, keeping them appraised of all developments, if any. Colonel Stuart is well aware that if the CDC fail, the president will have no alternative but to authorise a nuclear strike on US soil, killing many millions of innocent Americans. The stakes could not be higher, if only one of those terrifying black monsters were to leave that godforsaken island, then the United States and possibly the world would be in dire peril, this is the greatest threat mankind has ever faced!!!

Tuesday morning ONLY 4 DAYS TO GO!!!

Tuesday morning was just like yesterday, the Kirk family were at home, Ryan was in contact with his friend Stephan, they were still sifting through the mountain of information on the world wide web, looking for answers. Young Charley was just happy having her dad home every day, kids are so very resilient. Richard and Shona were trying to be the best parents that they can be, helping their children get through this horrific ordeal, one day at a time. Madison,

Lily and Grace are in constant contact with their frantic dad, Erik. They are all praying that the quarantine zone will only last for 7 days as the government has promised and then they will all be back home together. Sally and Simone had become very close friends, spending all of their time in Sally's apartment, too scared to be alone, hoping that one day soon, they can put this horrendous nightmare behind them. Bradley and Gene, a very sweet and loving couple. Are just happy being together, having their daughter Ruby there is a lovely bonus. Ruby and Edward are still trying desperately to find a way to expose the government's lies. Most of the islanders are staying at home, all food stores are still operating, and emergency services are still on duty as normal.

Colonel Stuart had spent the morning going around the perimeter of the entire island with his lieutenants making sure that everyone is on their toes and all fences and concrete barriers are air tight. All bridges and subterranean tunnels and subways all have their explosive charges in place and are ready for detonation at a moment's notice. The quarantine marshals are out in force with their high visibility vests and clipboards giving the impression that they are here to help. The navy are patrolling the waters around the stricken island making extra sure that absolutely no one was slipping onto the mainland. Oil tankers are standing by, ready to release an oil slick encompassing the island in a ring a fire. The air force has stepped up their aerial presence, strictly enforcing the no fly zone.

Tuesday 11.00 am

Colonel Stuart has arrived on Roosevelt Island, personally overseeing all developments at the CDC. "Morning Mrs Hocker," "morning Colonel," "the president would like an update on your progress so far." "Well Colonel it's not good news, my team and I have been working around the clock trying to kill these evil, deadly creatures, not even anthrax has any effect. I think the time has come Colonel, to kill one of our two arachnid specimens so we can analyse its DNA, then hopefully we can find something that we can weaponize and use against them" ... "professor Henderson," "yes Colonel," "you are the expert on these terrifying things, have they changed since their incarceration?" "Yes, Colonel they have, our two specimens seem to have the ability to remember and learn. They are in constant communication with each other somehow. As soon as a poisonous substance is pumped into their chambers, they both curl up into a tight black ball, they will stay tightly curled up for as long as the gas is present in the chamber, but as soon as the gas is vented, they will both stand fully erect, strutting around in perfect unison. It's like they are marking their territory and telling us, we can't be destroyed" ...

"So, professor how do we kill one of them?" "Easy Colonel, we just squish one, they are as fragile as any other spider out there, but these ones are extremely fast and super intelligent. Killing one is easy Colonel, killing millions, is proving to be near on impossible" ... "So, Mrs Hocker, what is the next step?" "Henry, our chief lab technician has volunteered to kill our spider." Henry enters through the double toughened glass security doors and into the inner chamber. Directly in front of him are the viewing windows of the two small chambers containing our specimens. The black evil monsters are up on all of its hairy, spiny long legs, their terrifying spider eyes looking deep into Henrys soul. Taking a sharp intake of breath and gulping down his very dry saliva, Henry looks over his shoulder at his colleagues peering through the large observation window. Then giving a tentative thumbs up, showing he is ready to proceed.

"Janet, I am ready for you to flood chamber A" with poisonous gas. As the deadly substance infiltrates chamber, A, the hideous creature curls up into a tight black ball. The spider in chamber B is still up on all of its 8 legs rooted to the spot. Henry bravely stands in front of the curled up spider and puts his slightly shaky hands on the levers that control the metal arms within. Looking nervously through the small viewing window Henry guides the metal arms and lifts up the Perspex box, holding it way above the curled up spiders head. Looking once more over his shoulder towards the large viewing window, Henry looks straight at Mrs Hocker for guidance ... With a slight nob of her head, Henry knows what's got to be done. Tightly gripping the levers, Henry SMASHES down the Perspex box with as much downwards force as he can muster ...... straight onto the head of our unsuspecting curled up spider .... SMASH!!! lifting up the box once more .... SMASH!!! again, onto the spiders black gruesome head, its thick gloopy red blood oozing out of its body filling the chamber floor, its hairy black body flattened, its live force slowly ebbing away ....

SUDDENLY !!!!! the spider in chamber B starts going absolutely crazy, spinning around and around, bouncing off the walls, bearing its sharp pointy fangs, trying desperately to smash its way through the viewing window. Henry jumps back, his hands still shaking, sweat pouring down his brow, he quickly exits through the security doors and back into the safety of the laboratory. Everyone in the lab is transfixed, looking through their large observation window straight into the chambers. The spider in chamber B is still whirling around its isolation pod, banging off every surface, its black long pointy fangs dripping with venom ... "Professor

!! it looks like the spider is desperately trying to escape, because it knows it's their turn next," "no Henry, I don't think so. These creatures are telepathically linked somehow, and spider B is feeling the other ones pain." Then suddenly the whirling spider STOPS !! lifting itself up on its black hairy spiny legs to its full height, pointing its gruesome long pointy fangs towards the heavens. Its black hairy body shimmering against the electric lights, its torso violently pulsating as if it was trying to communicate the death of its fallen comrade!!! ...... "Colonel Stuart .... come in Colonel," the Colonels radio springs into life, it's captain Rivers, he is in charge of 100 marshals inside the quarantine zone .... "Colonel .. SPIDERS!!!!! ... thousands of them" ... the radio goes silent!!

The black evil spiders had sensed the passing of one of their own, out of their dark concealed Heidi holes they crawled. This time not to procreate, vengeance was the order of the day. Driven on by pure animal primeval instinct, these savage monsters wanted retribution ... the unsuspecting people in the quarantined zone are living life the best they can, mostly obeying the rules and staying at home. Police, fire and ambulance staff are out doing their jobs. The food stores are busy with people buying essentials, the marshals are out in force doing their duty, keeping everybody contained and calm .... THEN out they came, black hideous creatures with vengeance on their evil minds. A black wave of death, rumbling in the near distance like an old freight train!!!

Unaware families in the super store picking up much needed essentials ... SPIDERS!!! SPIDERS !!! leaping out of every corner, black hideous creatures, their sharp pointy fangs dripping with anticipation. Men, women and children screaming, running for their lives. The spiders jumping two feet into the air and landing on these poor souls, thousands of these black gruesome monsters scurrying all over their terrified bodies. Sinking their razor sharp fangs deep into their terrified flesh, again and again, injecting huge amounts of deadly venom, straight into their pulsing veins. The hysterical people falling to the floor in agonising pain, blood pouring out, all over their tortured bodies from the dozens of deep, jagged, Oozing puncture wounds, everyone screaming at the top of their terrified voices. The venom coursing through their contorted bodies feeling like sulphuric acid had been poured straight into their souls, as it quickly burns them from the inside out. Hotter and hotter they get as the spiders venom burrows deep into their bones, all of their terrifying, agonising screams echoing out simultaneously. The excruciating pain is too much to bear ... and still they come, hundreds of thousands of these black hideous creatures attacking all at once around the island. Jumping, scurrying, crawling, a black army of death overwhelming the poor citizens of Manhattan.

The young and the old, doctors, builders, police officers, families isolating in their own homes, even the quarantine marshals are running for their very lives ... their blood curdling screams could be heard from miles around. The blood in their battered bodies reaching boiling point as the venom takes hold, big purple blisters bubbling through their tortured skin. The unbelievable excruciating pain as their infected veins start to expand, swelling up to double their normal size. Their tormented bodies burning brighter than the sun, black hideous spiders still biting, crawling, swarming all over our lost souls ...... Then **BOOOOOM** !!!!! their veins EXPLODE blood gushing from every orifice of their violated bodies, their eyes popping out of their agonised, contorted faces as they ALL lay DEAD on the floor!!! Rivers of thick red blood flooding the streets, hundreds of thousands of innocent people have lost their lives, in the most horrendous way possible. These black deadly spiders vanish once more, scurrying back to their dark secluded Heidi holes, the spiders vengeance is undeniable. Not one person carrying their unborn offspring was harmed in this blood thirsty, vicious attack and all of the adolescent children were speared, not one hair on their young heads has been touched.

By the time Colonel Stuart had managed to contact someone on the radio who knew what was going on ... the attack was over. It took these evil, fast, intelligent spiders less than 10 minutes to savagely kill many thousands of innocent people, their blood soaked lifeless bodies lay all around the island. Everyone at the CDC was in total shock ... A shaky, terrified voice booms out over the radio … "SPIDERS !!! there are thousands of spiders everywhere Colonel, black terrifying looking things, they are biting everyone, they are all dead, the people are all dead sir !!" … "who is this?" "Sorry Colonel its captain Rivers," sounding scared and out of breath, "we were all running for our lives. These black, evil monsters appeared from out of nowhere sir, most of my men are dead Colonel, only myself and two other marshals have survived!!"

"It was a blood bath Colonel, we didn't stand a chance, they attacked with such ferocity. These black evil demons were in a frenzy, they swarmed over everyone's bodies like a plaque of locusts. Biting, snarling, jumping high into the air, sinking their black hideous fangs into anything that moved, God only knows why I'm still alive." "Captain Rivers, are the spiders still there?" "No Colonel, they have all disappeared, the onslaught only lasted for about 10 minutes sir, then they were gone. There are dead people everywhere, too many to count. Their eyes popping out of their contorted bodies …. there is blood everywhere, it's like they all exploded from the inside out, it's absolutely horrendous Colonel." "Captain I'm on my way to the central command station in the inner perimeter, keep me fully informed of any new developments, help is on the way soldier," "yes Colonel."

Colonel Stuart jumps into his command vehicle, the driver heads over the Brooklyn bridge, the soldiers on the well-fortified bridge open all the barriers to let the Colonel through to the forward inner command post .... "Mr president," "yes Colonel Stuart," "we have a catastrophic situation sir, the spiders have attacked hundreds of thousands of people on Manhattan Island, I am on my way to the forward command post to assess the situation. Initial reports indicate that we have thousands of people dead, Mr president, I will give you a sitrep as soon as I can ascertain what exactly has happened." "Very good Colonel. I will be leaving on air force one within the hour, I want a full briefing on my arrival," "yes Mr president, I should know more by the time you arrive sir" .. Colonel Stuart then gets on his radio ordering the commanders of the air force and the navy to meet him at the forward command post immediately.

Tuesday 12.30.pm

Colonel Stuart arrives at the forward command post, the place is in total disarray. "Major" ... "yes Colonel," "what do we know, is the perimeter still secure?" "At approximately 11.50 am Colonel, reports started coming in from the quarantine marshals on the ground that big black hideous looking spiders were attacking everyone, then the airways went crazy. Marshalls from all over Manhattan Island were radioing in that there were spiders everywhere, then for a short time the radios were silent. What we have recently ascertained from the limited resources on the ground is ... we have many thousands of people dead Colonel, most of our brave marshals have been wiped out. The evil spiders didn't just attack people this time, they annihilated them in the most horrific way. We have reports of people exploding, their eyes popping out of their heads and hanging by stalks, dangling down their terrified faces, with blood gushing out of every orifice of their poor distorted bodies, it's an absolute mess out their Colonel. As far as we can tell, all the attacks happened inside our perimeter, all perimeter commanders have reported, no incursions found at their locations, the inner perimeter is at present, secure Colonel."

Colonel Stuart blows a great sigh of relief ... "Major, can you get me professor Henderson on the phone at the CDC," "YES Colonel" ... "Professor, it's a total mess here inside the quarantine zone, we have many thousands of innocent people dead, in your opinion professor are the spiders on the move, are they heading for the mainland?" "In my opinion Colonel no, this attack was a show of strength, we killed one of their own and they wanted revenge. These are highly intelligent creatures, I don't think they consider us a threat, we are just hosts or food to them. As long as their unborn babies remain on that island, so will they ... but Colonel, as soon as the new babies are born, it will be an all new ball game." "Are you sure about this professor, will they stay on this island until then?" "Yes Colonel Stuart, I believe so ... but if any of those infected souls were to escape the quarantine, the spiders would most definitely follow." "Thank you professor Henderson, keep me informed on your progress with our last specimen" ....

"Colonel, the navy and air force are here to see you sir." "Thank you Major, show them in," saluting, "gentlemen," "Colonel, as you are already aware, we have a serious situation on our hands. At the CDC earlier today killing one of our arachnid specimens so we could analyse its DNA. Within minutes of the spiders death the remaining spiders unleashed a wave of devastation destruction that we have never seen before, killing many thousands of our fellow Americans. In only 10 minutes they had decimated our population, leaving thousands of blood soaked bodies lying in the streets." "Gentlemen, the president is on route as we speak, he has given me full authority to use all and every means at my disposal ... No ONE and I mean no ONE will be permitted to leave that godforsaken island. We still have many rich and influential people on that island, and they will use any means possible to leave ... You WILL shoot down any aircraft that tries to take off and you WILL sink any craft that takes to the water, regardless gentlemen, of whoever is on board. Let's not pull any punches on where we find ourselves today, many thousands of people are dead, we are in for one hell of a shit show. There are way too many cameras in New York city to contain this horrific situation, the internet will be full of horrendous videos showing these deadly black hideous creatures. Within hours every single person in Manhattan and the world will know that the spiders are real, and they are sinking their black hideous fangs into people and killing them. Millions of terrified men, women and children in the quarantined zone will be heading for the exit, gentlemen we can't let them leave. Your orders still stand, shoot on sight, the fate of the country lies in your hands, may God have mercy on us for what we are about to do!!" ....

"Yes Colonel" ..." God speed gentlemen, dismissed." "Major," "yes Colonel," "inform all forward commanders on the perimeter to expect reinforcements within the hour, as soon as the news of what has happened sinks in, millions of terrified people will be heading to the inner perimeter fences trying desperately to get off this ungodly island, they must not breach our defences, Major. All of the soldiers under your command MUST do their duty, these hideous spiders don't just infect people, they savagely kill them too. We must stand fast Major, we must stay the course. Men, women and children will die today by our hand, but we do this for the good of the nation and possibly the entire world. We have primed all bridges and tunnels to blow at a moment's notice, totally cutting off Manhattan Island from the mainland but we are still hopeful that Mrs Hocker and her team will find a solution."

Colonel Stuart and the Major leave the command post and walk onto the parapet overlooking the barbed wire fences and concrete barriers, what greets them is utter chaos. Thousands of terrified people have charged towards the perimeter, trying desperately to escape the black evil, deadly spiders. The high density double steel wire fence with barbed wire on top stretches out in both directions as far as the eye can see, with interlocking concrete security barriers set directly behind. All the soldiers are entrenched with weapons at the ready, flamethrowers are positioned every 20 feet, all pointing inwards towards at the baying crowd. Thousands of screaming men, women and children are desperately trying to break through the fence. They are shouting, screaming at the soldiers to let them out, spiders, the spiders are real, they are killing people, let us out. More terrified people come, scared, terrified people. Most had seen the horrific videos, but lots were actually there, there when the black hideous spiders attacked, people's lifeless bloodied bodies falling to the floor in absolute agony, their eyes popping out of their heads, thick red blood awash on the streets.

This horrific scene was being replicated all along the entire perimeter, thousands and thousands of screaming, terrified people clawing at the thick steel fence, trying in vain to break free. The soldiers gripped tightly onto their weapons, not wanting to shoot innocent civilians, especially children ... but they knew the gruesome truth, the babies buried deep within, ready to explode into the world .... BANG ... BANG the sound of gunfire rings out, the crowd is armed, hundreds of Americans with guns trying to set themselves free!! Two young soldiers fall from the dugout, shot dead by the ravaging terrified crowd … The soldiers open fire, bullets flying left, right and centre, the hordes dropping to the floor to avoid being shot but still the gunfire is returned. Bullets whistling through the wire fence, aimed at the military blocking their way.

The battle rages on, automatic weapons pinging from both sides of the fence. Americans killing Americans, the world is watching, as the battle intensified, people shouting, people screaming, people dying, all live streamed in this technological society. The hundreds deep crowd baying for blood, trying desperately to destroy the barriers blocking their way to freedom. Hundreds lay dead, or dying, possibly thousands, traumatised screaming children cradling their dead or dying parents, to very young, to understand what is going on. For at least 30 minutes the bloody struggle continued, the sound of gun shots being heard in all directions … The fences are still secure, the soldiers calmly held their ground, the battle won for today, but the war will definitely continue on ......

Earlier today, the Kirk family were all at home. Ryan and Charley were in their bedrooms, Richard and Shona were in the kitchen, then suddenly a tearful Ryan burst into the kitchen. "What's the matter son?" "Mom, dad the spiders ... the spiders are back, they have been killing people!!" Shocked they both leapt to their feet. "What do mean Ryan?" "I was talking to one of my school friends online when the internet went crazy, hundreds of people started posting stories of big black hideous spiders attacking everyone all around the island .... Then the videos started to appear, there is one inside a food store, mom its absolutely terrifying." Ryan's eyes starting to well up, tears trickling down his scared face. "They lied to us dad, they told us that the army had killed all the spiders 10 days ago, they are not dead, those hideous monsters are back." "I know Ryan, I think the government has lied to us from the start, what videos!!"

Ryan then shows his distraught parents the newly posted horrific videos. Richard and

Shona watched in horror as hundreds of black evil spiders swarm the innocent families doing their food shopping. The black deadly creatures leaping onto the screaming bodies of the helpless shoppers, dozens of them scurrying onto each person, sinking their long pointy fangs deep into their tortured flesh. Everyone shouting, screaming, running in all directions ... running for their lives. Then the victims falling to the floor in complete agony, their twisted bodies violently convulsing as their red hot veins begin to explode!! Their eyes popping out of their terrified heads, dangling down their deceased faces, buckets of thick red blood covering every inch of the dirty, cold floor, then the spiders were gone, crawling back to their hiding places ... "Oh my god!!!" Shona's face crumples, shaking, crying, she quickly raps her frightened arms around both of the men in her life. The three of them hugging tightly, their skin tingling, their breathing fast and shallow, all their senses heightened, scared to death of what might happen next. Lots more gory videos are posted, on the streets, in people's homes, all around the city ... but one thing remains the same, children, terrified screaming children, standing right amongst the carnage, the black hideous spiders right there and still they continue to be untouched, why?? "I don't understand it Shona, why leave the children alone and they didn't go down the people's throats this time, the spiders just killed them in the most horrific way possible, why are we not dead?" ...

"Ryan, where is your sister's phone?" "In the living room I think dad," "go and get it for me son." Ryan hands his father Charley's phone. After taking out the battery Richard tells Ryan to put it back exactly where he found it, looking puzzled, Shona asks "why take the battery out?" "Charley will think her phone is broken because it won't turn on, if I hide it, she will nag the guts out of me to give it back. Charley can't find out what has happened, she thinks the spiders are all dead, we must keep it that way." "What are we going to do dad, the soldiers won't let us leave the island, people are trying but there is no way through." "I don't know Ryan ... keep looking at the internet and let us know, quietly, what you find out," "ok dad I will."

Over in Harlem Edward has just phoned Ruby on her dads phone to tell her about the spiders attack that happened only moments earlier. "Ruby … are you ok?" "Yes Edward, I've been in my parents apartment all day. Turn on your TV, you were right Ruby, the spiders do exist, they have been killing people. Every news channel is inundated with stories and live streaming videos of the black hideous spiders attacking screaming terrified people. The images have been subdued, much to graphic to be shown in full." Ruby is in total and utter shock watching these horrendous images, the spiders are far more gruesome than she had ever imagined. "Ruby you were right, the government has been lying to everyone. The world is watching, and the world is going crazy, spiders are most people's biggest nightmare but black hideous ones with enormous pointy fangs that kill people. Where did they come from? are those terrifying spiders coming here? Millions of people around the world Ruby people are really scared, the president and the military have blood on their hands and questions must be answered."

"Colonel Stuart the president is here." "Mr president," "Colonel, I have been watching the internet coverage on my way over, my phone has been ringing off the hook from all the dignitaries wanting answers from all around the world. Where did the spiders come from? why are we imprisoning millions of Americans behind an impenetrable ring of steel and concrete? Why are we shooting scared, terrified people who just want to leave the island? The crowd is live streaming every gunshot, the dead are paraded like martyr's splashed across our screen, blood soaked orphaned children whaling beside their dead parents. The world thinks we are the monsters, killing our own citizens. We have hundreds of millions of ordinary Americans screaming from the rooftops watching their soldiers shooting innocent new Yorkers dead in the streets. Congress is up in arms, Colonel, I am the president, and I cannot justify any of this .... but what if they all knew the terrifying truth??"

"Yes Colonel, what if we leek poor Tina Smith's autopsy report and the horrific statements of the doctors on duty that awful day. The realisation that millions more black hideous monsters are going to spew into the world in a matter of days!! They then might understand that we were trying to safeguard hundreds of millions of Americans lives and stop this black deadly horrific plague from spreading around the world" … "Mr president sir, if we leek this devastating information to the world we will make an impossible situation into a catastrophe. Everyone wants to evacuate the island now … but if they know that their friends and neighbours are carrying unborn baby spiders deep inside their bodies and they are going to explode into the world in a matter of days, then, there will be total and utter pandemonium. At the moment everyone on this island is in the same boat, they are all working towards the same goal, getting off the island but Mr president if the people know the truth it will be dog eat dog. Families turning against families, friends turning against friends, people will try everything and anything to leave this island, not because they are scared, just because they have nothing else to lose. Please think very carefully Mr president before you decide."

"Ok Colonel we can discuss my proposal later, what has been happening on the ground since the spiders attack." "Well Mr president as you have seen from the internet, thousands of scared, terrified people have swamped our perimeter trying desperately to leave the island. There were many gun battles up and down the fence line but no one was able to breach our defences. We have 41 dead and many more injured, reinforcements have been steadily arriving, but it is impossible to say how many civilians have been killed or wounded sir" ... "Colonel Stuart," the president drops his shoulders and breathes in deeply, "between you and me and these four walls we should of done more. Many people in the government were urging me from the outset to evacuate as many people off that stricken island as possible, especially the poor innocent children. I should of listened, most of the joint chiefs of staff were urging caution, the CDC will find a way out of this unprecedented situation. They are just spiders, how has it come to this Colonel, we are too far down this rabbit hole now to dig ourselves out. The die is cast, we have no alternative but to continue on our regretful course. These deadly creatures are like nothing we have encountered before, at our peril we have underestimated our foe. What we do in the days to come will determine if mankind has a future on this Planet, we call home!! The burden of responsibility falls to us Colonel, we must now sacrifice millions to save billions. If we fail in this gruesome task, humanity will become lambs to the slaughter, we must convince the world that what we do here today, right now, is for the greater good."

"Colonel Stuart !!" "Yes, Mr president," "I leave the protection of this great nation in your hands, you know what needs to be done. I will try to convince the American people and the world that what we are doing here is for the safety of the human race. Once again Colonel I reiterate, you have full presidential authority to do whatever is necessary to safeguarding this proud nation. I am now heading to the CDC to see if Mrs Hocker and her team are any closer to finding a resolution to this horrific situation. Carry on Colonel, please keep me informed of all developments," "yes Mr president.

Tuesday 18.00 pm

"Mrs Hocker, the president is here." "Mr president," taking hold of her hands, "Janet,

please tell me that you have some good news?"
"Sorry Mr president NO !! we have been working around the clock pumping our remaining specimen with the deadliest substances known to man, but nothing seems to kill it. We are in the process of combining lots of different toxins and nerve agents to see if they have any affect. Our brightest toxicologist have been frantically deconstructing our dead spiders DNA to determine what course of action we need to take next. We won't get the full toxicology report until early hours tomorrow morning. Mr president, I assure you that my dedicated team and I am doing everything humanly possible to get this job done" ... "I am well aware of that Janet, but may I remind you that the clock is ticking, we have a little over 3 days before all hell breaks loose. If you don't succeed, my only choice will be to authorise nuclear thermal devices to be used. These bombs won't just kill the spiders and the good citizens of Manhattan, their blast radius will also obliterate nearly everything and everyone in New Jersey, the Bronx, Queens and Brooklyn, many millions of hardworking Americans will be killed because we

failed!! We can't afford for even one of those hideous monsters to crawl its way onto the mainland. Mrs Hocker, you must succeed, the world is praying you don't fail!!" "Yes, Mr president, I am confident we will have an answer very soon."

Tuesday has been a shocking, violent, horrific day. Who would of thought just killing one solitary spider would have such horrendous consequences. The millions of scared, terrified people incarcerated behind barbed wire and concrete barriers are being treated like human mushrooms, kept in the dark and lied to again and again by the very people who were elected to protect them. The government had set a course down this unprecedented road, lying their way through the never ending streets. Twisting and turning, deceiving themselves as well as the American people, totally underestimating their black deadly opponents. The new arachnid species are far more intelligent than their predecessors, they are fast, very strong and highly organised. They seem to operate as one complete entity, if one bleeds, they all bleed, they are subconsciously connected somehow. Trying to find ANYTHING that kills these black, hideous, killing machines seems futile but try we must, the fate of civilisation depends on it. Wednesday night fades into obscurity, lots of scared, terrified people are still trying to claw their way to freedom. The soldiers on the front line beating them back at every turn, sporadic gunfire can be heard ringing out throughout the night along the entire perimeter of their incarceration. The population are in total shock, terrified that the hideous black demons will come back for them, scurrying over their tormented bodies, sinking their horrific black razor sharp fangs deep into their innocent flesh. Men, women and children to afraid to close their weary eyes just in case they never wake up again. Those black evil monsters dominating their every thought, where did they come from, what do they want, how can I keep my family safe ....

Wednesday 06.00 am ONLY 3 DAYS TO GO!!!

After only a couple of hours of sleep Colonel Stuart is personally inspecting the perimeter. There have been many incursions throughout the night, many brave soldiers have lost their lives trying to stop the black wave of terror from escaping the island and descending on their poor defenceless families safe and sound back on the mainland.

Colonel Stuart enters the perimeters command post. "Morning Major Simpson," "yes Colonel," "how was your night, Major?" "We had many desperate people, with their frightened families trying to escape the island sir but my men made sure no one succeeded. The crowd all around the perimeter were angry and scared, many with automatic weapons. They kept charging the wire fence, spraying bullets everywhere as they went. We have sustained many casualties throughout the whole perimeter" ... then a dirty, bloodied young lieutenant enters the room, teary eyed the young lieutenant straightens his weary shoulders, saluting, "sorry Colonel, I didn't know you were in here sir. Major," " yes lieutenant," " when we were collecting up our dead and injured I found this photograph on the bloody, dirty floor, handing it to the Major," it shows a pretty young woman on the front, with blonde wavy hair and on the back is a very poignant personal message, "I thought you should see it sir, it has touched all the men's hearts, it has made them realise why they are here" ..

The Major then reads out the heart felt message ... To my darling Sheena ... if anything may happen to me ... just see, for you I have done my best ... and now I may rest ... for the rest ... of eternity ...!! it was just signed, love you always RB xxx, "sir ... Major," "yes Colonel, that was beautiful, one of my OWN has written that." "Please find out who that brave soldier was and make sure the lady in question receives her photograph," "yes Colonel I will see to it personally" ... The Major turns to the young lieutenant, "thank you lieutenant for bringing this to my attention," saluting, "carry on lieutenant," "yes Major" ..." As I was saying Colonel, many more people lay dead and injured on the other side of the barricade, the situation seems to be a little calmer at the moment sir." "Very good Major, I have ordered more reinforcements to replenish your ranks, make sure the troops are well rested as I don't expect this terrible situation to come to an end any time soon. The longer this goes on, the more desperate the people will become. They will go to extra ordinary lengths to escape, we must be ready Major. I have an idea that I need to run past the president and if he agrees, I'm hoping that my idea will give us the time to reinforce our barricades … Major I am now going to the CDC to meet with Mrs Hocker, please keep me updated on my radio, yes Colonel."

Later on, that morning Richard and Shona are sat in the living room watching the horrific coverage on the TV of all the terrified people with their crying families trying to smash their way through the impenetrable ring of steel. Most people have their phones on, streaming live pictures to the world. Desperate screaming people giving live running commentary as the bullets fly over their terrified heads … "I am at the barbed wire with my wife and young son, all we want to do is get off this godforsaken island, but the soldiers won't let us leave." Hundreds of terrified people are pulling furiously at the thick steel wire fence, screaming at the soldiers to "let us go!!" The armed soldiers inside the perimeter pointing their weapons in our direction, keeping calm but every now and then they fired warning shots above out heads. Then suddenly automatic weapons fire rings out, the bullets flying straight towards the waiting soldiers. The crowd panics and fall to their knees, women and children crying frantically in terror as the military returns fire. Bullets pinging out in all directions, Americans killing Americans ....

"Shona, those poor frightened people," "yes Richard, they must be desperate to have a gunfight with the army. Look, there are thousands of them, up and down the entire island, all trying to break through the fences to freedom" .... "Mom, dad" an excitable Ryan enters the room, "yes Ryan what's up?" "A Colonel has just appeared on the internet, saying ... saying the spiders are dead, a soldier was stood next to him holding a dead one" .... The news on the TV suddenly stops, BREAKING NEWS ... the spiders are dead!! "There he is mom, that's him." We bring you breaking news, Colonel Stuart is holding a special news bulletin ... My fellow Americans, my name is Colonel Stuart, I am pleased to inform you that all the spiders on Manhattan Island are dead!! A crack unit of the green berets tracked the spiders to their nest deep under the city, I can confirm approximately 30 minutes ago that all the spiders were gassed to death ... "look dad, there's a man stood next to the Colonel, he's wearing a full body suit and he's holding a dead spider in his hand" ... we don't know where these hideous creatures came from, but the CDC is doing its utmost to determine what happened. I urge everyone who is at the perimeter fence to go home, the deadly threat to human bird flu still remains. The president assures me that the quarantine will be lifted in a few short days, so please go home and let the military and the CDC do their jobs ... That was a special news report from the Pentagon!!

"I told you mom, the spiders are dead." "Yes, Ryan you did, go and see if your sisters is ok in her bedroom for me Ryan," "ok mom." "Richard, this doesn't sound right, they told us last time that the spiders were dead ... but they lied to us, I think that they are lying to us now but why?" "Yes, Shona I think your right, none of this makes any sense to me, surely the government is there to protect us, not to lie to us. Where did the spiders come from, what do they want, why are we still alive, why didn't they attack the children." "I know Richard, all I want is answers, I just want to keep my family safe …"

Ruby calls Edward .. "Edward, I'm guessing you have seen the news report," "yes Ruby it all sounds very dodgy to me. Everyone here on the mainland thinks the government is hiding something, everything they have done up until now doesn't make any sense. If deadly human bird flu existed, why the barbed wire and concrete barriers? Where are the hundreds of dead bodies, why haven't the CDC been on the island testing people" … "I know Edward none of this makes any sense, my parents and all the people I have spoken to who were in the first quarantine zone, have told me that the soldiers had gassed the spiders days ago, not today. I think the spiders are still alive Edward and I think the bird flu is a cover up, but I don't know why?" "It doesn't make sense Ruby, if the spiders are still alive, barbed wire and concrete won't stop them getting onto the mainland. I'm hitching a ride on a news helicopter on Saturday morning, we are flying over to New Jersey. I will get the pilot to fly as close to the Hudson River as he dares, so we can zoom into Manhattan and give you an update on what we see." "Ok Edward that sounds good, we have lots of questions but no answers at the moment, we will just have to keep digging. Speak to you soon."

As Wednesday draws to a close the people believed the Colonels broadcast, slowly and surely, they start to make their way back home, beaten by the military's resolve and the impenetrable ring of steel. The air force had kept the sky clear, the navy patrolled the murky waters not letting anyone pass. The CDC are working tirelessly, around the clock but sadly to no avail, nothing seemed to be working.

The black hideous spiders lay in wait, hundreds of thousands of these black evil monsters lying just beneath the surface, just out of sight. Waiting patiently for their new blood thirsty offspring to spew into the world. The poor unsuspecting infected people above with only days left to live, their inner bodies aching, their Intestines slowly swelling with faint movements coming from within ...!!

Thursday morning ONLY 2 DAYS TO GO!!!

The president is under huge pressure, in fact his whole administration is creaking from inside out. The world is intently watching ... why is he incarcerated millions of Americans behind an enormous ring of wire and concrete. The world had watched in horror as the black hideous spiders viciously killed thousands of innocent people in their homes and on the bloodied streets. The entire population is scared to death, billions of frightened people, are the black evil monsters coming for me and my family. The internet is awash with the vilest imagery imaginable, fast evil demons scurrying all over peoples screaming bodies, sinking their long, pointy, razor sharp fangs deep into their helpless flesh. Screaming people falling to the floor in absolute agony, their terrified eyes popping out of their heads ...

The worlds governments wanted answers, show us proof of the deadly human bird flu, tell us where the deadly black spiders came from?? The American government had no answers, only lies. We can't tell the American people, let alone the world, the terrifying truth. Slowly but surely, Congress is turning against the president, the American people are protesting in the streets. Many of their friends and family live on the island of Manhattan, everyone is worried senseless. The unbelievable gory images of the spiders attacking and American soldiers shooting people dead on the streets. These savage, unprecedented pictures slashed across the entire internet and the world is watching their television screens with bated breath …

The president calls an emergency meeting with all departments, the CDC, the army, the navy and the air force … "Settle down everyone, right people, time has nearly ran out. The odds are stacked against us, congress and the world leaders are baying for my blood, I can't hold them off for much longer. They are not buying our human bird flu story, they all want answers. I think by tomorrow morning I will have no alternative but to tell everyone the truth, the terrible truth that sometime on Saturday morning, millions of baby evil, deadly spiders will explode into the world!!" "Mr president," "yes Colonel Stuart," "may I speak freely sir," "certainly Colonel" …

Standing up and composing himself, "morning everyone, Mr president, I have just managed to calm the chaotic situation down a little, I announced on all media outlets that the spiders are dead. I even had one of my captains hold up the dead spider from the CDC's laboratory to reinforce my message ... Mr president most of the people on that godforsaken island believed me, nearly all of them have abandoned the perimeter and are making their way back home. We have led the people to believe that the quarantine zone will be lifted in a couple of days. I think Mr president, it would be unwise to expose the truth to the world at this time. I spoke to you a few days ago about the ramifications of releasing this damaging information, the utter chaos that it would cause, the whole island will go up like a tinder box. Can I be totally candid with everyone in this room, if we announce to the already scared, frightened people on that island .... that millions upon millions of black evil baby spiders will explode out of their terrified bodies in less than 2 days .... There will be total and utter carnage, friends will turn against friends, families will rip themselves apart, people would turn against each other in the most savage way. Can you imagine waking up tomorrow morning and finding out from social media that you have got thousands of black hideous baby spiders growing deep inside of you and there is nothing … absolutely nothing that you can do about it. The mental trauma would be excruciating … and you only have 24 hours left to live!! The sense of self-preservation will be overwhelming, millions of screaming, desperate people will turn head long for the exit … but we have closed all the exits, we have caged them all in …. and the SPIDERS are coming!!!"

"I implore you Mr president, please change your mind. We have a little calm at present, we … I don't need absolute chaos inside the quarantine zone, I am personally responsible for thousands of military personnel. I have to write many letters of condolences, please do not make me write hundreds more." The room is silent, everyone is sat there with their eyes wide open and their mouths slightly a jar … "Thank you, Colonel Stuart, I will take on board everything that you have said. Professor

Henderson," "yes Mr president," "in your professional opinion what do you think the spiders will do next?" "Well Mr president this is only conjecture, but I think the spiders will stay out of sight until their offspring are born sometime on Saturday morning. They will then reappear and start to feed their ravenous hungry newly born babies" ...

"Feed !! professor," "yes Mr president, as I have already said, I believe that the hungry baby spiders will start to feed on our young adolescent children!! The adult spiders will attack the children, wrapping them tightly with their Webb, leaving their pray alive but unable to move, ready for the ravenous babies to suck dry at their leisure" ..." professor, Charles, do you think this will really happen, it is too unspeakable to contemplate." "Yes, Janet I believe so, the evidence speaks for itself. The children on two separate occasions were not attacked, we also have thousands of young prepubescent cocooned rats with hundreds of tiny puncture marks and their carcasses were totally drained of all their blood. I can only conclude from this that the children are food!!" "My god professor," the president sinks his head in shame, "what have I done to those poor innocent children? I shouldn't of listened to the many voices, I should of got the children out of there" ... The room is sombre, the enormity of what they have all just heard slowly sinking in ...

The president stands up, his arms slouched by his side, his heart heavy, carrying the burden of responsibility. "On reflection I have decided NOT to release any information to the public, I have doomed the citizens of Manhattan Island to a gruesome, hideous death but hopefully we can save the rest of this great nation we call America. I hope and pray the historians will look favourable on my tenure as president ... Mrs Hocker," "Janet," "please tell me some good news." "Sorry again Mr president my team and I have been working around the clock, we have tried every poisonous substance known to man, but nothing seems to kill these ungodly creatures. We are in the process of mixing together the deadliest toxins and nerve agents to see if they have any affect. Mr president, you good people sat around this table, I am sorry to say, I think the CDC may have come to the end of its road but we I keep trying to the bitter end." "Thank you, Mrs Hocker," "we will keep trying Mr president."

"Right, back to business everyone, let's concentrate on the here and now. Just before we all get back to our posts, Colonel Stuart can you give everyone an overview of where we are on the ground right now." "Certainly, Mr president, at present the perimeter is fully manned, we have suffered minor casualties, but we have beefed up security where needed. All bridges are barricaded at both ends with explosive charges in place when needed. I have been liaising with the navy and air force command, gun boats are constantly patrolling around the water ways of the island, pushing back any incursions that may occur. Oil tankers are strategically situated around the island, ready to encircle the whole island in a ring of fire. Apache helicopters are imposing our no fly zone. Mr president we are as ready as we'll ever be. When the world finally finds out what we have done here today, there will be hell to pay. We have left millions of Americans like helpless lambs to the slaughter, we will pay the piper but not today. We have a job to do, we cannot, we must not let these evil black monsters loose upon the world, this ends now. If the CDC fails in its mission to destroy these deadly creatures the president has authorised, as a last resort, the use of thermal nuclear weapons to eradicate all life on Manhattan Island. Once the ring of fire is established you will have just a matter of hours to withdraw your personnel to a safe distance. God speed everyone, let history judge us on what we do here today!!"

Everyone goes back to their departments knowing what needs to be done ... Mrs Hocker arrives back at the CDC, she gathers her extremely tiered team around her. Explaining what was said by the president and what needs to happen now. "We have only one more day before it's too late, if we fail the president is going to nuke the whole island. Not just killing them but millions of innocent people in the immediate vicinity, we must double our efforts, the clock is almost striking zero." Everyone hurries back to their mini labs to carry on working ... "Janet, can I have a word with you before I get back to work," "of course you can

Catalina," "what is the president doing about the children?" "I'm sorry Catalina we have disgust this numerous times, the president's hands are tied, there is nothing we can do for those poor children now but pray" ..." but Mrs Hocker ... Janet, surely, we can do something," "no Mrs Mendes the matter is out of our hands. Please Catalina time is of the essence, I know everyone is absolutely exhausted, but we need to push on" ...

The scene is set, everyone is staffing their stations. Thursday night is slowly drawing to a close, soon we will only have one day left. The citizens of Manhattan are drifting off to their beds, blissfully unaware of the unimaginable horrors that awaits them. The president's heart weighs heavy upon his soul, wishing he hadn't listened to the babbling fools who said the CDC will resolve this situation, they are only spiders, he should of evacuated as many people as he could ... Colonel Stuart, the long serving military man, protect and serve, etched into his very fabric. Duty and honour dripping out of every pour of his staunch body ... Mrs Janet Hocker, a woman of science, fact and investigation.

Protecting the world from microbes and organisms that might do it harm, her life's work hanging in the balance ... The spiders, acting purely out of instinct. Manmade evolution has elevated these super intelligent beings far above their station. Evolving, surviving the only way they know how ...

Friday 04.15 am ONLY 1 DAY TO GO!!!!!

"Janet ... Janet ... Mrs HOCKER," her eyes slowly open, she had only placed her weary head on that pillow an hour before. "Janet, wake up," her assistant Jenny is frantically trying to wake her leader. Coming too, Janet's eyes spring open, with Jenny's face only inches away. "Mrs Hocker," her voice shaking with fear, "the spider ... the spider is DEAD!!" Leaping out of bed ... "what do you mean Jenny??" "The spider is dead, I was preparing the next batch of toxins and when I went to the chamber the spider was lying motionless on the chamber floor, I thought it was dead!!" Her body is shaking, her hands are trembling, her voice crackling and very high pitched, tears welling up in her frightened face. "What if those hideous spiders attack again, it will be all my fault?" Taking Jenny firmly by the hand, Janet looks deep into her colleges confused eyes ... "NO Jenny none of this is your fault. Come on Jenny come with me, we will go together and find out exactly what's happened."

On reaching the main laboratory Mrs Hocker peers through the large viewing window, yes Jenny was right, the spider lay motionless on the chamber floor. "Quick Jenny, go and get everyone to meet me here in the main lab" ... moments later everyone is gathered, shocked at the terrible news that their prize specimen is dead. "What do we do now, how has this happened, what killed it?" ... "Calm down everyone, where is Catalina?" "I don't know Mrs Hocker, I'll go and look for her." As everybody starts milling around scratching their bemused heads, Mrs Hocker takes the initiative. She bravely enters through the double security doors straight into the inner large chamber, there it is, right in front of her, through the toughened viewing window, the deadly foe she had tried so hard to destroy. Taking hold of the levers that controlled the metal arms within, her hands sweating, her breathing becoming more erratic, Janet gives the motionless deadly spider a tentative poke ... NOTHING, she pokes it again .. but still nothing. Turning the thermal camera onto high density, she peers through the lens with utter trepidation. No sign of heat glowing outwards, the screen is in darkness, no signs of life emanating from within. After all the exhausted efforts of her dedicated team the spiders life force has been extinguish, lying dead face down on the chamber floor, after all their many hours of painstaking work had failed ...

"Right, everyone, I know your all exhausted, but we need to establish how this spider died. Go and check over every inch of your paperwork, then carefully scrutinize all video entries for the past 3 hours. The president will be phoning me shortly for an update, I need to have answers when he calls. I will arrange for an immediate autopsy to be carried out so we can establish the course of death." Everyone has a second wind, spurred on by the catastrophe that has just happened. What are we going to do now, no spider to run tests on, no possible way of destroying them. The citizens of Manhattan Island have only 24 hours before millions of baby spiders are born, everyone is running around the laboratories like crazy trying to solve this unprecedented situation .... "Mrs Hocker, everyone !! it was me, it's all my fault." Everyone stops what they are doing and files back into the main laboratory.

Stood before them is one of the junior lab technicians, looking so very apologetic and dead on his feet. "I'm so sorry everyone, about an hour ago when I was decontaminating the chamber ready for the next toxin to be administered, I accidentally turned off the oxygen supply. I think when you do the autopsy Mrs Hocker, you will most probably find that the spider was simply asphyxiated. I'm so sorry everyone, I have no excuses." All his exhausted colleagues gather around him, "it's not your fault, we are all tired, we are all dead on our feet." One of them even says, "what are we supposed to do now, suffocate the evil bastards!!" Professor Henderson stops in his tracks, stroking his chin he tells Mrs Hocker that he will see her later ... Everyone in the CDC is shell-shocked, they have all just become redundant, what is the president going to say now.

Friday 06.35 am

Young Ryan burst into his sleeping parents' bedroom, he is crying uncontrollably, tears are pouring down his young terrified face. His body is shaking from head to toe, his gaze transfixed at the unbelievable gruesome images on his phone. "Mooom, daaad," his crackling tearful voice trying to wake his parents … with a start, Shona is awake, she takes one look at her traumatised, babbling young boy and she is up like a shot. "Richard wake up, its Ryan, there's something terribly wrong." The two of them try to console their frantic, hysterical young son. They gently sit him down on the edge of the bed, sitting either side, holding a hand a piece. Squeezing his hand ever so gently, "what's wrong Ryan, come on son, you can tell us anything." The tears are still rolling down his horrified face, snot is bubbling out of his nose, his whole body is aching from the unbelievable horror he has witnessed on the internet.

"Moooom," slowly his voice becomes a little clearer, sniffling back the tears, wiping his soddened face. "Dad, the spiders .... the spiders are inside of us!!" "What do you mean Ryan, inside of us?" Still crying, his poor young body continuing to shudder, Ryan turns his forearm over, revealing his phone, someone had leaked ALL the terrifying information about the black hideous spiders to the world!!! As Richard and Shona watched in absolute horror, the full extent of what happened to them in the cinema that fateful Saturday afternoon suddenly dawns on them. Watching the horrendous footage from the shopping mall, of black evil spiders descending down people's gagging throats, their eyes wide open, frozen solid, unable to move. Helpless children screaming at the top of their terrified voices, hysterical people running in all directions, running for their lives ... It was too much for Richard and Shona to bare, they leapt off the bed, clawing frantically at their stomachs, the sight of poor old Tina's autopsy sending them both over the edge. All three of them looking at each other in total disbelief, their brains couldn't comprehend what their eyes were seeing.

Shocked and utterly confused they all sat on the edge of the bed, in silence they sat, their grey ashen faces looking far into the distance, their minds whirling around at a million miles an hour ... Then suddenly Richards terrified face starts to crumble, tears welling up in his saddened eyes, his traumatised body beginning to shake. His throat burning from the inside out, his breathing quick and shallow. Tears start falling, down his heartbroken face, sobbing uncontrollably, the top half of his tortured body being crushed by an invisible menacing force making it almost impossible to catch his saddened breath, his heart beating so fast, nearly bursting out of his chest. Richard has never cried so hard in his entire life ....

"Richard, you're scaring me, are you in pain?" Putting her loving arms around her heartbroken husband shoulders, squeezing him tighter than she had ever done before. Richard was inconsolable, he was broken inside, his tears were flooding down his expressionless face, his frantic sobs getting louder and louder. Shona kneels down in front of him, lifting up his sopping face, trying slowly to wipe away his tears, looking deep into his bloodshot eyes. "I've never seen you cry like this before?" Fighting back his sobbing tears, "I'm not crying for me Shona .... I'm crying for Charley, how do we tell our little Charley that we are all going to die tomorrow!!" The terrible realisation hits home, my little girl, Shona too starts to cry, tears of overwhelming sadness pouring down her face.

"How do I tell my little sister mom, dad what do we do?" The three of them hug deeply, crying on each other's shoulders, they are not crying for themselves but for poor little 9 year old Charley ... The floorboards begin to creak, the sound of little footsteps can be heard, its Charley, she's awake. Quickly jumping to their feet and wiping the tears away the best they can, Charley bounces into the bedroom. "Morning guys, what's all the noise about?" Spotting everyone's sad faces and the remnants of tears in their sad eyes Charley realises something was wrong. "What's wrong dad .. mom .. Ryan, please tell me what's going on?" None of them could hardly speak, especially with sweet little Charley looking back at them. Charley walks over to her big strong father, taking hold of his loving hand, she gazes up into his saddened tearful face. "Come on dad, you can tell me, I am a big girl now, I'm nearly 10." Unable to control himself, tears once more start rolling down his heartbroken face. Looking deep into his beautiful little girls sweet face is almost too much for him to bear. Sitting little Charley down on the bed next to him, fighting back his stuttering sobs and wiping away his tears.

"I have something very upsetting to tell you my darling little girl." Shona and Ryan were holding each other, still quietly sobbing, to upset to speak, Richard at any moment now was going to rip Charley's little heart out of her fragile body and shatter her innocent world forever!! "Charley" .... "Wait Richard, Charley," "yes mom," "it's your grandmother, I'm afraid she has died darling, she died peacefully in her sleep last night, that's why we are all a little sad today." Feeling a little teary as she looked around at the weeping faces, Charley felt even more sad for her family than for herself because she didn't really know her grandmother that well. She lived in Canada and Charley had only met her twice before. Her dad was still quietly sobbing sat on the bed next to her, Charley lifts up his head, wiping the tears from his upset face Charley says, "I know she was your mother dad," as she stroked his soddened brow, "your Charley is here, and I'll make it all ok for you," " you always make me feel better when I'm feeling sad, now it's my turn to make you feel better."

Richard couldn't contain his emotions any longer, he reached out scooping his thoughtful, considerate, beautiful daughter into his aching arms, squeezing her ever so tightly. Shona and Ryan joined in and the four of them are hugging, crying, squeezing together so compactly, the Kirk family United. This is the last time they will all be together like this, in a matter of hours they will all be dead!!! .... "Dad, mom, I can't breathe, let me go." Letting go of their loving grip Charley flops out of the foursome. Smiling, her hair all tangled, "guys you nearly suffocated me then, I need food" ... A little 9 year old Charley then bounces off to the kitchen to see what she could find. Richard, Shona and Ryan all look at each other, "what do we do now??" Richard reaches down and pulls furiously at his stomach, "I can't believe those hideous things are in there. The government had lied to us all along, they knew, and they did nothing." The three of them hold hands once more, shell-shocked and terrified, they looked into each other's frightened, weeping faces, "what do we DO NOW!!!" If they only knew that their beloved little Charley is going to be the FOOD that will sustain these hungry, insatiable creatures when they explode out of the very loins that bore her 9 years ago.

Friday 06.55 am

Colonel Stuart is woken from his slumber, he had spent most of the night personally making sure everything and everyone was in its place ready for whatever happens next. "Colonel, Colonel, its going crazy out their sir." The Colonel quickly jumps from his bunk and heads for the central command post which is located between Manhattan and Brooklyn bridge on the inner perimeter. Thousands of scared, angry people had gathered along the fence line, many are trying to force their way across both bridges, but the wire and concrete barriers are holding fast. The terrified but professional soldiers are well dug in, with their weapons pointing outwards to protect the nation at any cost. The hysterical crowd are shouting and screaming, the spiders are coming, let us off this fucking island, we are all going to die.

From his advantage point the Colonel could see right up and down the containment area, there were many more hordes of screaming terrified people heading for the closed, barricaded bridges and any hope of freedom. "Captain," "yes Colonel," "tell your men to hold the perimeter, with their lives if they have to, we know what's at stake if they fail." "Yes Colonel, my men will defend the perimeter at all costs, they will do their duty sir." Colonel Stuart heads back to the command centre, "lieutenant," saluting, "yes Colonel," "what the fuck is going on??" "It's the internet Colonel, someone has posted pages of video footage, showing spiders going down people's throats, they have even posted Tina Smith's autopsy report. Everybody knows, the world knows that millions of baby spiders will be born tomorrow morning, Colonel sir, the whole perimeter is under attack." Colonel Stuart gets straight on the blower to the president. "Mr president, its Colonel Stuart, have you seen the internet?" "Yes, Colonel we have, someone has leaked classified information regarding the spiders. The leak didn't come from the Whitehouse Colonel, but we will leave no stone unturned until we have discovered the culprit." "As I predicted Mr president, the quarantine zone has gone ballistic, millions of scared, terrified people are heading for our ring of steel. My men will hold them for as long as we can, but we will desperately need reinforcements, the whole perimeter is under attack" … There are many bridges that cross from the mainland onto Manhattan Island, both ends have been heavily fortified with reinforced barbed wire fences and thick concrete barriers. The inner perimeter totally encompasses the whole island, nearly right up to the water's edge. Thousands of soldiers with their automatic weapons and flamethrowers are entrenched in their dugouts, ready to repel anyone who tries to escape. The outer ring of steel is on the mainland, heavy artillery, 50 calibre machine guns, rocket launchers. With many thousands of soldiers based on New Jersey, the Bronx, Queens and

Brooklyn, all looking across the water directly at their deadly foe ...

As more families wake this morning, the horrifying gruesome truth, is there for everyone to see. Hundreds of thousands of families just like the Kirk's now realise why THEY are still alive and not dead like the poor souls in the food store. The utter despair of knowing that within 24 hours your body is going to explode, and you are going to die in the most horrific way possible. The affected people are crying, whaling, screaming out in total disbelief to what will happen to them. How do you tell your friends, your family, how do you tell your children!!

The hideous black spiders are hiding just below the surface, never a stone's throw from their unborn hungry monsters. These intelligent creatures are patiently waiting, collectively anticipating the utter terrifying carnage that is to come. Mankind's meddling has elevated these horrific deadly killing machines to the top of the pecking order, we are now the food. If we don't stop this black army of destruction here and now, they will descend upon the earth like a terrifying black shroud, engulfing everything in their path ... The American military are on the highest alert possible, its them or us, there is NO middle ground. Yesterday the world was against the president and his military envoys for keeping their innocent citizens caged up like wild animals but today since all the new horrifying revelations were released, the world is shiting itself ... Bomb them, nuke them, don't let those hideous black creatures off that island, poison them all, destroy the monsters ... All the world leaders have rallied around the president ... How can we help, what can we do, we will send our best people. The world's population watches in ore, petrified, scared out of their tiny little minds of what might happen. The images of those poor defenceless people screaming in absolute agony as their veins exploded with their wide open terrified eyes popping out of their blooded faces. Or worse still, being impregnated by those hideous beasts, then waiting for two very long agonising weeks before the terrifying baby's violently erupted out of every orifice of your rupturing body. Your very life blood spewing out in all directions as you are ripped apart from the inside out by these ravenous infants ...

BOOOOOM!!!! The command centre rocks from the shockwave of the deafening explosion!! "Colonel Stuart, someone from the quarantine zone has fired a rocket launcher, its partly destroyed our defences on the Brooklyn bridge." There are hundreds of heavily armed screaming, terrified people trying to cross, "tell your men to hold them captain, I will radio through for more reinforcements." Hundreds of hysterical men, women and children are desperately trying to cross the bridge to safety, shooting anybody who stands in their way. Every bridge on the island is under attack, millions of new Yorkers are heading for the boarder. Flames with thick black smoke can be seen from all four corners, automatic gunfire can be heard ringing out from all directions, millions of terrified, angry people are trying to smash their way out. The soldiers in the dugouts firing back with their submachine guns, cutting through the baying crowd like fodder. Men, women and even children's bodies are piling high, their fruitless attempt at freedom snubbed out, as their blood trickles onto the chaotic streets below.

Apache helicopters circle overhead, spraying bullets at anyone who tries to escape. A small helicopter makes a break for it, no match against the Apache, only one air to air missile needed as the poor souls in the craft plummet back to earth, smashing headlong into central park, exploding into a million pieces, the fireball ascending high into the sky … The radio crackles, "Colonel Stuart, this is captain Shore on the gunboat intrepid, you have a breach on the Hudson River sir," just below the George Washington bridge. A large dinghy has just been launched off the island and is heading for New Jersey, "we have tried in vain to push it back sir, but it won't stop. They are just families Colonel, with many small children on board, they are screaming at us to save them sir." "Captain Shore," "yes Colonel," "this is a direct order, do not let that boat reach the mainland, use any means necessary to stop it, I will send reinforcements to contain the breach" …

"PEOPLE in the dinghy, you must turn back, or we will open fire. Captain" "Shore, the dingy won't stop sir." "Sergeant, you have your orders ... open fire" ... "but sir there are children and small babies on board." The desperate people in the inflatable dinghy are holding up their phones with their flashlights shining, live streaming everything to the world, in the hope of freedom, the world is watching. "Sergeant I am giving you a direct order" .... Automatic gunfire shooting out of the gunboat, 50 calibre rounds screaming their way to the hapless lost families on the doomed inflatable dinghy. The bullets cutting through their innocent bodies like paper, men, women and children being cut to shreds as the world watched on in horror. The small craft slowly sinking to the depths as the dozens of dead bodies float face down, bobbing up and down on the waves ...

The island has descended into chaos, friends fighting friends, families ripping each other apart, screaming, desperate people running headlong straight into the waiting arms of the military with their automatic weapons pointing in their direction. As the battle continues,

Americans killing Americans, all in the desperate hope of saving the world.

"Mom, dad, I need to see you in the kitchen." "Charley," "yes mom," "you sit and watch your cartoons and we'll be in the kitchen if you need us, ok darling," "ok mom." "What is it Ryan," as they close the kitchen door firmly behind them. "Mom, dad, I don't know how to tell you this … A new report has just been leaked onto the internet, the detailed report is from a man called Professor Henderson" … The Kirk's had decided to stay at home, they still didn't know what to do for the best, who would, they watched, as the world watched, in absolute horror at the thousands of desperate people trying to flee the island. The aircraft being shot out of the skies, the boats being sunk in our waters, the screaming, terrified people being cut down in their prime along miles of razor sharp barbed wire fencing … "professor Henderson is saying that the children are going to be eaten by the baby spiders when they are born, that's why they weren't attacked by the adult spiders, because they are food."

Richard and Shona's pupils dilate, their shocked mouths spring open as they read every word of the damming report. Their scrambled brains trying to digest yet more horrific information but this time it's about their beloved little Charley. Sat at the kitchen table, Richard and Shona hold hands as they stare into each other's numb, blank faces. Their minds finding it impossible to compute exactly what they had just read. Richard sits back in his chair ... "what the fuck, I can't get my head around it." His brain is spinning wildly around in his head as he tries to make sense of any of it ... NO .. NO, I'm not having it, as he stands up pounding the table with his fists. "I am not leaving my little Charley here to be food for those hideous monsters. I am her dad, it's my job to protect her, I'm getting her off this godforsaken island." "What do you mean Richard?" "Shona, I can't, and I won't leave our little baby girl here. I will get her off this island to safety, or I will die trying." After giving his family a massive hug and lots of kisses, especially Charley, defiant Richard marches out the door. Luckily his friend from work, Stan only lives in the next block over.

The inner streets are quiet, most people are at the wire and concrete trying desperately to leave or they are at home not knowing exactly what to do … "I'm so glad you're in Stan," "come in Richard." Stan had never been married or had any children, he is a good friend to Richard and his family, the kind of man you can always rely on. After the two men had dissected all the horrifying events of the past few days, Richard explains his plight. "I need to get my little Charley off this bloody island, I am not leaving her here to be sucked dry by those hideous monsters. I have only hours at best to get her to safety, what can we do Stan?" "Richard, I have an idea, I have access to all the keys in the office … Go home Richard, get yourself and little Charley ready to leave and I will see you at yours in a few hours." "Ok Stan I am relying on you, please don't let me down," "do I ever Richard," "no Stan you never have." The two men embrace, slapping their backs as men do. Richard then makes his way through the mostly deserted streets heading quickly homewards.

Ruby is with her parents talking to Edward on the phone … "I know Edward, it's totally shocking, the whole place has gone absolutely mad. My parents are in total disarray, how can you get your head around the fact that tomorrow morning thousands of baby spiders are going to explode out of your body. This whole situation doesn't feel real, everyone is totally numb. My parents and everyone I have spoken to have sort of know for a couple of weeks that something wasn't quite right, they felt different somehow. Over that time, they have all gone through many different emotions, panic, terror, anguish, unbearable pain, a sense of loss, torment and disgust. After watching those poor innocent people being savagely bitten to death in the most horrific way, the affected people here seem to have a sense of acceptance, there is absolutely nothing that they can do about it, and they do not have any more emotions to give. Who can they speak to, where can they go, the place is surrounded by heavily armed soldiers intent on shooting them. With those awful terrible images on the news showing men, women and children being gunned down in the streets. A war has erupted and according to the world's media, everyone on the planet wants us dead."

"Your right Ruby, everyone on the mainland is terrified, those terrible, agonising, disgusting videos are etched into their very souls, they are totally petrified. I have heard rumours that nuclear weapons might be used to stop these demonic demons." "That would be a good thing Edward, at least the people won't suffer, at least it will be quick" … "Ruby, I need to try and get you out of there before it's too late, I'm going up in the news helicopter tonight, surely there is a way of getting you out." "No Edward my fate is sealed, my poor old parents need me more than ever, I can't let them go through this terrible ordeal alone. It's strange Edward, I too have accepted my fate, when all is lost and there is nothing more that can be done, you strangely except the inevitable. A warm calm floods over you, like a fluffy comfort blanket wrapping around your entire body, the pain, the terror, the absolutely paralysing panic is gone, just a quiet peace remains." "Please Ruby, I need you, I'm falling in love with you, let me try and get you out of there." "No Edward, it's just too dangerous, I'm falling for you to, I can't let you risk your life on a suicide mission. Thank you,

Edward, for coming into my life, you made me smile every day." "Ok Ruby I do understand where you're coming from, my heart will always be yours, I will call you tonight when we are in the air, love you Ruby," "love you too Edward."

Richard arrives home and an anxious, worried Shona is waiting for him. "I was scared Richard, the streets are not safe, where have you been?" "I went to see my mate Stan, he has agreed to help us get Charley off this godforsaken island." "But how Richard, the island is totally cut off, all the bridges are guarded by soldiers with guns, how are we supposed to get her out?" "I don't know Shona, but Stan said he would help, I have to trust that he will find a way ... Shona its Friday afternoon, the clock is ticking, we have only hours left before" .... "I know Richard, what are we going to tell our beautiful little Charley?" "We have to tell her Shona ... but how, what the hell do we say??" "Yes, Richard your right, our baby girl needs to know, can you tell her, please Richard, I can't do it, every time I even think about it, I burst into tears. Thinking about poor young Ryan is pure torture but what is going to HAPPEN to our precious little funny, sweet girl is unspeakable, I'm starting to choke up just talking to you about it ... Please Richard, you have to," the tears start rolling down Shona's distraught face, she buries her head in Richard's chest, "please Richard, please !!" as she starts to sob uncontrollably.

Richard raises his hand and starts stroking his heartbroken wife's face, "yes, my darling, I will tell her, I don't know how but I will. You and Ryan stay down here, I will take our little Charley into her bedroom. How do I tell her Shona, what do I say?" The tears starting to well up in Richard's eyes. "This is the hardest thing I have ever done in my entire life, Shona I can't!!" "You have to Richard, we have only hours left, our little baby girl needs to know the truth" ... Squeezing his distraught wife ever so tightly, breathing deeply in and out, his cheeks bellowing with every exhale. Tears starting to slowly dribble down his cheeks, a painful hard lump appearing at the back of his throat as he tries to swallow spit that isn't there. Staring into the far distance, his broken mind spinning at a million miles an hour .... straightening up his shoulders and blowing his cheeks once more, "ok Shona I will go and get Charley."

A very sombre Richard opens the living room door, sat in her usual spot is Charley, with her little head buried into the TV. "Charley … Charley," "sorry dad," "I need to speak to you about something," "what have I done this time dad," "nothing my darling girl, I just need to talk to you. Just me and you in your bedroom, your mother and brother are going to stay down here." "Ok dad," cheekily smiling, "but will you get straight to the point this time dad, my favourite program is coming on next." "Come on, me and you up the stairs, I promise Charley, you're not in any trouble." As father and daughter climb the stairs, mother and son comforted each other on the sofa, their muffled anguish kept to a minimum. "Come on my darling girl, let's sit on your bed, I have something very important to tell you." Sat cross legged and facing each other, Richard takes hold of his daughter's hands. Charley's eyes wide open with anticipation, she always loved having her dad all to herself. Squeezing her little hands, a bit tighter and looking deep into her beautiful, innocent face.

"Charley" ... Richard pauses for a moment, trying desperately to compose his thoughts, his whole body is stiff and aching, that hard lump in his throat has not gone away, he can feel the tears getting ready to gush down his agonising face, all Richard wants to do is run away screaming but he can't. He knows, he can't fall apart, this little beautiful girl looks up to him, he is a god in her very young eyes. Richard knows he must hold it together for the sake of his precious little daddy's girl ... "Charley," "yes dad," "you know I have always tried to teach you to be a strong independent little girl and I always tell you the truth if you asked me a question," "yes dad." "Well Charley, I need you to be very strong for me today, I am going to tell you something that is really going to upset you and I need you to use that inner strength deep within you, so we can all get through this thing together." Charley's mouth begins to quiver, her worried crumpled face begins to cry ... "Ok dad," her little voice starting to croak, "I'll try and be strong dad." Sitting there holding hands and gazing deep into one another's eyes, Richard takes a big deep breath, trying desperately to stop his tears from exploding down his heartbroken face.

Richard begins ... "Charley, my darling little girl, when the spiders went down my throat in the cinema, they laid lots of baby eggs in my tummy, those eggs are going to hatch tomorrow, and little baby spiders are going to come out of my body." Looking worried and confused ... "But dad can't the doctors make you better dad," "no Charley, there is nothing that the doctors can do." Scratching her head and looking a little dazed, "what about mommy and Ryan?" "They are the same my darling, both of them have baby spider eggs inside of them as well." "Why didn't they put spider eggs into me to dad?" "Because your too little my darling, your belly isn't big enough." "Are you and mommy going to be ok after the baby spiders come out of your body tomorrow?" ... Richard raises his head to the ceiling, taking a very large intake of breath and holds it ... should he tell his little girl the terrible truth, or should he lie to her, they will all be dead in the morning ...... Charley knows nothing about what is going on outside these four walls, the hideous spiders, the soldiers, the war raging all around them, what should Richard do?? ....

Richard slowly lowers his head, still tightly holding his little daughter's hands, he looks longingly into her sweet innocent face ... "we don't know what is going to happen after the baby spiders come out but that doesn't matter right now Charley, I am getting you off this island tonight," "you are coming to dad" .... "Yes, my darling girl, your dad is coming to. So, Charley, go and pack your little rucksack with some clothes and don't forget your toothbrush," "ok dad." Charley skips off, thinking that they are going on an adventure, the talk of baby spiders pushed to the back of her mind. Shona and Ryan are still sat on the sofa when Richard walks in. "I couldn't tell her Shona, Charley looked at me with them little puppy dog eyes and I melted. All I wanted to do was cry my eyes out, I couldn't destroy our little girls life, it would of broken her little heart and mine to. What was I supposed to say to her, your mom and dad are going to horribly die in the morning with thousands of terrifying baby spiders spewing out of our bodies ... She thinks we are going on some kind of adventure, I have told her to pack her little rucksack because we are leaving tonight." "Richard, you promised me that you would tell her," "I really couldn't Shona, I sat there holding our little girls Hopes and dreams in my hands, her little innocent face looking up at me. I just couldn't do it, what parent could. All we can do now is hope and pray that Stan will come through for us, I can't leave our beautiful little girl here to die a horrible, gruesome death, I would rather die trying" ...

Many thousands of families are facing the same god awful dilemma, what do you say to your children, do you tell your children? Most of the infected people have come to terms with their fate, they all seemed to know from the outset that something wasn't quite right. They have had longer to ponder their mortality, making a bee line for the heavily guarded boarder doesn't seem a possibility. Watching thousands of screaming, terrified people getting gunned down at the perimeter on your computer screens is reason enough to stay home. From the beginning, only two short weeks ago!! The government has lied to us but to be honest, in retrospect what could they have done. They couldn't remove the infected people, the black hideous spiders would of followed. How do you evacuate nearly 20 million people without a good reason and without causing a panic ... plus keeping the existence of the spiders out of sight. The whole situation was a catastrophe waiting to happen...

It is mid-afternoon now and Colonel Stuart has been summoned to the CDC, waiting for him with some good news is Mrs Hocker and professor Henderson ... "Colonel, before we start, I have just found who leaked all the sensitive information online about the spiders earlier this morning. I'm afraid to say Colonel, it was one of my own, it was Catalina Mendes, no one has seen her since the early hours." "I had a strange feeling it was her Janet, that do Gooder has cost hundreds of soldiers their lives. Because of her selfish actions my men are dying needlessly, what did she think people were going to do when they knew the terrible truth. As I predicted the whole island has gone ballistic, millions of terrified people with their families have rushed to the boarder, most of them are heavily armed. Its mayhem all around the perimeter, scared, hysterical people trying anything to get to safety. All the people on that godforsaken island were unfortunately dead already, there was no need for all my brave soldiers to die in vain too. When we find Mrs Mendes, she will get what's coming to her" ...

"We have called you here Colonel, because we think, it was actually professor Henderson who has come up with this daring and audacious plan to kill all the spiders on Manhattan Island, we are all very excited about it." "I am sorry," the Colonel bows his head, a sense of defeat written across his face. "When you informed the president this morning that your arachnid specimen was dead, he was forced to ordered a nuclear strike, this is strictly confidential at the moment. The bombers will be taking off at 06 hundred hours in the morning, obliterating everything within a 10 mile radius, unfortunately also killing many millions of innocent Americans" ... "No Colonel, we have a solution, I'll let the professor explain our plan to you." "Colonel, when I heard this morning that our spider had been suffocated it got me thinking .... Cast your mind back to the 1st world war. The German army started using chemical weapons, namely mustard gas. It was designed to infiltrate the enemies eyes, lungs and skin, of course blistering inside and out, there for, impeding your enemies ability to fight. The gas was designed to sink to the bottom of their trenches, giving the soldiers nowhere to hide. I have been working closely with my colleagues from England and here in Berkeley, we have reformulated this particular toxin, dramatically increasing its volume and density ... In plain language Colonel, we can suffocate those black evil demons. Our new and improved mustard bombs will descend deep below the city, then as it works its way up, the gas will infiltrate every nook and cranny until it has totally in cased the whole of Manhattan Island, right up to the highest skyscraper. The thick yellow gas will suck out all of the oxygen, leaving everyone and everything beneath it to suffocate. The gas will take at least 24 hours to dissipate and by then there will be nothing left alive. We have to try this Colonel, it's got to be better than using nuclear weapons, the amount of plutonium needed will make the ground radioactive for many years to come" ...

"How long do you need professor?" "We will need at least 24 hours or less to get the bombs primed and on the ground." "Your plan on paper seems very sound but I don't know professor if the president will give you the extra time, 24 hours takes us into Sunday morning. The spiders will be here for a full day before we reach your deadline." "Colonel, we have crunched the numbers backwards and forwards, this plan will work. I estimate once the baby spiders are born, they will need to feed, luckily, they have an ample food supply at hand, and I am hoping that they will not want to venture to far in the first couple of days. If we can keep them fully contained on that island for that time Colonel, I think we have a chance of destroying them. I implore you Colonel, give us the green light so we can get started right away, time is of the essence" ... "ok professor, you have your window, get started, I will somehow convince the president that your audacious plan is better than nuking the whole of New York state. A full evacuation of all military personnel from the inner perimeter coinciding with the demolition of all bridges plus the ring of fire in the waters around the island will commence at 04 hundred hours tomorrow morning, hopeful professor totally isolating the island will give you the extra time you need." Shaking their hands, "thank you Janet and Charles for your dedication and professionalism over the last several weeks. Whatever happens in the days to come I hope and pray that historians will look favourable upon us, for what we do now is for the good of mankind." "Yes Colonel, let's hope history reveals that we did the right thing here today. As a very proud Englishman, if someone ever decides to make a movie about what happens here today, let's hope the bulldog spirit wins through." Mrs Hocker and the professor quickly head off to get their plan into action as soon as possible, the Colonel heads back to the command centre to have a heart to heart with the president, let's hope he succeeds.

ONLY HOURS REMAINING!!!

"Dad, dad, there's someone at the door," "ok Ryan," Richard goes and investigates, "Stan your here, quick come in." "I'm sorry Richard that it has taken me so long, but I couldn't get any keys until now." Both men look through the living room window and parked outside is a brand new snowplough, with big yellow tempered steel v-blades on the front. Richard looks a little confused, "listen Richard, I thought if you can get little Charley over the bridge and to the stockade on the other side, the soldiers have to take her. They know that the children are not infected, surely once your there, they can't in all good conscience leave her here to die an agonising death. The snowplough was the most armed machine I could find, hopefully with its thick metal v-plates on the front you can ram your way through." "There is no way off this island Stan, I have looked at every possible Avenue." "Thousands of terrified people are at the perimeter trying to smash and shoot their way to freedom, luckily for you Richard, a few bridges have already been compromised on the islands side. Washington, Williamsburg and Manhattan bridges have all been smashed open, hundreds of screaming people are trying to cross to the other side but soldiers with machine guns are blocking their way. Hopefully Richard, the thick armoured plate on the snowplough will give you both enough protection against the bullets for you to reach the other side."

Giving his good friend a big hug, a good bye hug. "Thank you, Stan, you have been a good friend. I am so grateful that you have given me the chance of trying and save my little Charley. We have only hours left in this world, my little baby girl has the rest of her life to live." The two men part company and Richard prepares to go and see his wonderful young son for the last time, taking him into his bedroom so no one else can hear. Little Charley is sound asleep in her bedroom, her little red rucksack tucked up in the bed next to her. As soon as the door is closed Richard flings his arms around his heartbroken son, their weeping tears dripping onto both their shoulders. Their arms so tightly wrapped around one another, no one wanting to let go. Frantically sobbing into each other's arms, this is not goodbye for now, this is goodbye forever ... Richard slowly pulls away, knowing he has to leave soon, still gripping his young sons hands, father and son gaze longingly into each other's distraught, sobbing faces.

No words are spoken at a time like this, two brave, strong men saying goodbye ... I love you my dear, sweet boy ... I love you to dad, always. As Richard turns away his fragile, timid son crumples to the floor, the father in him desperately wants to stay but he knows his time is fleeting. Richard gently closes the bedroom door behind him and goes in search of his devastated beautiful wife. Shona too is in her bedroom, already crying, waiting for her strong, handsome man to say goodbye. At the sight of one another they collapse into each other's aching arms, floods of wailing tears streaming down both their heartbroken faces. Sobbing uncontrollably as they wrapped their loving arms around one another, kissing so deeply their love filling the room ... Fighting back the tears, "its time my darling Shona, I have to go," looking deep into each other's loving eyes for the last time they knew this was the end. "Oh Richard," her heart breaking into a million pieces, "I love you so very much, you have made me the happiest woman in whole world. Please protect my little darling baby girl, I love her more than words can say. Who will look after our little ray of sunshine when we are no long here to love and comfort her, she is only 9. I hope she understands that we had no choice but to leave her all alone in this cruel world."

Husband and wife fall back into each other's arms, their bodies aching with agonising pain and loss. Sobbing uncontrollably knowing this is the end, they will never see one another again … "Come on my darling, it's getting late, I have to go." "I know my darling Richard," as she wipes the tears from his tormented face, sniffling back her own devastating grief. "Richard, you take Ryan down stairs, I will go and wake our precious little angel, I want … I need to say goodbye, as only a mother knows how." Sitting on the edge bed, her little baby girl is tucked up fast asleep, her little beautiful face oblivious to the horrors that awaits her in the hours to come. The tears won't stop gushing down her mother's face, her beautiful, funny little girl is leaving, and she will never see her again. Shona slowly raises her hand and carefully brushes a sleeping Charley's hair away from her face, her whole body is aching inside and out. Her painful tears will not stop her soft muffled sobs, her chest raising and falling as a mother looks longingly into her beautiful little daughters sleeping face ...

Beginning to stir, Charley slowly opens her weary eyes, with an enormous smile, "mommy is it time to go." Charley notices her mother's tortured weeping face, "are you ok mommy? don't be sad, me and daddy will be back soon, we are only going on a short adventure." Shona leans forward and scoops her little excited girl into her arms, mumbling through her devastating heartache. "I know my baby girl, these are happy tears, I will just miss you so very much." "Me to mommy," mother and daughter hug and squeeze each other so very tightly, the sad tears still pouring down Shona's devastated face. The two of them lovingly embracing, Little Charley saying goodbye for now, a mother saying goodbye for EVER. All Shona wants to do is run around the bedroom screaming at the top of her heartbroken voice and collapse in a quivering heap on the floor, but she can't. She must be brave, the bravest she has ever been in her entire life. Trying to desperately pull herself together, sniffing back her unbearable grief, "come on my darling girl, daddy and Ryan are waiting for you downstairs."

Excitedly Charley leaps out of bed, grabbing her little red rucksack, mother and daughter head down the stairs. Waiting for them both., are a very teary father and brother, Charley takes one look at a weeping young Ryan, "don't be sad Ryan," as she skips over to give her older brother a hug, she loves him deep down really. Wrapping her little arms around his waist, "you can come with me and dad next time, we will be back in a few days, so there is no reason to be sad." Brother and sister have a lovely hug, young Ryan's face is still crumpled, his devastating tears running down his face. Richard and Shona stand there holding each other's hands, watching their children saying goodbye for the very last time ... "Come on Charley, it's time to go," as Charley pulls away from her brotherly hug Ryan bends down and kisses his little sister on the cheek, "yuck," as she wipes her wet face, but she is smiling inside to ... "No Richard, not yet, mommy needs a family hug first," as a desperately sad mother opens up her aching arms all the Kirk family embrace for the very last time.

Shona and Ryan are in bits, sobbing heavily, their grieving tears cascading down, engulfing the whole family, as if to keep them all safe. Richards heart is also breaking, all he wants to do is stay with his entire family until the bitter end, but he can't. He has to try ... he has to try with all his might to save his beautiful, darling little girl, the one who changed his life all those years ago. "Charley," "yes dad," "can you go into the kitchen for a minute while I say goodbye to your mother and brother." "Ok dad, can I grab some chips while I'm in there, I'm starving," "of course you can my darling girl, daddy won't be long." As little Charley enters the kitchen the three of them burst into tears, trying very hard to muffle their absolute agony, the loss they all feel is unimaginable. No words are spoken as the three of them huddle closely for the last ... the final time!!! Little Charley comes strolling out of the kitchen eating her chips, "are we ready to go dad." "Yes, Charley we are, it's getting late, its after midnight already." "Wait Charley don't go," Shona quickly returns from the living room,

"I have something for you, turn around." Shona unzips Charley's little red rucksack and slips a photo album inside. Spinning her back around, Shona gives her little precious daughter a big monster hug and a deeply loving kiss on the lips.

"You know mommy loves you, don't you. I've put something really special in your little rucksack, it's yours to keep forever and ever my darling little girl. You won't understand right now but, in the future, if your ever feeling sad and mommy and daddy are not around, you can look at the lovely photos of us all and remember the happy times we all had together. Ok my little baby girl," looking a little bemused, "ok mommy." "Come on, we need to go. Right, give Your brother and mommy one final kiss," Charley runs over and gives Ryan and her mommy one last kiss. Richard firmly takes hold of Charley's hand and out the front door they go.

"Where are we going dad?" "I will explain everything later Charley, I have a surprise for you." As they walk hand in hand around the corner ... "wow, what's that dad?" "it's a snowplough Charley" "but dad, it's not snowing, are we going in that?" "Yes, my darling girl, I have to make sure it's working ok for the guys at work." "What's those yellow metal bars on the front for dad?" "They are made from extra thick steel, they are called v-blades, for pushing the snow out of the way. Right Charley, strap yourself in, it's time to go" ...... As a very excited little Charley sits in the passenger seat waiting to go on her adventure a very sullen Richard glances over his extremely heavy shoulder towards the house, he once called home. In the big bay window looking out at him are the rest of his doomed family. Shona and Ryan are holding hands, their tears are streaming down their heartbroken faces as they watch the other half of their decimated family driving away for ever, they will never see each other again.

Saturday 12.30 am ONLY HOURS REMAINING

"Hello Ruby, its Edward, I'm finally in the sky. How is your mom and dad?" "Not to good Edward, they have both been really ill today, terrible pains in their stomachs. There are no ambulances, no doctors and all the hospitals are abandoned, I have managed to get them some morphine to help with the pain but there is little else I can do." "I am sorry to say Ruby, there is nothing that can be done, I think we both know that." "I know Edward, but they are my parents" .. "We have finally been given permission to fly over New Jersey, away from the no fly zone. When we get level with New York I will zoom in using our high density news camera. It's that powerful, we can even see people's wrinkles on their face from this distance. We can't broadcast live because the government will know what we are up to. We are just coming up to New York now, I can see Amazon towers in the distance, just by central park, the tallest skyscraper in the city, it's a beautiful city at night, it's devastating to think it's come to this. Oh my God Ruby, there are fires raging everywhere, thick black smoke rising high in the sky in all directions. From here I can see the inner ring of steel, encompassing the whole island, my god it looks menacing, I'll zoom in." "How is it looking Edward?" "it's awful Ruby, the news feeds were right, there are thousands of screaming terrified people trying to, cut, smash, ram their way out. I can see lots of bright flashes of gunfire coming from both directions, there are hundreds of dead and wounded people lying everywhere, its chaos Ruby" ....

"Where are we going dad, we've been driving around for ages." "I know Charley, we are trying to get to Manhattan bridge, Stan told me that the barricade was down." "What barricade dad?" "I will tell you everything soon Charley, but we need to just get there first." Richard knows every back street and alleyway on the island, it wasn't long before they reached the top of Manhattan bridge. "Look dad, there are hundreds of people on the bridge, how are we going to get to the other side? Dad, dad, are you ok?" Awww my stomach, it's absolutely killing me. Richard tightly gripped the steering wheel, curling his toes inwards, arching his back, firmly clamping his teeth together. The pain is excruciating, it feels like his insides are being ripped out, if it wasn't for his little girl, Richard would be screaming out in agony.

"It's ok darling, daddy will suck it up, like I have always taught you my darling girl. Sometimes when life gets tough, you just have to suck it up and get on with it." "Yes, dad you have but are you ok?" "To be honest Charley, I'm not. I have always been honest with you all through your life, but I have been lying to you for these past few days. I have never lied to you before, I have always been as honest as I could be. I have something to tell you my darling little girl and its breaks my heart to have to tell you this." Charley's little face starts to crumble, tears welling up in her sad, worried eyes, "what is it dad?" As the chaos erupts around them, the fire, the screaming desperate people, the automatic gunfire, Richard has to be finally honest with his beautiful daughter. Tightly holding one another's trembling hands, father and daughter look deeply into each other's eyes. The heart-breaking tears start rolling down his face once more. An enormous hard lump appears at the back of his throat, the agonising pain within is tearing his body apart.

Charley too is crying, scared of what her super hero dad is going to say. "Charley" .... Richard raises his head and looks to the heavens, tears are still pouring down his face, that hard lump in his throat is now twice the size. Closing his eyes for a moment and continuously blowing out his cheeks .... oh god, how am I supposed to tell my beautiful daughter that I am going to die in a matter of hours, and she is going to be left all alone in this cruel world, please God help me be strong ... Richard slowly lowers his head and looks straight at his sobbing little girl. "Charley, those spiders that are inside of me, they are killing me, they will be coming out of my body very soon and I will be dead." "NOOOO dad, NOOOO!!" her whole little body erupts, crying, screaming, kicking her arms and legs out in front of her, crying uncontrollably ... "No dad, you promised, you promised you'd come with me." Her little heart is breaking ... sobbing, trying to get her words out, "what ... about mommy and Ryan?"

..." I'm sorry but mommy and Ryan will be dead to, my darling girl" .... "NOOOOOOO DAAAAAD" Charley falls into a hysterical heap on the seat, her little world has been blown apart. Her little 9 year old brain trying to make sense, any sense of what's going on, tears streaming down her heartbroken face ... Awwwww the pain deep inside Richard is getting far worse, he's having trouble thinking straight .... screaming out in absolute agony, putting his hands tightly around himself, my STOMACH ... "Charley it's nearly too late, we have to GOOOOO !! get down into the foot well and stay there until I tell you to come out!" Richard lifts the thick steel v-blades half way up the windshield, protecting himself and little Charley in the foot well. Revving up the engine, Richard pulls out onto the start of the crowded chaotic bridge ...

"Ruby, I can see a big yellow snowplough pulling onto Manhattan bridge, it's going to drive over it !! there are hundreds of terrified people in its way. It's going, oh my god, its smashing into people, Ruby, I can't believe what I'm seeing" ...

Richards foot is flat to the floor, the v-blades are cutting through people like butter, their bones crunching and snapping like twigs, thick red blood splattering up the windshield. Many people are lying on the floor in absolute agony, clutching their belly's. The snowplough is bouncing over them like speed humps in the road and Charley is still sobbing her little heart out in the foot well ...

Ruby it's not stopping, the poor people on the bridge don't stand a chance, there are dead bodies everywhere ... The soldiers are firing, their brightly lit muzzles lighting up the nights sky, bullets are pinging off the snowplough in all different directions ...

Over half way down the bridge and the bullets start flying, "stay down Charley," Richard keeps his foot to the floor, the thick steel v-blades doing their job, keeping them both safe, keeping them both alive, for now. Gripping the steering wheel with all his might, doubling over in agonising pain, Richard's whole body is almost ready to explode but still he ploughs on. The bullets are coming thick and fast cutting deep into the body of the snowplough, big jets of red hot steam are pouring out of the engine but still it keeps going, cutting through everyone in its path .... **BOOOOOM** with a defining smash the battered snowplough plunges straight into the concrete barriers, thick black smoke bellowing into the nights sky as the yellow beast comes to a grinding halt, the shocked soldiers taking cover as the big yellow machine finally runs out of road ...

"It's crashed, its crashed, Ruby the snowplough has made it to the other side, there is smoke everywhere, the soldiers have stopped shooting … there are bloodied dead and dying bodies all over the bridge, its carnage Ruby" …

As quick as a flash Richard was out of the battered snowplough and on his knees in front of the thick wire fence. "Don't SHOOT, don't SHOOT, I have a child, Charley quick, come here." Richard knew his time was up, the black hideous baby spiders are on their way, he had to act now, if he was to have any chance of saving his beautiful little daddy's girl. Most of the people on the bridge were either dead, injured or too dazed to care, so Richard took this small opportunity to try and save his little girl. As the smoke slowly dissipates a brave young lieutenant, his shaking hands still holding his rifle peers through the thick wire fence. "Don't shoot, I'm unarmed, I have my little girl with me." "Get back, or I'll shoot," "please take my daughter before it's too late, she's only 9, you know that she's not infected, the spiders didn't attack our children." Pointing his rifle, "get back, I have my orders, no one is allowed through."

"PLEASE, PLEASE, I beg you, do you have children, please help me save mine" ... The immense, unbearable pain returns, Richard screams out in agonising pain, his whole body shaking and going into fits of spasms. Gritty his teeth and somehow standing to his feet, Richard picks up his little girl and holds her out in front of him. "Please take her, please." Charley spins around and puts her arms around her dads neck, "no dad I can't leave you, you are my dad, I love you so very much, I can't live without you. Dad, please don't leave me all on my own, please dad." Little Charley's tears and heart-breaking cries were too much for the young lieutenant to bare. He had noticed a small hole in the thick wire fence, it had happened when the snowplough had hit the concrete barriers .. Putting down his rifle, "quick ... quickly pass me your daughter, I will save her for you, there is a small hole above the concrete" .. Pulling Charley away from his neck, Richard looks for the last time upon his beautiful little girls face. "I love you my darling girl, I have from the very first time

I saw you, you have given me the best 9 years of my life, just remember, your dad loves you always." With that Richard lifts a screaming, sobbing Charley high in the air. Taking 3 steps forward and squeezing her through the small gap in the security fence and into the arms of the young lieutenant. A kicking and screaming little Charley fights and scratches trying with all her little might to get back into her dads loving arms, her little heart breaking into a thousand tiny pieces ...

"Who is in the snowplough Edward, what's happening?" "There is a man and a little girl in the snowplough, I think they are father and daughter. The man pushed the little girl through a hole in the fence, he has saved her life. I have captured it all on camera Ruby, it was heart breaking." "Edward ... Edward, my parents, they are" .... "Ruby are you there, Ruby ... I don't know if you can hear me, but I will keep filming" ...

Richard could bare the agonising pain no longer, falling to his knees, his body slowly being eaten from the inside out. His deafening screams could be heard for miles around, more soldiers begin to muster behind the barbed wire fence. Heartbroken little Charley manages to wriggle free, out of the arms of the lieutenant and pushed her way to the front, past the gorping frightened soldiers. Gripping the thick wire fence, her little sobbing face peeping through the wire at her Grief-stricken dad on the other side. At sight of her, Richard's terrible, agonising screams subsided, father and daughter's gaze transfixed, looking deep into each other's heartbroken faces for one last time. Simultaneously thousands of blood curdling deafening screams could be heard crying out around the city, the baby spiders are nearly here ...!! All around the island thousands of people are falling to their knees, their twisted, agonised bodies are in absolute agony ...

Richard begins to writhe around on the floor in unbelievable, excruciating pain. Charley is hysterically screaming at the top of her little voice, "NO dad, NOOOOO!!! Don't leave me, I love you DAD, I will always love you." Trying with all her little might to rip apart the thick wire fence so she can hold her dying dad once more, her gut wrenching tears pouring down her heartbroken face. Then they came, the first appearing in the corner of Richard's eye, then another, then another. The little black baby spiders burrowing up through his eyes, then dropping onto his cheeks. The pain is unbearable, Poor Richard let's out one final agonising scream, "I love you too my little baby girl" as the baby monsters pour out of his tortured body. Thick red blood spurting out of his nose and mouth as the new born monsters ejaculate into the world .... Little Charley is absolutely hysterical, kicking and screaming, MY DAD, MY DAD, NOOOO!!! The young lieutenant scoops an utterly broken Charley up into his arms and carries her away to safety .... SPIDERS ... SPIDERS !!! the terrified soldiers behind the wire start shouting for their lives ... WHOOOOOSH a flaming hot jet of fire streams out from a flamethrower instantly incinerating the baby spiders, WHOOSH, another jet is fired totally encapsulating poor Richard's dead body, burning him to a crisp. All around the island baby spiders are spewing into the world, millions of them ... Colonel Stuart's radio springs into life, "SPIDERS Colonel, the SPIDERS are here, BLOW the bridges!!!" As all the terrified soldiers run for their lives ..

Poor Shona and Ryan were on their knees on the living room floor, screaming out in absolute agony, the unbelievable pain they felt was excruciating. They didn't know that their beloved Richard was already dead, but their beautiful little Charley was safe. As their pain intensified, they managed to grip each other's hands, "I'm scared mom, the pain, ahhhhhh the pain." "I LOVE YOU SON" was the last word that was spoken as their tortured bodies exploded, splattering thick red blood all over the room. The newly born spiders pouring out of their dead bodies like a black avalanche of death and destruction ...

BOOOOOOMMM!!! Manhattan bridge explodes into an enormous fireball, the CRACK of the explosion sending brick and concrete high into the air, along with all the poor souls that were still on the bridge ... BOOM .. BOOM .. BOOM ...!!!

"My god Ruby I don't know if you can still hear me, but Manhattan bridge has just exploded into a thousand pieces, the fireball is nearly as high as the helicopter. **BOOM .. BOOM**, Williamsburg bridge is gone, so is Brooklyn bridge, the explosions are enormous, shrapnel is being flung high into the nights sky, there are thousands of people on those bridges, and they are being blown to Smithereens. The huge fireballs are spectacular, like ALL the fourth of July's rolled into one. **BOOM .. BOOM .. BOOM**, The George Washington, Henry Hudson and Madison Avenue bridges are all gone, the shockwaves from the explosions are rocking the helicopter, we can barely stay in the sky. **BOOM .. BOOM ..** All the bridges on the island are exploding, millions of terrified people are running away from the perimeter and back into the centre of the city ... WHOOSH!! There is fire, it's on the Hudson River, there is fire on the Harlem River, the flames are spreading around the island like a huge wall over 20 feet high. From up here it looks like the whole island is burning, the water, the bridges even the streets are on fire, there are millions of screaming, terrified people everywhere" ...

At the exact same moment, the baby monsters are spewing into the world their black hideous mothers have reappeared. Millions of hysterical, screaming people are running for their lives, they have nowhere to run, and they definitely have nowhere to hide. The big black ugly spiders are everywhere, scurrying around at a hundred miles an hour. But this time, they are after our young, adolescent children. Jumping 2 feet into the air and landing on their young terrified, screaming bodies. Sinking their razor sharp pointy fangs deep inside their small hysterical bodies. Injecting just enough venom into their young fragile victims, just enough to paralyse them. Their little terrified eyes are still wide open, their bodies are stiff and rigid, but the young children can still see and feel everything. The spiders quickly wrap up their young prey, cocooning them tightly within their sticky web. Ready for their hungry, ravenous babies to feed on at their leisure ...

Edward can see everything from his helicopter, millions of black baby spiders are spewing into the world, like a black evil shroud covering the bloodied streets. Terrified, screaming people are frantically running for their very lives. Ravenous hungry babies are pouncing onto our innocence cocooned children sucking them dry ...

Colonel Stuart is back at central command in Brooklyn at the old naval yard .. "Captain," "yes Colonel," "did we get all our soldiers off the island before the bridges were blown?" "Not all Colonel, we are still waiting for all the reports to come in sir, but we do know that a lot of our brave soldiers were trapped on the perimeter when the bridges exploded. The navy has successfully encircled the whole island in a ring of fire, it is now totally cut off from the mainland. I am sad to report Colonel, that professor Henderson was right, the adult spiders have re-emerged, and they are attacking the children, the baby spiders are having a feeding frenzy" ... "Get me the professor on the phone," "yes Colonel." "Professor Henderson, its Colonel Stuart, the spiders are here, you were right professor, they are feeding on our poor defenceless children. How long before your bombs are ready to go, we have totally isolated the island. All bridges have been blown and we have a flaming wall of fire encircling the whole perimeter. In your opinion professor, how long do you think we can keep these hideous monsters caged up until they want out?"

"I predict Colonel, we have several hours before the spiders start looking for a way off that godforsaken island. At the moment the adult spiders are busy scurrying around wrapping up our innocence children for their offspring to gorge on at their convenience, once they have done that, the adults will turn their attention to the islands adult population. Going down their rasping throats once more, impregnating them with their tiny eggs ready for the whole gory cycle to start all over again. There are hundreds of millions of ravenous hungry babies to feed, the food supply will only last so long, then these evil black killing machines will want off that island and they will try every avenue possible to achieve their goal. I assure you Colonel, all the counter measures we have in place will hold. Your engineers have told me that the new mustard bombs will be operational within a couple of hours, they should be airborne soon after. I am making my way back to your location,

I should be back with you within the hour. ""Very good professor, I will see you shortly ..."

Her devastated body is broken, her many tears have washed her into a sea of terrible grief, poor Ruby's precious Bradley and Gene are no more .. Covered in her dead parents blood Ruby wanders the streets in absolute shock and horror ... Ring, ring, "Edward, can you hear me?" "Oh Ruby, I feared the worst when the phone went dead earlier. Are you ok my darling?" "No Edward I'm not," as she fought back her painful, tears, "my beloved parents are gone. It was terrible Edward, they had been in excruciating pain for hours. In the end I had to overdose them with the last of the morphine, I lay them on the bed semi-conscious holding each other's hands. Their terrible pain had finally gone, my wonderful parents spent the last moments of their lives holding hands and smiling as they looked deep into each other's loving eyes. But then they started convulsing on the bed, blood pouring out everywhere. Little baby spiders appearing one by one .. then all of a sudden, their fragile old bodies exploded, thick red blood along with the newly born baby spiders were spewing out in all different directions, covering the bed." "Are you ok Ruby? did they harm you?" "No Edward, the baby spiders just vanished into the night. I had to come outside Edward, I couldn't stay in my parents apartment any longer." "Are you safe on the streets Ruby?" "I don't know Edward, I'm just numb, I suppose I'm in shock, I just don't feel anything. The spiders are everywhere Edward, the big ones are attacking the children and the babies are feeding on the children, they are all leaving me alone, I don't really care anymore." "Don't say that Ruby, you know I love you." "I know Edward, I have to go now" ... Ruby hangs up the phone her mind is scrambled, her terrible grief has overwhelmed her. Lost and alone she wanders the streets ...

The remaining islanders are in total shock, bird flu they were told, now black hideous terrifying spiders, quarantine. It has all happened so very fast, out of nowhere. One minute we were all living a normal life, then this .... how did it all come to this. Hundreds of thousands of American citizens are dead, their souls savagely ripped away by these hideous black monsters.

Our poor defenceless innocent children are fodder for these newly born insatiable ravenous beasts. Many more thousands of innocent people have died, treacherously gunned down by the very people who swore to protect and serve, their only crime .. being in the wrong place, at the right time!!

"Colonel Stuart, professor Henderson is here," "very good captain, show him in." "Colonel, we've done it, the mustard bombs are being loaded as we speak. The bombers will be over their targets within 90 minutes." "Well done professor," "it was a team effort Colonel, everyone has worked through the night to get the job done." "How confident are you professor that these mustard bombs will do what you say they'll do?" "Very confident Colonel." "Just to be sure professor, the president has ordered that the nuclear bombers will be 30 minutes behind, just in case you fail. He has given me full presidential authority to order a nuclear strike on Manhattan Island if your plan does not succeed. Our helicopter will be taking off in 60 minutes so we can see first-hand if your audacious plan has worked ..."

"Colonel, Colonel Stuart, sorry to interrupt sir," "what is it captain?" "We have a survivor sir, a little girl was pushed through the wire on Manhattan bridge, we think she might be the only person who has successfully escaped from the island." How old is she captain?" "About 8 or 9 Colonel, she has just arrived at the command centre and the little girl is being looked after by my personal staff." "I must see her captain, please lead the way. Professor be ready to leave on the helicopter within the hour," "yes Colonel, I will be ready …"

In a room adjacent to the command centre is poor heartbroken little Charley, she is sat in the corner of the room holding tightly onto her little red rucksack. Her heart breaking tears streaming down her sad, lonely face, the captain escorts the Colonel inside. "Colonel, this is lieutenant Cooper, she has been looking after this little girl." Talking quietly in the opposite corner, "how is she lieutenant?" "Not too good Colonel, she hasn't spoken a word since she was brought in sir. Lieutenant Rosewood is the officer who brought her in from the perimeter, he told me that a man, who he thinks was her father, drove the yellow snowplough that crashed into the barricade on Manhattan bridge. The man then pushed the little girl through the wire to lieutenant Rosewood just before the baby spiders exploded out of his body. Her little sad crumpled up face Colonel, all I want to do is cry with her."

"Ok lieutenant Cooper, I will try and talk to her, be on hand if I need you," "yes Colonel." Colonel Stuart walks slowly over to poor little Charley and sits beside her. "Hello, my name is Colonel Stuart, what is your name?" nothing .. Charley doesn't say a word, just a faint sound of her heart breaking sobs echoing around the cold, white room .. "Are you hurt?" .. nothing .. "Are you hungry?" .. still nothing. The Colonel spots her little red rucksack, "shall I look in here little girl so I can see who you are." As the Colonel touches the little red rucksack, sobbing Charley pulls away angrily .. "NO, it's mine!!" But as she pulls away the photo album fall out onto the floor. Poking out of a corner of the album is a white envelope, the Colonel leans down and picks up the photo album off the floor and retrieves the white envelope poking out.

Little Charley snatches the photo album out of his hands and holds it tightly to her aching chest. Her agonising tears still streaming down her devastated little face .. "NO, I said, this is mine." As the Colonel turns the white envelope over, he notices a name written on the front, "is your name Charley?" ... she nods, as she holds the precious gift her mother had given her. "Shall I open the letter Charley, it could be important?" Through her heart breaking tears Charley mumbles .. "Ok." Colonel Stuart carefully opens the envelope ... "It's a letter from your dad, would you like me to read it to you?" Charley sits upright for a minute, slowly wiping the tears away from her little sad, confused face. "A letter from my dad!!" ... putting her precious photo album down on her knees, Charley opens it to the first page. Staring back at her are four happy smiling faces, the beautiful, loving family that she had lost. The painful tears begin to fall once more, the hard lump in the back of her little aching throat making it impossible to swallow. Her whole little body is screaming inside as poor lost and alone little Charley looks at the family that is no more ..

Be brave, she thinks, my dad always taught me to be brave. Turning to the next page was too much for little Charley to bear, looking out are two incredibly happy faces with their smiling cheeks touching, this was the last selfie that Charley had ever taken with her and her dad, on the morning of the cinema. Looking at this amazing image Charley goes into meltdown, sobbing uncontrollably, her sad and lonely cries filling the room .. The Colonel tries to console our little Charley but first he must put her precious letter away .. "No," she screams through her agonising tears, "I want you to read my dad's letter, I need to know what he said." Unfolding the letter once more, the Colonel begins to read.

My darling little Charley

Firstly, I want to thank you for being my beautiful little daughter, the day I stood there watching you being born was the happiest day of my life. You changed me inside, I cried as I watch the midwife bringing you into this world. We have this connection you and me, I know you feel it too. Love is not a strong enough word for what we share. You made me a happy man, a better man, a man you were proud to call your dad. Writing this letter is the second hardest thing I have ever had to do in my entire life, leaving you my darling little girl is the first. You brought so much joy into my life and for that I am truly thankful. I hope in the future, my beautiful little girl, you will find someone who truly loves you and when you have your little children, you will understand a parents love for their child. Please show them photos of me, their grandad, I would of loved to be there and hold them in my arms, like I first held you. Be happy my little daddy's girl, no more tears, your daddy loves you so very, very much.

Goodbye my beautiful little girl, daddy will shine down on you always. XXX

As the Colonel finishes reading her dads letter Charley is still crying her little heart out, looking intently at the photo of her and her wonderful dad. This little daddy's girl is only 9 years old but listening to the words of her super hero dad makes her feel a little bit better inside ....

"Colonel Stuart, sorry to disturb you sir but your helicopter is ready," "thank you captain. Lieutenant Cooper, please make sure this little brave girl is well cared for, I will look in on her later." Colonel Stuart and professor Henderson board the helicopter and head to their vantage point high above the city, waiting for the bombers to arrive. From up here they can see the whole island, it is chaos down there. Millions of terrified, screaming people are still running around for their very lives with no possible way of getting to safety. The government has forsaken them, the world has turned their back on them, they must die so the world has a chance at living ... "Professor, do you think the people of the world will forgive us for not doing enough to help those poor souls trapped on that godforsaken island, especially the children?" "No Colonel, the world will say that we didn't do enough. I have been here from the very beginning, and I don't think we did enough, but I am talking retrospectively. Let's just hope Colonel that when the dust settles here today, the rest of the world will still be here tomorrow to judge us ..." "Here they come professor, the bombers are here, let's hope and pray your plan works." The sound of the jet engines is deafening as the 5 bombers with full payloads circle the island. The order is given and the first aircraft leaves formation, the others follow suit as they all descend below the clouds to make their final approach. The bombers carrying their nuclear payloads are only 30 minutes behind if all else fails .. The world is watching, this is mankind's last hope of destroying these hideous, deadly creatures. If we fail today, this black wave of death and destruction will sweep the world killing everything in its path ...

BOOOOOM !!! the first bomb explodes in the middle of central park, BOOOOOM, BOOOOOM then other and another enormous explosions are seen up and down the island, monstrous mushrooms of thick yellow gas erupt skywards. BOOOOOM, BOOOOOM, the last of the mustard bombs are dropped, the whole island is covered in a sea of thick yellow mist, hopeful choking to death everyone and anything still left alive on that godforsaken island ... "You've done it professor, your plan has worked, your mustard gas has enveloped the whole island" ... "What's happening professor, your gas is starting to dissipate, its slowly disappearing, you have failed professor, we have failed. Call in the nuclear bombers, we can't let those hideous monsters off that island." "NO Colonel wait, call off the bombers, the gas is designed to sink to the depths, then rise up like the phoenix. Engulfing the whole island; then choking to death anything still left alive down there, just wait Colonel" .... 10 minutes .. nothing, 15 minutes still nothing. "Professor your plan has failed, the nuclear bombers will be here imminently," "but Colonel," "no professor we had our shot, it's time to accept defeat. Let God have mercy on our souls, the nuclear blast will not just kill everything on that island, it will decimate every living thing within a 10 mile radius."

The pilot of the helicopter, "Colonel Stuart, the nuclear bombers are awaiting your orders sir to start their final dissent" .... Colonel Stuart gives the order, and the nuclear bombers start their final dissent. Passing over the island, then breaking formation to commit to their final run .... "WAIT Colonel, call off the bombers, the gas, the yellow mustard gas is rising, look it is working Colonel. Call off the bombers" ... Millions of screaming, terrified people are running frantically around the decimated island. Thick yellow gas rising up slowly above their ankles, starting to engulf their traumatised, battered bodies. Spiders running in all different directions, millions of them, trying desperately to escape. Colonel Stuart calls off the bombers !! telling them to circle the island in a holding pattern, they may still be needed. "I told you Colonel my plan would work, the mustard gas is starting to infiltrate every building." Slowly the thick yellow gas starts rising up from the depths, scared, terrified people have come out of their hiding places coughing and spluttering, gasping for air. The black hideous spiders and their ravenous offspring have also piled onto the empty streets.

The whole island is covered in thick yellow smoke, fires are burning out of control in every corner of the city. The thick yellow gas continues to rise, slowly sucking the oxygen out of the atmosphere. Scared, frantic people are starting to fall to the floor, their faces turning purple as they gasp their final breath. Spiders are everywhere, lying on their backs with their long legs pointing skywards as the life is being sucked out of their hideous bodies. Thicker and thicker, higher and higher the mustard gas climbs, engulfing the whole island in a yellow blanket of death, suffocating everything before it!!! .... WAIT .. on the top of the city's tallest skyscraper, there is movement. On the very top of Amazon towers the last surviving spider is taking its last fateful breath. lying on its black gruesome back with it long spiny hairy legs pointing skywards, its life force slowly draining away .... What's that flying above the spiders dying head, it swoops, pinning down the last dying spider with its RAZOR SHARP talons. With one sharp, stabbing movement, it sinks its long pointy BEAK deep inside the spiders dying FLESH!! .... Instantly it was off, flying around in the sky like a mad thing. Its eyes are spinning out of its head, whirling around and around in the sky, like some kind of demented lunatic. What the hell is it, what could it be .... oh no, It's a BLACK .... UGLY .... CROW!!!!!!!!!!

Written by Bernie Unwin Spencer.

Lightning Source UK Ltd.
Milton Keynes UK
UKHW012011150822
407336UK00001B/243